P9-DFW-665

THE BATTLE FOR NEWFOUNDLAND

by

Herb Sakalaucks

Copyright 2018 © Herb Sakalaucks
Published by Eric Flint's Ring of Fire Press
East Chicago, IN, U.S.A.
http://www.1632.org
All rights reserved.
ISBN:9781976994371

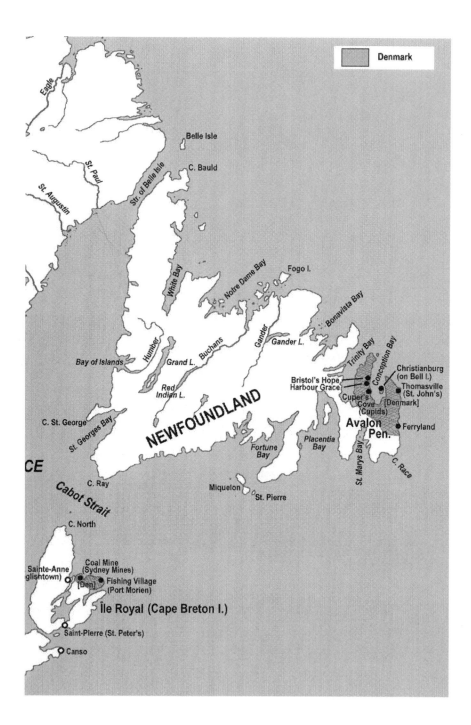

PREFACE TO THE BATTLE FOR NEWFOUNDLAND

Herb Sakalaucks approached me a few years ago and raised the idea of turning his serialized stories in the *Grantville Gazette* magazine titled "Northwest Passage" into one or more novels that we could publish through Ring of Fire Press. What I found intriguing about the idea was that it raised the possibility of showing an alternate historical path from the one that actually happened, which is sometimes called the American Holocaust.

The "holocaust" referred to was the destruction of indigenous American societies under the impact of European colonization and settlement of the New World. The subject is a contentious one among historians, and spreads across a wide range of disputed topics. On the most basic level, for instance, there is sharp disagreement concerning the size of the populations of the Americans on the eve of Columbus' arrival in 1492 and the death rate produced by diseases.

But leaving aside the specific disputes involved, what is unquestionably true is that the overall impact of the Old World upon the New World was to crush out of existence the cultures which had arisen in the Americas prior to 1492. Whatever percentage of the existing population survived, the societies themselves all perished in the course of the centuries following 1492.

Could this have been prevented, or at least ameliorated? This is a question that was first raised to me by Del Rey's editor Steve Saffel more than a decade ago, when he asked me if I could write an alternate history in which the Trail of Tears never happened. My first response was that I could—provided I could start with the era of the Vikings. If the initial Norse settlements in Newfoundland in the 10ᵗʰ century had become permanent, then the populations of the Americas would have had almost five hundred years more than they actually had to adapt to Europeans along with their diseases and their technologies.

That wasn't a story Steve was looking for, however. He wanted something set in a much later period: specifically, the beginning of the 19th century. The end result was the Trail of Glory series I began with *1812: The Rivers of War* and *1824: The Arkansas War.*

What Herb was proposing was an alternate way of depicting the historical possibilities, one which began with the premises of my Ring of Fire setting in the first half of the 17th century. What if the colonization of a large portion of North America had been dominated by one of Europe's *small* nations instead of, as actually happened, by the great powers of France, Britain and Spain?

Specifically, Denmark. In real history, Denmark did have a few small settlements in the Caribbean, but they never amounted to much. But what if, given the very different parameters of the power equations produced by the arrival of Grantville, Denmark had been able to dominate a large portion of what is today called "Canada"?

The possible ramifications were fascinating to me. A nation like early 17th century Denmark didn't have the military power or the population to simply overwhelm the indigenous peoples of North America. Willy-nilly, whether they wanted to or not, Danish settlers would have to develop a *modus vivendi* with the people they encountered in the New World. The hybrid societies which the French settlements originally produced such as the *metis,* which were cut short by the British victory in the Seven Years War, might have emerged and become more stable and long-lasting.

Who could say? It seemed to me that Herb's project was interesting enough to support—and no matter what the final outcome, was bound to produce a number of good stories.

So, here we are, with the second volume of that project. I hope you enjoy it.

CHAPTER 1

March 1634, Paris

The early spring showers left a tattered, evening fog over the streets of Paris. A lone pedestrian looked back, over his shoulder. Captain Rene Roussard breathed a sigh of relief. The last barge he'd ridden, from Giverny, had been refused entrance to the city due to past *indiscretions* by her captain. The city guards had been ecstatic as they escorted the barge captain off in chains. The passengers had been left, unmolested, to complete their journeys. As a result, Rene had been left to his own resources to finish the last two miles of his journey. The shadowy figures that had been following him, since the city gate, had finally disappeared at the last intersection. He pulled a worn, knit, stocking cap from his head and mopped the salt soaked rain from his eyes in relief. Either they had just coincidentally been traveling the same route he was taking, or they had finally decided he was simply not worth the effort of robbing.

Now he could concentrate on the *real* problem that had brought him to Paris. He had to report to Cardinal Richelieu the calamity that had befallen the mission he'd been given personally by the cardinal. It had been a fast return voyage from New France, after he'd been boarded by the Dutch privateer in the Cabot Strait. With the forged papers he carried, he had managed to convince the Dutch that his was a Dutch ship. Ever since he'd made port at Le Havre he'd been in mortal fear of this impending meeting.

His ship was safe, but the other ship he'd sailed with from Quebec had been taken. Some would view his release as a failure, and that was the nub of the problem. People who failed the cardinal sometimes wound up dead. Simply sailing away had been considered. However, those who failed to report at all could depend on reaching that fate when the cardinal's men caught up with them. He shook his head. *The gold had seemed so good at the time!*

He continued walking as he mulled over his possible fate and suddenly realized he'd arrived at his destination. The doorway was barely visible in the reflected candle light from the windows at the front of the structure. The light notes of a *sarabande* escaped from an open second floor window. Two rats stood near the door, watching him and guarding their piles of trash, challenge reflected in their red eyes. They stood their ground, snarling, as he stepped up to the door. *They're braver than I feel.*

He knocked on the kitchen door and a small viewport opened. The guard growled at him, demanding what his business was at this hour. "I'm here to give a message to His Eminence. Tell him it's a *brevet* message."

The cardinal's guard stared at him in doubt, but it was one of the code words on the list. He decided that the visitor probably was legitimate. There was a load snick as a bolt was thrown back and the door opened.

"Follow me," was all the guard said. The aura of menace precluded any thought of refusal. Although the guard's hands were empty, Rene could see that the sword was free in its scabbard. As they walked through the kitchen, Rene's stomach rumbled at the aroma of roast duck and fresh breads. It was well past his usual dinner hour. Even before he had entered the gates of Paris, he'd decided that promptness in reporting to the cardinal was preferable to a last supper. His stomach wasn't as sure.

After only a few strides, they reached a small room at the head of a long corridor awash in candle light. The quantity of candles being burned could have fed a sailor's family for a month. The guard paid the light no attention and simply opened a door and motioned Rene in. "Wait here. I'll see if his Eminence knows you and wants to see you. He has guests here tonight." The door shut and the sound of a key turning in the lock was loud in the silence. Rene wasn't surprised. The cardinal had many enemies that wanted him dead and a password could be obtained in many ways.

The light from the enormous ballroom chandeliers lit up the street in front of the *Palais-Cardinal*. This was the first party hosted in the new residence Cardinal Richelieu was building in Paris. Based on the boisterous crowd in attendance, it promised to be the site of many future galas. The residence wing was still under construction, but the main ballroom, kitchen and meeting rooms were complete enough to host a royal ball. No expense had been spared to decorate the new *Palais*. Tapestries adorning the walls were reflected in the mirrors, which also reflected light for the rooms. Inside, the party celebrating the last day before the start of Lent included all of the court nobility who were in town, since Queen Anne had chosen to attend. The king was not present. He had decided to remain in the country until after the Easter season. Court gossip hinted at a scandal that *didn't* involve the queen.

The smell of fresh paint and oils mixed with the scent of beeswax and perfumes from the gentlemen and ladies in attendance. As the musicians finished a *sarabande*, Etienne_Servien made his way through the dancers toward the group of men gathered in the far corner of the room in attendance on the queen. Cardinal Richelieu stood out as the taller of two somber, scarlet figures in a crowd of brightly clad court sycophants. Servien tried to pass unnoticed through the crowd, but failed. The cardinal's attention was drawn toward the swirl in the crowd as Servien passed. He noticed that Servien was making a straight line toward him. *Not a good omen. He usually only does that in an emergency.*

"Your Eminence?" Servien bowed to the cardinal as he arrived. "There is a matter in the kitchens that requires your attention before the banquet is served."

Cardinal Richelieu hesitated just a brief second, as if from irritation at the interruption for so trivial a matter. "Oh, very well!" he said in a huff. Servien nodded slightly. To those nearby, it appeared to simply be a fit of pique on the part of Richelieu toward a servant, but long years together told Richelieu what he needed to know. *So something untoward has come up. And it's important enough that he doesn't want anyone here to find out.*

Once outside the ballroom and alone in the corridor, Richelieu confronted Servien. "Etienne, I do hope this is something more than just a problem with the meal. Her Majesty expects that I will pay close attendance on her. With Louis out of the city, she has to be careful of who she is seen with."

"Your Eminence, there is not a problem with the meal. A *Compagnie* problem has come up and I didn't want your guests to know. A messenger has arrived and is waiting for you in the guard's room off the kitchen. He had the proper code word." Without waiting for an answer, Servien bowed and gestured toward the kitchen area. The cardinal preceded him toward the kitchens. Servien's silence portended ominous news if even a chance passerby was too dangerous to overhear a remark.

A few moments' walk brought the two to the guard room. The guard preceded Servien and the cardinal into the room and waited at attention next to the visitor. He was a short, fat man. The cut of his clothes suggested a merchant ship captain or first mate. Servien introduced the messenger. "Your Eminence, this is Captain Rene Roussard, out of Le Havre. He has news of the Compagnie fur shipment."

As Servien mentioned the fur shipment, the temperature in the room seemed to drop. The cardinal waved, motioning the guard to leave. When the guard started to protest, Richelieu said, "It's all right; he's known to me." After the guard left, Richelieu asked, "And what is the news, Rene?"

Servien stared at the visitor. Evidently the cardinal was very familiar with him. He always had a guard present with strangers. Since he knew just about everyone that the cardinal employed on the king's business, this must be one of the cardinal's *special Compagnie contacts*.

Captain Roussard removed his stocking cap and bowed to the cardinal. "As His Eminence knows, I sail between Le Havre and New France, trading timber and sundries with the colonists." He looked at Servien, as if to apologize for not telling Servien more when they spoke earlier. "When I sailed this last time from New France, I sailed in company with the *Compagnie's* fur ship, as you had directed. Three days out from port, we were attacked by two Dutch *fregate* that had been laying hove to, seemingly waiting for us. When we split up, the Dutch gave chase to both ships. My ship was captured immediately, but the Dutch papers you had supplied, added to my passable Dutch, saw to our release. They seemed to want to avoid any possible entanglement with their own countrymen. The *Compagnie* ship's captain made a good run, but I fear he set too much canvas to try and out run the *Dutchman*, or he may have been hit by the *Dutchman's* bow chaser. In either case, he lost his foremast and was captured. I didn't know what to do. We were unarmed, so as soon as I was released, I sailed on. When we reached Le Havre I came straight here, without telling a soul what had happened."

Captain Roussard appeared much calmer than most agents reporting bad news to the cardinal. Servien pondered what the captain had left unsaid. *Why had the cardinal given a timber ship* false *papers?* Something didn't add up. If the fur shipment had been intercepted, the cardinal should be livid.

Richelieu's calmly asked the captain, "Were you able to do the transfer as I had directed?"

The man nodded vigorously. "*Oui,* the first night from Quebec, we anchored and transferred most of the cargo, as your orders directed. Captain Gilbert was angry, thinking you didn't trust him, but I reassured him that was not the case. As events turned out, your fears were well placed. The Dutch were definitely expecting us."

Richelieu broke into a wry smile. The man had done well to bring the news. The *Compagnie* was in dire financial straits and had been depending on the funds to be realized from the sale of the furs to stave off bankruptcy. But three-fourths of a loaf was better than nothing. His finances and political position would suffer in the short term, once news of the capture became common knowledge. Knowing that *most* of the shipment had made it through safely, before others did, might help him recoup his losses and mitigate the political aspects.

He turned back to Servien, who had waited quietly by the door to make sure they weren't interrupted. "See that this man is rewarded." Roussard's stomach chose that moment to rumble loud enough for all to hear. "And see that he is fed before he goes. He has done me a great service."

Richelieu continued, "Just remember the second half of my instructions. Make sure no one goes ashore with this information for at least a week, and hold off unloading the special cargo until then, too. I'll know who'll have spread the word if this gets out before then." Rene's smile disappeared quickly as he nodded acknowledgement.

"I'll see to it at once, Your Eminence." Servien started to show Roussard out.

6

As they reached the door, Roussard turned to add, "I almost forgot the most important point, Your Eminence. When the Dutch ships left with their prize, they headed north, toward Newfoundland."

"You're positive of this?"

"We kept watch until we lost sight of their sails." Rene then preceded Servien out. They left the cardinal to gather his thoughts before returning to his guests. Servien handed Rene a weighted bag that clinked delightfully and ordered the guard to see he was fed well. As Servien stepped back into the guardroom to see to his master's needs, the cardinal said quietly, in a voice still as death. "After the party, Servien, come to my quarters. We will see what can be done with this opportunity! The time has come to strike back at that Danish drunk."

It was three hours past midnight before the final reveler left the *Palais*. Servien had waited in the study, dozing, until the cardinal could safely break away. When the cardinal entered, foot sore and weary, Servien almost blurted out his question, "Your Eminence, please don't think me presumptuous, but how did you know that the shipment might be intercepted? I've seen nothing in your normal correspondence that even hinted at such a possibility."

Richelieu stroked his beard, debating the wisdom of revealing a source. "I had heard rumors that Dutch ships might be raiding the fishing fleets off the Banks. Given the richness of the prize, I took precautions to insure that at least part of the fur shipment would arrive. What concerns me more is the direction the raiders retired. It seems there is much more going on in the North Atlantic than we've been told. Perhaps our agents in Copenhagen were not as successful as we'd been led to believe in stopping the Danes from sailing. I want an armed trading ship or two dispatched to scout out the area and report back. If Rene is willing, send him as one of them. We may need to shore up our defenses in New France. Begin locating possible assets that could follow up, once we receive the report. Now, go get some rest! This can wait until the morning."

CHAPTER 2

July 1634, lower James Bay

Life had settled into the routine of summer for the Cree tribes around James Bay. Hunting and fishing, to gather and preserve food for the winter, occupied everyone's time from March through October. The long summer days, though, did occasionally leave some time for other activities. Today was a special day for one of the villages on the western shore. There was a coming of age event. Two fishermen paddled a birch bark canoe slowly downstream, still only a short distance from their village. The fishing spot they were headed to was at the mouth of the Cheepash River, but on the opposite shore from the village. The older man in the back used the short stroke of one used to covering long distances and old enough to know not to tire himself out. The young boy in front, already showing signs of tiring, paused to try to see where they were. From the canoe, neither shore of the river was visible. The early morning fog muffled sound and limited sight to mere feet. The summer sun was trying to break through, but the few clear patches quickly filled back in. The boy couldn't hold back his enthusiasm when a fish nearly leaped into the boat, trying to catch a bug hovering above the water. He turned and asked, "Are we close, Grandfather?"

Chief Luther Longspear paused in his paddling and tried to act like he wasn't sure. This was supposed to be Adam's initiation into spear fishing, and the boy still needed to learn patience. As Adam continued to squirm and started to reach for the iron fishing spear lying in the boat's bottom, Luther turned the question around. "What do *you* think? I've told you where we're going, and I've taught you how to find your way. We're not that far from the village. You tell me where we are, Adam."

The boy was so like his father at this age. Always eager for new adventure, but too excited to think. Too bad his father had died before he could complete Adam's training. James had shown a skill in raising Adam alone. Now that he and his wife were dead, and, with his brother missing on a long journey, it fell to the grandparents to raise Adam.

Realizing this was a test, Adam paused to take a deep breath and consider his surroundings. His father had always emphasized, 'Notice the small things and then think!' He noticed that the canoe was rocking on small waves. He reached over the side, dipped his hand in the water and tasted it. *Brackish.* Off to the north, the sound of nesting ducks was barely audible through the fog. "I think the island is somewhere over in that direction," he said, pointing to the north. "Since you've never shown me where your secret fishing spot is, I'm not sure just how far over there."

His grandfather suppressed a smile. The answer showed Adam had thought the question through. Behind the boy, the fog bank broke momentarily and Luther spotted their destination. He paused, trying to look thoughtful. He too tasted the water, just like his grandson, to reinforce the proper habit, and then cupped his ear. After a moment, he held a moistened finger in the air to test the air flow and then pointed the canoe toward the tree stump he'd seen earlier. "Should be just ahead. Prepare to tie us up." After three strong strokes, the dead stump broke through the mist.

Adam looked at his grandfather in awe. *The stories they tell are true! Grandfather always knows where he's at.* Quickly, Adam grabbed the rawhide rope at

10

the front and tied the canoe to the stump. The current slowly pulled the canoe away from shore until the rope was taut. They were about ten feet from the stump. The river bottom was just visible about four feet down, through the bottom growth, and small ciscoes and blue gill minnows seemed to be everywhere. Luther took the rock he used to anchor the canoe and slowly lowered it to the bottom. "We'll stay here until the sun reaches over head. This way the fish won't see your shadow." He pointed to the shadows that reached toward the shore. The sun had finally broken through the fog and was quickly burning it off.

Adam carefully picked up the spear and hefted it to gauge the canoe's reaction to the movement. He carefully wrapped the spear's retrieval strap around his wrist. He *really* didn't want to have to dive after it in the cold waters. He knelt on the furs his grandmother had sent along to ease the strain of the wait. Luther leaned back on his furs in the bow of the canoe and studied Adam's technique. Adam settled back on his haunches, carefully keeping his shadow away from his search area. It was only a few minutes before the larger fish returned to hunt the school of minnows darting back and forth among the rocks and plants. A trio of walleyes caught Adam's eye and he watched them as they stalked the minnows. They suddenly flashed into the school, intent on their prey. In his excitement, Adam cast the spear, neatly spearing the tail of a small ciscoe trapped in the middle of the trio of walleyes. As Adam retrieved the spear, Luther shook his head in amazement. "I don't think that will be much of a meal. Next time, focus on one fish. You focused on the group and missed all of them." Adam was downcast at the result. The small fish used the pause to wiggle off the spear and splashed back into the water. As it tried to swim away, one of the walleyes darted back and swallowed it whole. Adam settled back down to resume his hunt.

The walleye's success encouraged its comrades to return. This time, Adam tracked the movements of a single target, and when the spear splashed this time, he was rewarded with a walleye that was nearly as long as his arm. He carefully lifted the fish out of the water and set the spear and fish down in the canoe. Removing a stone knife from a sheath at his waist, Adam used it to free the fish from the spear tines and placed it in a wicker basket. After tying the basket to a lead, he set it over the side to keep the fish fresh in the cool water. Luther watched, with frequent nods of approval, as Adam finished his tasks. The boy's actions had been swift and precise. Luther settled back on the furs to enjoy the warm sunlight. The slow rocking from the waves promised a quiet, relaxing day of fishing. "Wait a few minutes for the fish to calm down and let the big ones return. Then try again." Adam nodded quietly and resumed his watch.

Out on the bay, the fog banks were slowly dissipating in the east. Adam spied two walleye circling back into shore, seemingly unconcerned as to the fate of the third in their group. Hunger, and a ready supply of prey, drove out all thoughts of danger. Luck, though, was on their side. The school of minnows stayed just far enough away from the canoe that Adam didn't want to chance a throw. Finally, one of the walleyes darted in for a strike and the school broke back toward the shore. The other walleye tried to cut them off but came into range. Adam cast the spear and was rewarded with his second catch of the day. As he held it up, he cried out, shaking the spear, "Look grandfather!"

Luther had been dozing and was startled by the cry. "Be careful! You'll lose the fish shaking it that way."

Adam dropped the spear into the canoe. "No grandfather, look!" He pointed with his arm, past Luther's right side. "There's something out on the bay."

Luther turned and nearly upset the canoe. Far out on the bay, just emerging from a dying fogbank, were what looked like a grove of grey trees. Adam had stood up, trying to get a little better view. Luther quickly pulled him back down and hissed, "Be careful! We have no idea who they are or what they intend for us. Pull us back to the stump. I need you to carry a message to the village to warn them we have visitors."

Adam started hauling in the rawhide rope. "*Who, or what,* are they, grandfather? Have you seen them before?"

Luther tried to get a better sight, but the fog still obscured the visitors. "I saw something like them, a few years ago. *They* were friendly, but warned us that there were others like them that weren't to be trusted. I have no idea which ones these might be. I want you to run to the village and warn them to prepare to hide in the woods, if the visitors go upriver. I'll paddle out and meet them alone. Better that one old man should sacrifice himself than the whole village be destroyed if they are enemies."

Adam wanted to protest that he should stay and help, but Luther's glare left the protest unspoken. The canoe bumped up against the stump and Adam slipped over the side into the cool, knee deep water. The bottom was sandy and he was able to quickly reach the shore without losing his moccasins. He started to turn once more to protest, but Luther pointed at him with his paddle. "Get to the village as quickly as possible, but don't take foolish risks. Your grandmother should be on this side of the river, helping gather berries. Tell her what you've seen and that I said to gather up all those that are nearby. Take as much food and tools as they can and go to the forest, south of the village. They should also try to hide any canoes, if there's time, so that the village isn't easily spotted from the river. If these men are friendly, I'll be back before sundown. If I'm not, you must not try to rescue me. Now go!" Luther grabbed the rope and loosened it from the stump. He pushed off with his paddle and turned toward the open water. Without a backward glance he started paddling toward the visitors.

With his grandfather's injunction for haste still ringing in his ears, Adam broke into an easy lope along the riverbank. Thankfully, the shoreline on this side of the river was mostly sand, and he could follow it until just below the village. He'd have to head inland when he reached the stream, and pick his way across on the tangle of trees that had washed upstream in the spring flood. The slight bend in the river at the stream had allowed the current to deposit debris there, during the previous spring flood, which formed a precarious crossing. As he jogged along, he worried about his grandfather. If these were the same people that had visited before, he *should* have recognized them. The tales he had heard mentioned only one of the large canoes. Those visitors had spent the winter with his village and had brought them many gifts. His grandfather's spear was a token of their friendship. One of the visitors had told his family about their gods. Grandfather had been impressed by the stories, and had been baptized and changed his name. He'd also had his sons and grandson baptized, and had given them their new, Christian, names. He was just barely able to recall the face and kindly voice of the white man who had baptized him, but that was all he could recall about the visitors.

His day dreaming almost landed him in the trouble his grandfather had warned him to avoid. He managed to stop just short of the embankment that dropped precipitously down to the stream. Only the shadow of the old tree that anchored the soil and kept the stream from cutting down the bank saved him from a cold, wet swim. Adam paused to catch his breath. The run had gone faster than he'd expected. The excitement had added speed to his pace, but was beginning to tire him out. He leaned against the tree trunk to catch his breath. *Grandfather trusted me to be smart! I have to make sure I get there in time.* He pushed off and headed upstream to the logjam, where he could cross.

As he approached the tangle of debris in the stream, he surveyed the site carefully. At first, nothing appeared to have changed since he had crossed it the previous week. Then a movement caught his eye. On the far bank, the large birch tree that anchored the jam on that side had finally been undercut by the stream. It was still holding the neighboring branches and logs down with the weight of the remaining dirt at its roots. But if you watched closely, small quivers ran through the branches when the current hit the roots just right. He could go a little further upstream, but he would have to swim and the water was still *really cold*. He eyed the jam again and decided. *It* should *still hold him*. Adam carefully slid down the bank to the rocks on his side of the stream. An old, weathered tree trunk was firmly buried in the silt, offering a solid footing to reach the nearest tangle of branches. This wasn't like the spring, when they tried to see who could be the fastest across. He was heavier now and the jam was starting to untangle.

As if on cue, a small tree just ahead came loose and was swept away by the current. The branch he was balanced on started to shift. A loud snap underfoot signaled that the time for caution was past. He leaped to catch the next snag just as the center of the debris broke loose. He took three quick steps toward the birch roots, when his foot slipped and was trapped in between a crotch in a pine limb and a branch underneath. Reaching down to try to free his foot, he couldn't get a strong enough grip on the lower branch. The bark had rotted away in the water and left a slimy coating on the wood. More ominous rumbling warned that the jam was ready to break free. If he couldn't free his foot quickly, he could be swept under as the jam broke. He kept trying to pull the foot free, but it just pulled the lower branch tighter to the crotch he had slipped through. Another small tree broke free as he struggled. As it was pulled from the tangle, a weathered branch fell from the pile overhead and almost brained him.

As he went to push it away, Adam realized he had just been given the means to his escape. He took the branch and shoved it between the restraining branches. With his other foot, he stomped on the lever and forced the lower branch just far enough down to release his foot. He twisted quickly and reached the birch roots and safety. As he pulled himself up the tree to shore a loud crash announced the final breakup of the logjam. Adam flopped on the ground and took a deep breath in relief at his narrow

15

escape. The birch tree remained; but even as he watched, the stream was already eating away at the remaining earth. He levered himself up and resumed his jog toward the berry grounds.

CHAPTER 3

Captain Luke Foxe surveyed the approaching shore. The copies of up-time maps he had, showed that the river ahead should be the Cheepash River, where one of the original Hudson Bay Company forts had been located. It was also the site where Captain James had over wintered with the local tribe on his last voyage. Hopefully, the tribal leaders would welcome his group as much as they had Captain James. Otherwise, it was going to be a *really long* trip back to Newfoundland. A shout from the crow's nest drew his attention to an approaching canoe.

Luther slowly approached the lead ship. There was a flurry of activity at the bow of the ship. As he paused to consider which side to approach, the large hook on the far side fell noisily into the water. A man, who was hanging over the front of the boat, was busily coiling up a rope with a weight on it. The nearer side seemed to offer the safest approach. Nearby splashes signaled that the other ships had dropped their hooks too. From his past visits to his friend's ship before he left, Luther recognized the battens on the side of the boat where he could tie off his canoe and board.

Strange, white faces of men with beards and women with head coverings lined the side of the ship as he paddled up to the battens. Now would be the best time if they simply wanted to kill Luther. A large rock over the side into the canoe and he would freeze in the water before he could reach the shore.

A young, red headed man leaned out of an opening above the battens and called out, in passable Cree, that he was welcome to come aboard. Luther fumbled for a moment, trying to secure the hide line. As he climbed very slowly up the side, another voice in Cree called out, "Surely you haven't aged so much that we have to send a rope chair to help you up, *father!'* Luther missed the slime covered batten with his foot and almost fell into the water. A desperate grasp at the edge of the entry port above him saved him and the redhead helped pull him up the last steps. The smile on the young man's face and evident concern helped reassure Luther that he probably was among friends. Looking around frantically, Luther tried to locate the source of the earlier comment that almost caused his fall. A large crowd had gathered to catch a glimpse of the visitor. Pushing his way through was an older, white man who had the look of a leader. He was dressed in a linen coat and breeches, a broad brimmed hat clutched at his side. The young man who had saved him was still at his elbow and said in halting Cree, "Chief Longbow, this is our leader, Captain Foxe. We welcome you on board the *København.*"

The older man extended a hand in friendship. He said something quickly to the younger man that Luther couldn't quite make out completely. It was a name and then something about meeting. One thing was certain, though. They spoke English, just like his friend Captain James, so they were probably friendly. Or at least they weren't the Spanish or French he'd been warned about. The younger man, whose name sounded like Svend, nodded and motioned for the crowd to clear back. He started to try and stammer something out in Cree, but Luther said, "I do speak English. Captain James taught me when he stayed with us."

Svend looked relieved. "That's good. I had just about exhausted my Cree. I think there's someone here who's anxious to see you." As the crowd finally parted, a young Inuit woman slowly helped a young Cree male across the deck. He was wrapped in bandages around his back and shoulder, and his steps were very wobbly.

"Father, your son has returned, as Captain James promised." Joseph Longspear smiled at his father's astonishment.

Luther was so stunned he couldn't move. A tear slowly trickled down his cheek. As it hit the deck, the reverie broke and Luther rushed over to embrace his son. The young woman intercepted him before he could crush his son in a welcoming embrace. "Please be careful. You'll undo all the healing in one hug."

Luther finally *looked* and the extent of his son's injuries stopped him dead in his tracks. "Joseph, what happened to you?"

Joseph finished hobbling up and very carefully hugged his father. "It's a long story, Father. Can I find a comfortable place to sit before I start?" Luther nodded, still dumbfounded at his son's unexpected return. The young Inuit woman went to find some seats.

The first mate, John Barrow, and two sailors, soon produced, like magicians, three legged stools for the group. John motioned for the group to sit. "Here you go. It's way too nice of a day to spend down below." Then, in direct contradiction of his comment, John proceeded to shoo the onlookers below decks to offer the group some privacy.

As the crowd thinned out, Luther had a chance to study his surroundings. The ship was very similar to the one Captain James had sailed. The other ships anchored nearby appeared smaller, but the bustle of activity on their decks continued. People had gathered at the sides facing the ship he was on, presumably to catch a glimpse of him. Captain Foxe finished giving orders to his crew and slowly eased himself down on the stool.

He appeared to be close to Luther's age, with a mustache and a thinning hairline. His clothes and boots were salt stained. The cloth was much finer than any he'd seen before, and the metal buckles brought an unexpected surge of envy. Metal among the Cree was a rare commodity. He turned his attention back to the group around his son. The young red head seemed to be a good friend of his son and hovered close in support. Joseph was dressed in the pants of the white men, with his upper body still wrapped in dressings from the bear attack, and a light blanket draped carefully around his shoulders to fend off the light breeze that had sprung up.

The Inuit woman who sat by his side was definitely more than a friend. The looks she kept giving Joseph were very proprietary. As soon as he could get Joseph alone, he would find out what their relationship meant. In the meantime, the ship held many clues as to the visitors' intentions. This ship, unlike his friend Captain James' ship, carried many women. From the description of the voyage his friend had given him when they wintered together, it was very unusual to see women on ships, unless they were planning to stay. His plan for Joseph to accompany Captain James to learn about the white men may have been more important than he had realized when he sent Joseph on the voyage.

A slight cough from Captain Foxe interrupted Luther's musings. "I'm delighted that you were the first person to meet us. Had you received some advance notice of our arrival?" Captain Foxe paused to remove his hat and wipe his brow. "This weather is a definite improvement over the earlier part of our voyage. Your son was telling me about his home, but he never mentioned that the weather was so fair." Luke seemed to be uneasy and paused, waiting for a reply.

Luther let the pause stretch out. Experience had taught him the first one to break a silence generally lost the negotiations and this session had all the signs of an important outcome. Luke finally continued, "I suspect you're curious as to why we are here?"

"My friend, Captain James, warned me that white men might come with bad intentions. Are you one of those? He said they would come to steal, rape, and murder my people. That the French and Spaniards were not to be trusted"."

Luke took a deep breath. "Your friend was wise, but we are not French, nor Spanish. I'm an Englishman, but our group is from Denmark, a small country far to the east, across the great sea. Captain James sailed with us when we left Denmark, but he stayed behind at our last stop to lead the people who remained there. We seek trade and friendly relations with the tribes in this land. Your son has told us much about you. He said that you are a peaceful and honorable people. I would like to speak to you and your tribe on these matters."

Luther held up his hand. "There will be time for this. But for now, my son, who was thought to be lost, has returned. I would like to return to my village to give them the news and rejoice." He smiled before continuing, "And to tell them that the warning I had sent was unneeded. You are welcome to accompany me with a small party of your own people. It is just a short trip by small boats up the river."

"Chief Longspear, I would be delighted." Luke turned to his first mate. "John, please prepare the longboat for a short trip. You'll be in charge while I'm gone. Svend, you'll come with, along with Joseph and Karima and the doctor."

John leaned close to whisper to Luke. He looked fit to be tied. "But, Captain, what about guards? If they mean you harm, you'll be unprotected. Please take at least two or three men."

"John, we're here in peace. If they are hostile, two or three wouldn't make a bit of difference, and they would be an insult if they are friendly.

21

We want to live here, and they'll be our neighbors. It makes no sense to start off on the wrong foot. Just have the boat ready in fifteen minutes."

"Aye, aye Captain."

Luke walked over to where Joseph and his father were catching up on events in the village. "We'll be ready to leave in a short time. I suggest that Joseph ride in my boat. It will be safer as far as getting his wounds wet."

Luther nodded agreement. "I should start now. I sent my grandson away earlier to warn the village that strangers had arrived. I may need some time to round up everyone from their retreats. Joseph can give you directions to the best spot to land near the village."

Luther gingerly embraced Joseph again, and then padded across the deck to the entry port. As he turned to descend, he spotted Captain Foxe standing near the boat that was being prepared to be lowered. An unspoken thank you passed between them, for the safe return of his son. After the barely perceptible nod, Luther turned and carefully descended the battens to his canoe. A quick tug untied the line and he settled down in the rear and shoved off. His powerful strokes helped hide his sobs of joy as the canoe headed upstream. *My son lives!*

Captain Foxe watched enviously, as Chief Longspear paddled away. The chief just had to let his people know all was well. Luke's months-long voyage was at an end, but a new world's problems were about to land squarely on his shoulders. Ever since the loss of Sir Thomas Roe when the *Hamburg* was lost in the storm, he had gone from crisis to crisis and the weight of leadership had grown heavier. Now he had to negotiate with the natives to secure a living place for his people. Failure in the hours ahead meant ruin for many and possible death for those around him. For the first time in his life, his sailing skills couldn't save him. He needed to be a diplomat and, at this moment, he truly missed Sir Thomas. Polished speech was not something he was any good at. He'd always been gruff and unpolished in dealing with people, but at least he'd been honest. Hopefully that would be enough.

A loud squeal broke Luke's reverie, as a spar was swung around for the bosun's chair to assist Joseph into the longboat. *One problem at a time. First I've got to convince the chief we're* worthy *to be his neighbors!* One of the sailors grabbed a frayed rope and started to run it through the block on the end of the spar for the chair. John Barrow noticed it even before Luke could shout a warning and read the sailor the riot act for his negligence. Luke let John handle the sailor's error. Years together had taught Luke to trust John's judgment. He sighed, trying to ease the knot of fear in his stomach. *Just what I need. Having to tell the chief we'd let his son drown would not be a good way to start the meeting.* The chair was finally secured with a new rope and swung out to the rail where Joseph was waiting with Svend and Karima. Svend assisted Joseph into the seat and Karima gently tied down the rope fastenings to secure him for the short ride down to the longboat.

John double checked to make sure everything was secure and then leaned over the side to make sure the boat hadn't drifted out of position. A quick spin of his hand and the sailors standing nearby hauled away on the lines. The chair rose smoothly into the air and the spar was swung out. With the practiced eye of a cargo loader, John gauged the position and motioned for a slight adjustment further aft. Luke stood by, not saying a word. John was the best on board for this work and jiggling his elbow would only have bad results. Joseph was laughing and said something to Karima in Cree that made her blush and sent Svend into a coughing fit. That started Joseph laughing and the chair swinging.

"Hold!" shouted John. He had seen the look of surprise, mixed with fear on Luke's face and realized things were getting out of hand. "As soon as you three can compose yourselves, we'll try to finish this job. That water's a might cold for swimming." The sailors holding the line stifled their laughs and waited for John's signal. Once the chair quit swinging, John motioned for them to pay out the lines and lower the chair. It settled squarely in the center of the longboat without raising a ripple. Joseph unfastened the restraining rope and shifted to the nearest thwart. Once he was clear, the chair was hoisted back on board.

Svend started to reach for a rope that was still dangling over the side to help Karima down the battens but Luke called out, "Don't forget your drawing paper and pencils. I want this meeting recorded for posterity." Svend mumbled an apology to Karima, handed her the rope and then hurried past her to the nearby hatchway. He returned a few moments later, still trying to adjust his backpack of drawing supplies. Captain Foxe was descending via the battens, so Svend simply grabbed the rope that was still hanging there and went down hand over hand like a monkey. As Luke settled himself on a thwart with his back to Svend, he yelled up for Svend to hurry. Svend's quiet reply from just behind him of, "I'm already here, father," resulted in Luke jumping two inches off the thwart. He turned and glared at Svend, but the stifled laughter of the boat's crew ended in a father's simple shake of the head. *My stepson is growing up so fast.*

Luke gave a quiet order to shove off and then turned toward the aftercastle, where John was leaning over the rail. "Mr. Barrow, I'll be back by nightfall, or will send the boat back with word on how things are progressing. Let the other ships know where we stand. In the meantime, start crews to sweeping the river for hidden obstacles. If we're going to settle here, we need to know as much as we can about the waters hereabout." John still looked pained about the captain's decision to leave the guards behind, but acknowledged the new order with a nod and turned to tell off the crews for the charting work.

As the rowers gave way, Luke reached for the spyglass he'd brought to study the river banks. The shore to the north was a marsh, with low sandbars marking the shore line. Suddenly, a white cloud of tundra swans rose into the air. Something had spooked the flock, but Luke couldn't see whether it was a human or some predator. The graceful birds circled, but then settled back down. Evidently it was a false alarm. Luke turned the glass toward the southern shore. A brief flash of brown among the bushes hinted at a bear on a foraging hunt. The southern river bank seemed to hold the best promise for a watch tower site to provide an early warning post for the new settlement.

Captain James' notes said the best anchorage he'd discovered lay on the south side of the islands upstream from the river's mouth. As he steered the longboat to port, Luke scanned the approaching islands. They were covered in low brush to the shoreline, with Tamarack pines covering the interior. The trees were a distinct change from the pines of his childhood. These trees were tall and spindly, with short branches that seemed ready to fall off at the slightest touch. *It's a good thing I had John load the sawmill for this voyage. There are enough trees that we should be able to erect adequate shelter for the winter. I just wish we hadn't lost all the heating stoves with the* Hamburg. *The loss of those, and the foodstuffs she carried, may come back to haunt us.* Sounds from the rowers broke his concentration. The current had picked up as they cleared the island's protection. "Put your backs into it, lads. It's a good sign that we should have an adequate depth for the ships here. Hopefully, that's our new home off to starboard." The rowers seemed to dig in and the rhythm of the stroke increased, even while they took furtive glances at the passing shoreline.

Up front, the three young folks were avidly discussing plans for the coming days. Luke listened for a moment and then broke in. "That's all very well and good, but what if they don't want us here?" That had been Luke's hidden fear since they had left Copenhagen. He watched Joseph to try one more time to get some sense of where he stood on the issue. "I'll respect your father's decision, no matter which way it goes. There is so much we can do for each other. I'm just afraid I'm not the best spokesman for us. Sir Thomas had such a way with words and could express the matter so much better."

Joseph held up his hand. "Captain Foxe, I'm sure you've guessed by now that my father sent me to study your peoples because of that very question. The one thing I can say with certainty is that I believe you are an honorable man and will try to keep your word. I did learn about what history says would have happened to my people without the city in Germany. I also have an inkling of what the knowledge they brought back could mean to my people. If the Ring of Fire didn't prove anything else, it proved that nothing is so written in stone that men of good intentions can't change the future. Your treatment of Karima's people, to whom you owe nothing, speaks well of your intentions. I will report to my father what I have learned. Rest assured, you will be listened to with an open mind."

Joseph pointed toward an island ahead, off the starboard bow. "There's the island our village is on. You'll need to steer around the smaller island beyond to reach the beach that's hidden around that spit of land. You should be able to see some boats soon." As if at Joseph's bidding, a small group of canoes appeared, heading towards the longboat. Leading them was Chief Longspear, with a younger boy at the prow of the canoe, waving wildly. The reception by the others, all males with weapons just barely visible, resting in the canoes, was more restrained, but still apparently friendly.

CHAPTER 4

Luke studied the approaching flotilla. The first thing he noticed was that the chief was *not* carrying a weapon. While it was evident that the other canoes had weapons, none were being displayed. The decision to leave the guards behind was looking better all the time. Less chance of some idiot causing an unnecessary incident; and while they might have weapons, it said their new allies weren't prone to foolish risks either.

Chief Longspear's canoe was the first to arrive. The young boy at the prow was so excited that he jumped in the river and swam up to the longboat. The rowers tossed the oars so he could grab hold of the side safely. The youngster shook the water from his head and called out, "Uncle, welcome home."

Joseph stared in amazement. "Adam, is that really you? You've grown since I've left." He turned to Luke. "This is my brother's son. Can he come aboard? The water's cold and he's just a foolish boy *who should know better!*" The reproach was softened by a smile and a soft laugh. Luke motioned for the two sailors to help him aboard, but Adam was up, over the side, before they could even sort out who would hold their oars. Dripping water, he gingerly gave his uncle a hug and started telling him news of the family, in Cree. When he got to the news on his father, Luke sensed that something was wrong. Joseph told Adam to wait, as he explained to the others.

"It seems that my brother and his wife have both died while I was gone. Adam's mother died in child birth last year and James was bitten by a wolf and died of the slobbering sickness this past winter." Karima reached out and slipped her hand into his to comfort him. Joseph smiled at the act, then continued, "It seems we're even more in need of your medicines than even I imagined."

He seemed to give himself a mental shake before continuing. "Enough of family reunions for now. It seems my father was able to gather the other leaders of the tribe to greet you." While they'd been talking the other canoes had reached the longboat and now surrounded it.

Chief Longspear spoke loud enough for all to hear. "Please accept my apologies for my grandson's exuberance. I hope he was no bother."

Luke clapped the boy on his shoulder and chuckled. "None needed. If he's brave enough to endure the cold water, I'm proud to meet him." The reply was translated and was met with a chorus of laughs and nods of approval from the others.

Luther pointed back the way they'd come. "If you'll follow us, I'll show you to the landing by our village. The women have returned and are preparing a feast in honor of Joseph's return." Luke called for the rowers to give way and steered the boat toward the channel between the islands. The fact that Luther had not mentioned their staying was not lost on him.

As they approached the clearing where other canoes were already beached, Luke noticed the signs of recent flooding. He called out to Joseph to make himself heard over the celebration noise that was already coming from the village. "Does this site flood often? It looks like there was high water here recently."

"Oh yes! At least every three or four springs we have to move to higher ground if the ice piles up where the river meets the bay. It usually only lasts for a few days, and then we move back. It helps to clean out the garbage around the village." Joseph turned quickly away as a friend hailed him from the beach. The longboat chose that moment to run aground about five yards from the shoreline.

Captain Foxe sized up the distance from the bank and weighed it against Joseph's need to stay relatively dry. He reached a quick decision. "Ship oars and over the side. Pull us up as far as possible. We're at low tide and we need to make sure it doesn't float off while we're here. Set a stake at least a boat length up the bank and tie us off."

Captain Foxe reached down for the small sea chest he'd brought along. "William, be careful taking this ashore. It contains gifts for our friends and I don't want them to get wet." He heaved himself over the side and helped stabilize the boat as Svend and Karima helped Joseph disembark. They then had to keep the well-wishers back so they wouldn't accidentally re-injure Joseph.

As Luke stepped through the debris piled up along the water's edge, he paused to study the crowd that had gathered to celebrate Joseph's return. More people were coming down the path that led to the village. The Cree appeared to be well fed and were clothed in mostly furs and skins, decorated with quills and feathers. The men were in breechcloths and leggings, with the women in dresses. There were a large number of children hanging back toward the tree line, with a few mothers carrying babies on backboards standing guard, keeping the youngsters out of the crowd. The chief was speaking to Joseph, along with Adam and an older woman, who was undoubtedly Joseph's mother. She was crying and praising Jesus for the return of her last son. Svend and Karima hovered nearby, trying to remain inconspicuous. Luther spotted Captain Foxe and motioned for him to join the group.

"Captain Foxe, this is my wife Ruth. She has the women preparing a welcome home meal for Joseph. Please extend an invitation to your sailors to join us. It will be ready by the time we have finished our discussion with the elders." He indicated the path leading into the trees.

Luke nodded, "My thanks. Svend, let the crew know they can come up and join the feast. Remind them they are to be on their best behavior!" Svend took his leave of Joseph and Karima and trotted back to the long-boat to let the crew know of their good fortune. Fresh food would be a real treat for them.

Luke walked up the path, trailing the chief and his family. As they broke through the trees, the village spread out before them. There were numer-ous tepees scattered throughout the clearing, with two larger frame houses covered in bark. A large cooking pit was being attended to by the older women of the tribe, just in front of what turned out to be the village's meeting house. Ruth shooed Joseph over to the family's quarters, but he demurred. "I'll have to help translate for the captain at his meeting." He walked gingerly over to the meeting house door and waited. Ruth took Karima under her wing and the two women stepped over to the cooking pit.

Introductions were started. The chief held aside the hide door on the meeting house and Luke and Joseph entered. Svend came trotting up the path and Luke motioned for him to join them. They all entered the house and waited for their eyes to adjust to the dim light and fire smoke. The elders that had greeted the longboat were all gathered, waiting expectantly.

Luke took a deep breath and then bowed to the assembly. *This is it. Relax and do your best. I still wish Sir Thomas was with me, but Joseph and Svend will have to do.* "Svend, please bring me the chest." Svend hoisted the chest and set it in front of Luke. Keeping eye contact with the elders, Luke reached down and unhooked the catch and opened the chest. Lifting the top tray, he showed it to his audience and then launched into his prepared speech in Cree. "We are here to fulfill Captain James' promise to return Joseph to his people. We wish to be friends with the Cree. These gifts are a glimpse of a possible future for our peoples." He passed the tray to Lu-ther, who proceeded to show the tray to the others. Luke turned to Joseph,

"Will you help translate the next part. I'm afraid I've used up all the Cree that I know."

"You did well Captain. I will do my best. Just remember to keep it short and give me enough time."

As the first tray finished its round, Luke brought the chest over for the elders to view. While the tray had included some items for home use, the rest of the chest was composed of metal tools. "These tools are readily available in my country. If we work together, these can help make your work easier too." He waited for Joseph to translate. "There are many deposits of metal to the south that would be useful in developments that are coming in my home country. What we hope to do is work with the peoples that are here to form a partnership to develop these metals. It will take many more people than we have to make this happen. I am asking you if you will accept us as neighbors and partners." He turned to Joseph and nodded that he was done. Joseph stumbled over a few words that had no Cree equivalent, and even asked for help on developments from Svend, but seemed to feel that he had gotten the gist of the intent across.

Luke took a deep breath and proceeded to ask the important question. "We are interested in settling on the larger island to the east. Would you be willing to let us settle there?" As Joseph translated, he studied the faces of the elders. Outside of some looks of surprise, the elders hid their thoughts well. Chief Longspear looked around at the others and got a solid endorsement of silence. No one appeared to want to be the first to speak. After a long, awkward moment of silence, he finally decided to speak.

"Captain Foxe, it seems I'm left to speak for my people. As you no doubt have realized, I sent Joseph with Captain James to learn more about your people. I suspected that this moment would come someday. I have not had a chance to speak with Joseph about what he learned, but I am prepared to make this concession. You and your people may disembark and build on the island you've mentioned. After we have had an opportunity to see if your deeds match your words and you show you are good neighbors, we will then discuss a long term arrangement. In either case, you will be permitted to build a trading post and maintain it as long as you comport yourselves as good neighbors. Is that satisfactory?"

Luke paused to consider the offer. What was left unsaid was that Joseph's report would play a major part in the tribe's decision. From the hints Joseph had dropped earlier, that shouldn't be a problem. As long as some idiot didn't do something stupid and offend the tribe, it should work. He'd just have to make sure that the chances of that happening were minimized. "I agree. I will want to work with you as soon as we can to make sure that our customs and laws don't give offense and that we understand what you expect in those same areas." He held out his hand to Luther and a simple handshake was good enough.

Chief Longspear studied Captain Foxe and hoped he'd read the man correctly. The future seemed to hold much promise if the man was sincere. His last words were more than he'd expected for someone who undoubtedly had the strength to simply take what he wanted. The discussion with Joseph would have to happen tonight. For the moment, there was a welcome home feast that was wafting fragrant aromas through the open door. Luther motioned to the source of the aromas. "Let us join the others in the feast for my son's safe return."

CHAPTER 5

The feast had lasted well into the night. Captain Foxe had sent the longboat back to give the fleet the good news, but had stayed overnight with Svend in a tipi. Snores showed the toll the long day had taken on them. In a neighboring tipi, Luther finally had Joseph alone to discuss the issue that was upper most in his mind. "So tell me my son, what did you learn about our guests during your stay with them? Are they good or evil, and can they be trusted?"

Joseph held up his hands to slow the avalanche of questions. He had been expecting these questions after the earlier meeting. "One question at a time father." He paused, staring into the flames. These were the same questions he had asked himself, over and over, during the voyages over and back. Each time he thought he had the answers, the questions changed. He took a deep breath and then started, "The answer is....complicated. Something happened which Captain James was not aware of when he visited us. There is a story, which sounds impossible, but appears to be true, that a city from the far future has appeared amongst these white men. It has brought back great knowledge and stirred up many new conflicts. Even the white men who have seen this city cannot agree why and how it appeared, just that it has. Those that I spoke to agree that it contains the knowledge of what was supposed to happen in the future, but now that future is changing because of this knowledge. Everything there is so different from what we are familiar with. The lands across the ocean are as Captain James said, large and heavily populated. Their sheer numbers raise questions I had never even considered. The main village I was in, for most of the time there, would extend from here to the river's mouth and be three times as wide. Simply feeding themselves is a major undertaking like we've never faced. They have wide belts of farms that surround their city. Maintaining order requires one special set of warriors. Keeping their enemies at bay requires another set. They have more warriors in just that city than our entire clan has people. They fight each other over issues than I cannot grasp. Many claim they are poor, but their poor people have more than most of the families here." He shook his head in bewilderment.

"I met with some men, who called themselves members of 'Committees for Correspondence'. Many of them are from the poor that I mentioned. They talked about the oppression their leaders inflict on their subjects. They told me tales of what will happen across these lands to our people, whom they call 'Indians', at the hands of the white men. In that other future, we were crowded on small parcels of land and lived at the white man's sufferance. But I also learned many of these stories were the result of Spanish, French and English actions far to the south. These Danes never were involved in that future.

"This is one of the changes that seem to be occurring. Their leaders include a number that are viewed as outcasts by other groups, just as we 'Indians' were viewed as outcasts by the English and Spanish. They seem to have some sympathy for what would have happened to our people in that other time. They also have knowledge that can help our people. Their doctor treated me after the bear attack and I tell you, if it weren't for his medicines, you would have no sons." Joseph paused to let the implications set in. He had been given the full story by his mother how his brother had died of the drooling sickness after he'd been attacked by wolves.

His father finally nodded for him to continue. "I've also seen what one white man was able to do for Karima's people. Her Inuit village is far ahead of any others I saw. Captain Foxe has promised to send a teacher there to help them even further. From all that I've seen, Captain Foxe is an honorable man who will keep his word, and he sits high in the council of this 'Hudson's Bay Company' that sent this group here."

Luther interrupted, "That's all well and good, as long as he lives, but what about the future? You said not all white men are honorable. What happens to us if one of them should succeed this Captain Foxe?"

Joseph sat silently, contemplating the flames and his father's question. *How do I answer without sounding arrogant or absurd? We have to change if we're to survive, but change is a frightening thing. This village, our clan, could never stand up to the white men in battle. But Captain Foxe has talked about needing allies and workers to overcome the obstacles he faces in taming this land and bettering the lives of all that live here. Education and medicine will go a long way to helping us survive the changes that are coming. We just need to stand together to reach our potential.*

An idea that he had discussed with Karima coalesced as he sat there. "Father, I have thought about your question long and hard. I think the answer lies in how Karima's people have worked with the white man who lived among them. The white men know much that we have never even suspected. This town from the future has brought back much knowledge that these white men from across the ocean never suspected. If we insist on being provided teachers to learn what we need to adapt and grow, we may be able to change our fate. The medicines they have mastered will change our people forever. If we have fewer deaths, we will need the new knowledge to grow more crops and catch more fish. Karima's people are already doing this."

Joseph stood up and stood by the fire. He stared down at his father, from a position of authority. "Most importantly, *we must become one people!* These white men have learned that lesson and practice it to extremes.

There is strength in numbers. The Cree people must become a united people and secure our lands. The white men have a strange notion that the land is owned by individuals. They raise crops and build permanent houses and take metals from the ground. To them, the land is something to be used, like a spear or a hoe. If they work the land, they expect they will reap the benefits of the crops they sow. Captain Foxe's request to settle nearby and explore for metals needs to be thought over very carefully. Where they settle will be their land for all time. You need to make sure that the Cree have their lands for all time also. You need to make sure he understands that you do not speak for all Cree, just this village. I think his main interests are in lands to the south. My friend Svend has talked about this often. There are metals there that the white men value highly. I think we need to summon the other clans to council to discuss how we will deal with the Danes as a Cree nation, just as the Danes are a nation. We need to be able to direct where this new future leads, not be dictated to by a stronger party. I think the Danes will be honorable, as long as we don't squabble amongst ourselves."

Luther sat and watched the fire's twisting flames. *I sent away a boy and he has come back a man.* His description of the white man's land seemed as twisted and shifting as the flames, but as Joseph said, there were many benefits to be had, just like the heat of a fire. Just so the tribe didn't end up being burned, getting too close to the flames. His back twinged from the exertions of the past days. He wasn't getting any younger. He stared for a few more moments, sorting out the choices. "I'll send messengers out in the morning. Where will you hold this council?"

◆ ◆ ◆

Svend woke up to see Joseph standing in the entrance to the tipi, holding the flap back to let in the early morning sun. "Rise and shine, brother, you need to help me write up a treaty for the captain to sign. As he said, you need to get the settlers landed quickly so that you can get started on your crops." Svend rubbed the sleep from his eyes and sat up from the fur covered bedding with a low groan. Joseph laughed, "You sound like one of the old men. Not used to sleeping on solid ground yet? You're going to be here for a while so you better get used to it quickly."

Joseph gave him a nudge with a moccasined foot to help him along. "The jakes are out behind the meeting house by the trees. As soon as you're finished, breakfast is cooking at my father's tipi. I'll see you there, and don't forget your paper and quill." Svend gave him a halfhearted salute and stumbled out to perform his morning ablutions.

An hour later, after a breakfast of duck eggs and venison, Svend perched on a stump on the sunny side of a small grove of trees with his pad and started to write out the terms Joseph and Chief Longspear laid out. Even with the shelter of the trees, there was a strong enough breeze to make writing difficult. Since he was working on a draft for the treaty, the smudges and smears were less bothersome at the start. As he went along, Svend noticed that more and more smears were showing up on the sheets. He paused and then realized his shirt sleeve had been dragging across the wet ink as the pages flapped in the breeze. Muttering imprecations under his breath, Svend reached in his pack and drew out some string to use as a page holder. The pad slipped from his hands and fell open to a picture Svend had drawn of Agnes.

Chief Longspear picked the pad up and asked who the lady was. "She and I were going to be married, but her ship disappeared during our trip across the ocean," Svend replied wistfully.

Chief Longstreet studied the drawing intently. "You sound as if you think she's still alive. Did you not see her ship sink?"

"No, we were caught in a severe storm. Our ship nearly sank. The last we saw of the *Hamburg*, she'd lost a mast and was in danger of capsizing. Agnes' father was the leader of our expedition. I suppose if they had survived they would have contacted us while we were still at our first stop. I know my father has agonized over the loss. He's no politician, but he did read the histories of what happened in that other time between my people and yours. He needs to make this expedition a success for our investors, but he also doesn't want the blood on his soul from the mistreatment the books describe may occur to your people."

Svend picked up the treaty they were drafting. "Please make this work! I couldn't stand to think my loss of Agnes was only the first of many." As he set the treaty down, he realized this was the first time he'd spoken of her in the past tense. A single tear started, until he braced himself up and vowed to still wait for her. "Let's get this finished right!" Svend rearranged the drawing pad and dipped his quill in the ink, which somehow had stayed upright during the episode.

By noontime, the rough draft was finished. As the morning had worn on, Svend had come to the conclusion that Joseph was much more than he had seemed during his acquaintance. The chief had offered an occasional suggestion, but the main body of the treaty was Joseph's work.

Svend rolled up the draft. "I'll take this to the captain so that he can read it before I do a fair hand final. If he has any suggestions I'll bring them back for your consideration."

Chief Longbow waved Svend on towards the captain's tipi. "Please proceed. I look forward to the captain's thoughts on the treaty." Svend bowed and hurried off.

Captain Foxe was not in the tipi. Luke stopped a nearby seaman and asked if he had seen where the captain had gone. "Last I saw of him sir, the captain asked to be rowed over to the proposed settlement site. Would you like me to get a boat for you to go there?"

"Yes, thank you. I'll meet the crew down by the beach."

Twenty minutes later, the gig rode up on the sandy beach at the proposed site, next to the captain's boat. Captain Foxe was visible, walking the site with Mister Barrow and Karl Andersen, the expedition's military commander. As Svend approached he could hear a heated discussion. "Karl, I think this site will meet our needs. I understand your concerns about defensibility from the sea, but if we are facing someone with enough power to capture a fortified position as you've suggested, we're in serious trouble. They would have brought enough firepower to defeat us, no matter what we build. This will be a trading post. If we face an attack, it will most likely be by a group that wants to steal our trade goods. I want our native allies to trust us, and the less obvious our site is as a fort, the better." Luke spotted Svend climbing the riverbank and waved for him to join them.

"Captain, Chief Longbow had me write out a proposed treaty for your review." Svend handed over the draft and then stepped back.

Luke unrolled the pages and started to read. The first thing he noticed were the smudges. "What happened? Did you write this with the feather end of the quill?" All three men laughed as Svend went red.

He held up his sleeve. "Close, the wind kept blowing the pages around and my sleeve served as a blotter."

Luke, Karl, and John all laughed at the offending sleeve as Luke turned back to the treaty. "Let's see what Luther is proposing." He started reading but Svend interrupted before he finished the first sentence.

"I think you should know that most of what's there came from Joseph.

"I have no doubt of that. I've come to suspect that Joseph was sent to learn about our customs. Let's see what he came up with." All four crowded together as Luke synopsized the treaty clauses. "It leads off by saying that this pertains to Chief Longbow's people only. It goes on to say that they want schooling for their youngsters, jurisdiction over their lands, and payment for lands we acquire. We will own this island in exchange for the trade goods we've shown them, doctors for their people, equality as partners on ventures, access to all goods including weapons, ten percent royalty on all exports, and assistance in building housing with modern heating stoves. There's nothing here I have a problem with. King Christian might object to the export tax, but I think that might be the best clause in the treaty. It will mean that the economy *here* will grow from our sweat and toil and not go to benefit someone across the sea. Svend, copy it out and set up a signing ceremony with Chief Longspear for tomorrow. He'll need to call a council of the other nearby chiefs to get their support for the overall proposals. We have to take this one step at a time. We need to start here as soon as possible to get our crops planted, so that we have some hope of them maturing before the first frost.

CHAPTER 6

August 1634, Copenhagen

The note that arrived carried the right code, but Bundgaard still waited across the street from the tavern to make sure it was his cousin who actually showed up for the meeting. The tavern was wedged in between a warehouse and an apothecary shop and offered three escape routes if they were needed. Ever since his escape from the king's prison in the Blue Tower, Gammel Bundgaard had survived by being extra careful. Being the subject of the City Guard's attention had a tendency to sharpen one's wits. Gone were his days as the richest ship's chandler in Copenhagen, with the fancy house and fine clothes. His tattered and soiled clothes helped him blend in as just another worker returning home from a long day's work on the docks. He fingered the soiled jacket in disgust. Someday, some way, he would find a way to get revenge on the Hudson's Bay Company. The fact that he'd tried to steal them blind never entered into his thoughts. *They* were the ones responsible for his fall.

He turned his attention back to the tavern. First things first. Make sure the meeting went safely. Five minutes before the appointed time, his cousin arrived, in the company of someone who was obviously a foreigner. Bundgaard waited an extra ten minutes to make sure no one was following them and then entered the tavern through a side door. As someone with a large price on his head by the king, patience could spell the difference as to whether one kept one's head. As his eyes adjusted to the dark taproom, he spotted his cousin seated in an alcove off to the side, away from nosey patrons. Bundgaard walked over and took a seat in the shadows, out of knife reach from the foreigner seated next to his cousin.

Bundgaard whispered, "I got your note saying this was urgent. It had better be. It's still way too hot for me to be seen anywhere down by the docks."

His cousin was sweating profusely, but managed to stammer out, "It's going to get even hotter. The king's gotten verification that you worked for the French and knows about the rotten supplies you sold the army. You're to be hanged if caught."

Bundgaard eyed his cousin's demeanor. "You should be sweating! If I hang, you'll be right beside me. You got just as much as I did on those deals!"

Asmund glanced at his companion. "That's why I've made arrangements to get you out of the country tonight. My friend here is the first mate on a ship sailing to Batavia. They have room for one passenger."

Bundgaard scowled, "And what am I to do for funds there? I can't get to my money in less than a week! Am I supposed to starve and save the king the cost of a rope?"

The clink of a large money bag was Asmund's answer as he tossed it on the table. The top was just open enough to show the color of gold. Bundgaard quickly swept it into his coat. A single gold coin could get one beaten severely in this neighborhood. What a bag could get you was dead. "That should tide you over until I can forward the rest of your funds to you." He pushed a document across the table. "Sign here and I'll be able to move your funds. Then all I'll need is to know where they are."

Bundgaard looked at the document for some time. It wasn't like he had a lot of options. The longer he tried to stay in hiding, the faster his money slipped away. Most of his associates were just as crooked as he was, and they were starting to sense blood in the water. Every time he'd contacted someone to furnish funds, they'd taken an extra percentage. It wasn't like he could take them to court! Finally he sighed and answered, "I suppose I should take a trip for my health."

He called the barman for a quill and ink. The quill was blunt, so he drew his dagger and sharpened the end. With a flourish, he signed his name and, on the bottom of the sheet, he left detailed instructions for how to reach his funds. When it was done he pointed with the dagger. "If you try to cheat me, cousin, I'll make sure my friends hunt you down!" The hollow threat still sounded real. He grabbed the sailor by the shoulder and pointed him out the door. "Let's go see this ship I'm sailing on."

It was almost pitch dark when they reached the docks. On the whole walk, the sailor kept to himself, mumbling half heard answers to Bundgaard's questions. The pier they approached was empty when they arrived. Bundgaard swung on his guide. "What type of treachery is this?" He started to draw his knife.

The sailor finally found his tongue. In an English accent he answered, "Your cousin told you we're sailing tonight! The captain shoved off to be ready to sail with the tide. I've a small boat below to row us out to the ship. This way there's even less chance of someone spotting you." He pulled away and climbed down a half seen ladder to the waiting boat. Once Bundgaard boarded, the two sailors who'd been waiting with the boat pushed off and started rowing.

Ten minutes later, the shadow of a Dutch sailing ship was visible in the starlight. As Bundgaard climbed aboard, the 'first mate' called up to the deck, "Here's your passenger, Captain." As Bundgaard turned to see what the sailor was doing, a blow behind his ear knocked him out cold.

When he awakened, the sound of a ship getting under weigh was evident. He had only been out a few moments! As he turned over, a short, stout Dutchman could be seen standing over him with a lantern. "Ahh, Fister Bundgaard, we meet again. I hope you enjoy *our* hospitality on this trip. We've saved some special provisions just for you!" In a flash, Bundgaard recognized the captain he'd scammed on a previous trip. He'd sold him short count and spoiled kegs of salt pork. The ship's crew had nearly starved on that voyage. The captain had tried to collect when they returned from the voyage, but Bundgaard's friend on the City Watch had squashed the complaint.

The captain had found a way to retaliate. Two sailors grabbed Bundgaard and shoved him down the nearby companionway toward the crews' quarters. The nightmare continued when they continued past the hammocks, shoved him into the sail locker, and locked the door behind him. The room was pitch black and rustling could be heard faintly under the discarded pieces of sail.

The ersatz first mate returned to the War Minister's residence, where two of his associates were detaining the Minister. "Your cousin is off on his adventure." The chuckle spoke volumes of Bundgaard's fate. "He's getting off far too lightly, given the attempt he made on my friend's life. But my employer insisted, so he will live. As I promised, no word of this will reach the king's ear, as long as you resign and turn over the funds we agreed to. Otherwise, you won't be able to run far enough and fast enough to avoid the king's displeasure."

Asmund was terrified and simply nodded and handed over the paper Bundgaard had signed.

As he opened the door to leave, Michael muttered under his breath, "Francisco will put these funds to good use." He abruptly spun back, pointing at Asmund, "Now start packing!" He left his associates to oversee the Minister's departure. As he walked down the empty street he whistled an old Irish war song.

Michael glanced at the authorization again, comprehension dawning as to what could come from it. The job had gone well. The former servant to Sir Thomas Roe was proud to be working for the up-timers. He and his helpers had accomplished everything, just as Don Francisco had hoped. They'd been able to break up the spy ring that had helped the French *and* not embarrass King Christian by exposing his Minister of War as a traitor. As an added bonus, Don Francisco now had enough funds to buy that tavern down by the docks as a clearinghouse for information coming in to Copenhagen by ship. And none of the spymaster's government funds had been used! *Talk about making war pay for itself!* Whenever Mike Stearns left office, there'd still be work for Michael O'Leary here in Copenhagen with Don Francisco.

"Oh, my goodness!" Mette Foxe stared at the contract and the bank draft that Factor Bamberg had delivered from Fransisco Nasi. He had paid her asking price for the tavern without even an attempt to haggle. She dropped the contract on the table and stared at Bamberg.

Augustus Bamberg was shocked that Mette would balk at the offer. "I assure you, Frau Foxe, the offer is a fair price! It *is* what you requested, yes? He will keep Frau O'Leary on to run the tavern once you've gone."

Mette picked the contract back up, hands trembling. "Of course it's what I *asked* for. I just never expected to get that much." The bank draft that had accompanied the contract was still clenched tightly in her left hand.

Augustus smiled and stretched out his hand in jest, "If you feel it's too much, I can return it!"

"No, no. I'll keep it." She quickly picked up a quill pen, dipped it in ink, and signed the contract. "It will help buy the extra supplies to help us re-settle in the New World. I'm sure the captain will put it to good use." *If he can't, I'm sure I can find a good way to invest it to see the children never have to want for anything again.* She handed the signed contract to Augustus. "Now all I need to do is break the news to Anna. I hope she doesn't turn down the offer to run the tavern now that she's married." She walked slowly down the stairs, still in a slight daze at the unexpected good fortune.

The sun was just setting as Michael O'Leary entered the tavern to have supper with his wife, Anna, in the back room before the usual supper crowd started to gather. Anna met him half way across the common room. "You'll never guess what happened today."

Without missing a beat he replied, "Mette sold the tavern and the new owner has placed you in charge."

Her jaw dropped in surprise. "But, but, how did you?"

"My new boss is the one who bought it. Remember the job I told you about the other day? That's where the money came from. You'll run the tavern and I'll be in charge of his 'information network' here in Denmark. With the shipping clientele that you serve, we'll have all the gossip as soon as it comes ashore."

CHAPTER 7

August 1634, Ft. Hamburg, South
end of James Bay

The new meeting house the expedition's sailors had erected was packed with visiting Cree leaders. Luke had offered to erect the first permanent structure for the Cree on the island to showcase some of the advantages that working with the Company could offer. Never in its history had the northern Cree met in such a council. Chief Longspear had invited Captain Foxe to attend as his guest. Luke's Cree was being taxed to the extreme, trying to follow the questions being politely asked by the visitors. Joseph stood at the captain's elbow, translating the more involved questions. Luke carefully watched the expressions of his questioners. Over the years as a ship's captain, he'd learned that the truth was harder to hide from the face than the voice. Overall, it seemed that the settlement, and the new council building, had made a good first impression on the visiting clan chiefs. Joseph's suggestion that a wooden meeting house be built to allow a neutral gathering place had been inspired. On the nearby hill, Mister Barrow was being kept busy showing a steady stream of curious attendees how the wood was cut and planed. In the next clearing, visitors were getting their introduction to sheep, which were also on the evening's menu. The aroma rising from the cooking spits had everyone drooling.

Luke turned his attention back to the pending meeting. The cast iron heating stove in the middle of the main room had a fire laid in, even though the day was a bit warm. The lack of smoke had occasioned almost as many comments as the sawmill's operation. Luke caught Joseph's eye and motioned toward his father. Luther had seated himself and was prepared to start. Joseph pointed in that direction and suggested that the chiefs join the circle that was forming and allow the captain a chance to refresh himself before they began. The steady whine of the sawmill continued on the other side of the hill.

Luke stepped out and headed toward the outhouses set up behind the council house. When he finished and started to walk back, he saw Svend hurrying up from the beach. Svend was trying to run and juggle his drawing case, drawing papers, and the gifts Luke had decided upon for the visiting chiefs. Those gifts were the result of some serious discussions among the colony's leaders. Arguments for and against weapons had been heated. Luke eventually reached a decision that seemed to please all concerned. Thinking back to a comment his wife, Mette, had made before he departed Copenhagen, Luke had asked Svend to prepare small parcels with sewing pins, skinning knives and bright beads. Some of the chiefs had traveled quite a distance and having something they could take home to their families seemed a very good idea for long term relations.

Luke hurried over and relieved Svend of the gifts. "Let me proceed in first," he said. "I want you to concentrate on recording the images of the meeting for posterity. Joseph is doing a good job acting as my interpreter. If you do hear something that seems to be in error, don't interrupt, but try and catch my attention. If I think there is an urgent need to confirm, I'll ask you to come speak with me in private. I want our guests to feel that they can trust us to behave respectfully and honestly. I may introduce you to the chiefs individually, after the meeting, and have you show them what you've done. Don't be surprised if you get requests for individual drawings. That may help us convince them we're civilized enough to be their neighbors."

Svend almost started to chuckle at the remark, until he saw Luke's expression. "You're serious, aren't you? My drawings might be that important?"

"I don't know, but sometimes it's the little things that can sway a person's opinion. Be courteous and understanding. Believe me; I'm having to learn a lot of this on the fly, too. Sir Thomas and I had a number of long discussions on how we needed to approach this issue. He was the one who had the training. I was just supposed to be along to answer questions. Now you've got that job. I'm just now starting to fully realize just what the loss of the *Hamburg* means to our future."

Svend opened the door, "Well then then, let's not keep them waiting. Here's to fair winds and a calm sea."

Luke stepped through the door and was met by Joseph. "The council is ready for your opening presentation, Captain. I've already recapitulated the summons that was sent for the meeting and we can now proceed with your introduction, as planned."

Luke took a deep breath and said a silent prayer that the Lord grant him the wisdom and serenity to do what was right for all parties. He stepped forward and Joseph began his introduction. After five minutes, Luke found himself blushing at the flowery compliments Joseph was bestowing on him. A soft throat clearing reminded Joseph that there was something else that needed to be said before the meal. Joseph wound up the introduction and motioned for the captain to proceed with his speech.

Luke stepped forward and executed a formal leg bow that would have been good form at any court in Europe. "I want to thank all of you for coming to this council to meet my people and help determine the direction we will all go in the future. It is my hope that our united wisdom can find a path that is one of peace and prosperity for all. As the summons said, my people come from a land far across the seas. What is important is why we have come." He paused, to focus his listeners. "An event occurred recently that may be as difficult for you to accept as it was for my people. A Ring of Fire brought to our land a group of travelers from our future, with knowledge and tools that have already changed what was to come in our history. They came from a land far to the south and were sent back by means no one knows, but they are here. Their knowledge of what would have happened in the lands on this side of the ocean was a tale of sorrow. Those white men that call themselves French, English, and Spaniards would have taken advantage of the natives of these lands and eventually would have subjugated them in their pursuit of riches. My chief, King Christian, has sent us here to try and change what that history said would occur. Rather than come as conquerors, we want to come as friends and allies."

"There are many things we can offer your people that can make their lives easier and safer. As some of you have remarked, the stove that heats this building does not foul the air with smoke. This tool has helped reduce the deaths among my people from the coughing death and made cold winters more bearable. To build these stoves, we need metals that we form into the parts needed. There are places to the south of here that contain metals that we use in our commerce. We want to reach an agreement on how we might work with you to bring workers here to mine these metals. We have new plants and methods to raise more food so that all will have enough to last even the longest winter. We have medicines that often defeat the coughing sickness and reduce childbirth deaths. Here, beside the great water, we would establish a center for trade, education and medicine. Our people would settle near here, or move south to where the metals lie. Before that can happen, we want your blessing on our endeavor and a formal treaty to govern how these events can happen so that you are sat-isfied of our worthiness to be your neighbors." He scanned the faces to try to gauge their thoughts. To his chagrin, a number of chiefs were more fascinated by Svend's efforts, quietly remarking to each other on the quality of the likenesses.

In a snap decision, he decided to depart from his prepared speech. "This is my step son Svend," he said, pointing to the busy artist. "I felt that this important occasion should be recorded for our descendants. Svend has a gift for recording events and I asked him to do so for this meeting. If anyone wishes a picture of themselves to take back to their village, please feel free to ask him. If you want pictures of the tools we've displayed, he can make those too." As he finished, Luke suddenly realized that he sounded just like one of the salesmen he'd seen on television when he had visited Grantville.

Luke's attention was caught by three older chiefs who had ignored his comments. They seemed to be bored and wishing they were any place but here. When they had been introduced earlier, Joseph had remarked that they were from the area south of his village, along the route they would need to travel for the gold field. *This is where I really miss Sir Thomas. His experience as a diplomat is what's needed now. Why did I ever consent to his sailing on the Hamburg? All I can do now....*

A shrill woman's scream focused everyone's attention on the door. The scream went on and on, finally ending in a shuddering sobbing. Luke's heart fell. His first thought was an assault by one of the sailors on a local woman. He'd warned them time and again against *any* unwelcome frater-nizing. This was the end for all the carefully laid plans for the expedition. All he could do now was try to minimize the damage. As the person closest to the door, he used the advantage to get outside first, to try and get some sense of the catastrophe that had occurred, before the rest of the chiefs. Looking around, Luke was startled to see the doctor tending to a young child on the ground, with Karima by his side. What they were doing was a mystery. They were supposed to be teaching the visiting healers the basics of sterilizing wounds. Instead, Doctor Mordecai Altstadt was pumping on the child's chest, while Karima appeared to be trying to blow in his mouth. The screams had probably originated from the older woman who was holding the child's hand and sobbing softly.

As he neared, Luke could see the child was dead. He was the shade of blue he'd seen numerous times before on heart attack victims. Why the doctor was wasting his time wasn't as serious as the impression he was having on the crowd that he *could* accomplish something. Much of their future depended on the tribes being willing to listen to his teachings. Failure at this critical time would damage his credibility. As he watched, one of the chiefs who had been ignoring his speech pushed through the crowd. When he saw who the victim was, he too let out an anguished cry and then started rapidly questioning the woman. Luke couldn't follow the conversation and looked around for Joseph. He spotted him at the rear of the crowd, trying to catch his attention. One more look convinced Luke of the hopelessness of the child's fate and he turned away, shaking his head in relief that at least the catastrophe he'd dreaded hadn't happened. Almost immediately, he was ashamed for the thought. The chief and his wife had lost a son. Compared to that, his problems were of little consequence.

Joseph elbowed his way to Captain Foxe and started to explain what had happened. "The child was playing with one of the lambs in the pen. Something irritated the ram and he head butted the boy. He went down immediately. As soon as the ram could be secured, they got the boy out but he'd stopped breathing. That's when the doctor appeared and he started CPR on him."

Luke frowned at the acronym. "What's CPR?"

"Cardio Pulmonary Resuscitation. The doctor told Karima and me about it during the voyage. It's a way to save someone who's stopped breathing. You…"

A multitude of shouts interrupted any further explanation. The woman was hugging the boy to her chest. He was struggling to speak but appeared to be all right. The chief had embraced the doctor and was crying, all the time repeating his thanks.

Luke simply stood there, slack jawed, trying to comprehend what it all meant. Joseph leaned in and whispered, "I think you have your treaty." He nodded toward the chief and his son. The chief noticed Luke and a smile split his face. He turned his son back over to his wife and hurried over to Luke. He pulled along the two other chiefs that had been seated with him, pointing toward his son with his chin, while he tried to make some point that Luke totally failed to translate.

Luke hurriedly asked Joseph what the chief had said. The chief stood there with his two compatriots, waiting for some sign from Luke that he understood. Joseph quickly explained, "Keme says that you are welcome to send a party to his tribe. He asks that you send a medicine worker, when you can, to teach his people. He understands now that you do come with good intentions."

Luke nodded vigorously, hoping it was a universal sign of agreement. Sir Thomas had told him there were many possibilities that could happen. This outcome had been in the realm of hopeful optimism. "Tell the chief I am happy the doctor was able to save his son. I accept his offer and will send a message to our people, asking that they send additional doctors to help train the clans." Luke surveyed the area. The crowd was starting to disperse, so he motioned toward the meeting house entrance. "Shall we resume our discussions? I'm sure others still have questions for me."

Joseph announced in a voice that would have done a drill sergeant proud, "Please return to council. We still have some time left before the feast can begin." Everyone filed back into the building. As they entered, Luke couldn't help but notice that there was a change in the atmosphere. Everyone seemed more relaxed. The bubble that had surrounded him earlier was gone. Joseph was kept busy translating requests and in small talk. While the accident had nearly ended in a tragedy, the final result could well go down in history as the start of a beautiful friendship. He called out to the doctor to accompany him into the final session. There was no doubt the other chiefs would have questions for him. He looked around for Svend, but realized he might be a little late returning. He was finishing a drawing of the young boy and his mother.

♦ ♦ ♦

As the feast finally broke up, Luke sat back in satisfaction. The day had gone gloriously. The tribes had agreed on adopting a Cree Nation council that would deal with the new settlers on an equal basis. Any new settlers would be able to claim ten acres of land, but the Company would pay the council for the privilege. A joint group would negotiate and publish for all parties a common set of laws and punishments. Joseph had played a major role in bridging the cultural differences that arose during the meeting. The young man definitely was going to be a leader for his people if things continued as they appeared to be heading. His friendship with Svend was another positive hope for the future. Luke chuckled at the thought of Svend. He'd last been seen at the table in the meeting house trying to turn all his notes into a fair hand draft for all parties to review before the final treaty was signed. Joseph's mother had taken a tray of food to him so he could continue to work through the feast.

A dance was underway to celebrate the events of the day. Chief Long-spear's people had their drums out and were being joined by the visiting Cree. Sailors from the ships were adding a new element to the Cree dances, hornpipes and flutes. The bosun was tuning up his violin and trying to find a suitable counterpoint. To Luke's ear, it was worse than the sound of a ship running aground, but the attendees seemed to be enjoying the new sounds. After a while, the three groups found a common timing and the sounds approached what might be called music. Svend finally emerged from the meeting house, haggard but triumphant. He waved the finished copy at the captain and strolled over with the document.

"It's ready sir." Luke solemnly pronounced. "What shall I do with it?"

"Hand it here. I'll retire to our cabin and read it over. If I find anything that needs correction, it can wait 'til morning. Now go ahead and join the party. You've earned a night's entertainment." He gave Svend a push toward the group of dancers around the fire and then headed off to quieter quarters. Svend grabbed up a mug of beer and then spotted Joseph and Karima off to the side. He decided to settle there until he had finished his drink.

As soon as Svend found an open spot to sit down, Karima immediately gave Joseph a sharp nudge in the ribs. "Remember what you promised!"

Joseph sighed, but nodded agreement. "I'm not going to get any peace until I ask you. Would you like me to introduce you to my cousin Hurit? She and Karima have been pestering me all week to introduce her to you. I think she's sweet on you." He turned to Karima. "Are you satisfied now? I've asked him."

Karima gave him the stare only lovers can have for someone who has said something amazingly stupid. "I hope you realize what you've just done?"

Joseph put on his best look of innocence. "What did I do? I asked just what you wanted."

Svend just sat there watching his friend dig himself deeper and deeper in trouble. Stifling a laugh he interrupted the pair before Joseph got into any further trouble. "Of course I'd be glad to meet her." He looked straight at Karima. "Just don't get your hopes up too high on your schemes," he laughed. "I'm still not sure whether my heart's ready to accept someone else in my life."

Karima's posture sagged, but she quickly replied, "Of course not. Just enjoy the dance tonight. Tomorrow will bring its own answers." She waved to Hurit, who'd been watching the interchange with anticipation. Karima gave her a sly wink as she sat down next to Svend. All Joseph could do was shake his head in wonder at the schemes of the two girls.

In the morning, Luke had Joseph join him in a closed meeting with the chiefs. Svend was summoned to make a number of minor changes and then write out a final copy of the treaty. The council emerged shortly before midday and Chief Longspear announced to the assembled gathering. "My people, we have considered well the requests our friends have made to remain amongst us. They have pledged their lives, honor, and sacred trust that our peoples shall live in harmony. We have pledged the same as the Cree Nation. This day shall be remembered to the seventh generation as the day the Cree people joined as one nation. We make our mark so that all future generations know that this is a binding promise." With that, Luther stepped over to the table with the treaty and wrote his name out, as Joseph had taught him. Captain Foxe and the other captains then signed. When they finished, Luke handed the quill pen to Joseph and asked, "Will you help the other clan chiefs sign? I believe they would appreciate seeing their names on the paper."

Joseph simply nodded and motioned for the chiefs to gather around the table. After about an hour the last chief had made his mark and Joseph tried to hand the pen to his father. "No, son. You sign too. If it wasn't for your efforts, this never would have happened." Joseph was dumbstruck, but proceeded to sign his name in a bold, flowing script, at the bottom.

When Svend saw the signature later he asked Joseph, "Why so large? Having trouble with the quill?"

Luke was nearby and eavesdropped on Joseph's answer "No, I just wanted to make sure my one chance at being remembered in history wasn't missed."

Luke muttered quietly, unheard by anyone, "I seriously doubt this will be the last time history hears of you. If you survive, I think your people will remember you for a long time."

Luke looked out across the fields that were starting to emerge from the island's undergrowth. Chief Longspear stood next to him, admiring the organized chaos going into clearing the fields. In the distance, John Barrow shouted a warning. "Stand by! Fire in the hole!" Ten seconds later, a series of small explosions rocked the ground as a small grove of tree stumps were cleared from the ground. Luke and Luther both held their heads. John noticed and walked over, digging in his pants pocket. "I thought you might have celebrated a little too much last night, Captain. I took the time to stop and see Doctor Altstadt this morning before I had the men start on the trees." He held out a handful of small blue pills. "These should cure what ails you, Doctor Gribilflotz's best. I've got enough to cover all your visiting dignitaries. It should help to cement their good opinion of you!"

Luke grimaced, but gladly accepted the aspirins. He handed the rest to Chief Longspear and managed to pantomime a reasonable approximation of what he needed to tell the other chiefs when they finally woke up. Luther very gingerly nodded and walked off to seek out the other partiers.

The next week was a frantic attempt to get as much land cleared and planted as the season and manpower would support. When it was done, fifteen acres of cabbage, peas, carrots, and beans were planted. Luke was kept busy explaining to the few chiefs who remained what would sprout from the gardens. Most simply shook their heads that anyone would be so foolish to spend so much effort to plant so late in the season. Even the farmers chided Luke that he was expecting too much. Luke's answer was always, "Just wait. Let's see what develops."

Even as the young plants began to sprout, so did the buildings for the new settlement. The ships' crews were put to work building the trading post and its stockade. John Barrow questioned Luke as to the need. "You yourself told me Captain, that we had to trust our new neighbors. Now you go and build a fort as the first building. Aren't you sending the wrong message?"

"I thought about it, John, but there is a good reason for it, and Chief Longspear agreed. We will have a lot of trade goods stored here and it creates a great temptation for those that didn't make the council meeting, along with the tribes further east. It will only take one bad apple and all of us here could be in serious trouble. It also will serve as a house of last resort if we have a fire in the village itself. The storehouse will also hold our food supply. If I'm wrong and the farmers are right, we may need to keep some of our own people this winter from raiding the supplies."

John's eyes widen at the comment. "So you aren't as positive as you tell everyone?"

"Oh, I'm positive John. But my job is to also be prepared for the worst. We lost quite a bit of our reserves with the *Hamburg*, and I have to face facts. It may be a long winter." His eyes brightened as a nearby shout heralded the successful hoist of a new house's roof pole. "That's almost as important as the crops." He pointed to the village that was starting to take shape outside the trading post. "Good shelter is important in this climate. I just wish we hadn't lost so many of the heating stoves with the *Hamburg*. The houses have chimneys for cooking and heating, but that may not be enough when the deep winter sets in. Tempers may get a bit frayed if we have to pack everyone into the meeting house to stay warm, but it will sure beat the alternative. Luke and John both laughed, thinking back to their previous winter visits to the Bay.

While Luke was busy supervising the construction of the settlement, Svend and Joseph spent the days wreaking havoc on the local schools of fish. Adam served as their 'guide' and got the dubious honor of cleaning the daily catch. This arrangement held until one night the two fishermen were bragging about their day's catch. When Karima heard how they were responsible for the evening's meal, she patted Adam on the back and said, "I guess you don't need to show these mighty fisherman any more of your secrets, though they did seem to be awfully slow in following your lessons on cleaning fish. Hopefully they won't hurt themselves tomorrow when they have to clean them by themselves." Hoots of laughter from around the fire sent Svend and Joseph off in embarrassed silence. The next morning, Adam joined in the fishing and got to have Svend and Joseph clean his catch, while Karima stood watch, offering pointed comments on the two's efforts. When the fish were cleaned, Karima made an exaggerated examination of the results. When she was done, she announced in a loud voice, "I pronounce Joseph Longspear as having met the minimum requirements to provide for me as a husband. I now accept his proposal of marriage. If there is anyone who will challenge this, let them speak now!" When she was done, she walked over to Adam and handed him a present. "Thank you for training your uncle properly. I hope he wasn't too much trouble."

Adam gave a slight nod. "My father taught him many things, and Svend has taught him more. I just hope he doesn't disappoint you on your wedding night. I'm too young and Svend knows even less than I do." He walked away as Svend nearly choked in embarrassment and laughter at the same time, watching his friend's imitation of a fish out of water as Karima's unexpected announcement sunk in.

Karima grabbed Joseph and gave him a long, lingering kiss and then walked off, following in Adam's wake through the crowd that had gathered. Svend leaned in to Joseph and quietly asked, "So, would today be a good day to go hunting, since I just had hunting lesson number one?"

Joseph frowned at the request, and then Svend's jibe slowly sunk in. "Alright, just remember that when you get caught. I think Karima is giving my cousin lessons."

Svend shrugged off the comment. "I'll see what happens if it comes. Right now, we have some caribou to bring home. Let's go get the spears and get started."

The stillness amongst the tamarack was barely marred by the two hunters searching for recent sign along the game trail. As they came to a clearing from a past lightening fire, Joseph raised his hand for a halt. "See the trail off to the right? If we head there, we'll spook whatever may be nearby. We can't make it through the new growth quietly. We'll circle around to the west and try to strike the trail there."

Svend nodded, but then waved for him to join him. "Let's break here for a quick bite. I don't think anything is near enough to matter. Besides, we need to talk." His serious demeanor warned Joseph that something was bothering Svend. "I know I'm not one to talk about love and marriage, but as your friend I think I need to ask, are you comfortable with marrying Karima? She seemed to be *forceful* with this marriage proposal." Svend tried not to smile, but the lips did quirk up a little.

Joseph stood there, carefully considering his reply. He knew Svend was trying hard not to intrude. "We will be married very soon. You must understand, our ways are not your ways. Karima is alone, without family to protect her and support her decision. What you heard today was her declaration to the village that I was acceptable to her and that she was making the choice of her own free will. I love her deeply and will do whatever needs to be done to make her transition into our clan as easy as possible. She has many ideas that I think can help both our peoples and we want to make that difference. So calm your mind. I am as one with her." He paused and placed both hands on Svend's shoulders. "I thank you from the bottom of my heart for your concern as a friend. I could ask you the similar questions about Agnes and what you intend. I think we both know she's not coming back, but I still see you with pain when the *Hamburg* is mentioned."

Svend turned away slowly, trying to gather his thoughts. "I know in my mind she's gone, but the grief is still with me. Just being at the celebration helped. Your cousin was nice to talk to, but I'm just not ready yet for someone new. Perhaps by the fall, the pain will be lessened and I'll be ready to move on."

Joseph sensed it was best to drop the thought, so he added, "In any case, will you stand as my brother at the wedding?"

"I'd be honored." After a short pause, he asked," So tell me, what do I need to know to keep from making a fool of myself?" On the game trail to the south, three caribou heard laughter and silently trotted away from the disturbance.

CHAPTER 8

August 1634, Christianburg

The anchorage off Christianburg was like a pebbled sheet of glass. It was also as bare as one. Not a ship was at anchorage. There was a palisade on the hill, overlooking the bustling village. A pile of iron ore sat near a formidable wooden dock that reached over a hundred feet into the harbor. A wooden railed track ran back into the center of the island to a mine entrance. A shot from the fort announced the arrival of the three ships, and a crowd started to gather at the dock. One figure was missing. Mette Foxe could not see any sign of her husband, Luke. She stood on the forecastle with her children, wondering why Luke was missing. Surely he would have been one of the first to greet the arriving ships, if he was alright. A sudden kick by the baby redoubled her fear that something had happened. Finally, she recognized Captain James, waiting at the front of the crowd. He was waving vigorously and didn't seem concerned. Mette descended the forecastle ladder slowly and strolled back to where Captain Bjornsen stood, directing the docking maneuvers. "Captain, how soon can we disembark? I really would appreciate footing that doesn't keep moving." Mette glanced down to her pregnant belly.

Captain Bjornsen chuckled. Mette had experienced a rough voyage. "I understand Milady. My wife had the same problem with our three. It should be less than half an hour. Don't be surprised if the land feels like it's moving once you land. It will take a day or so to get your land legs back."

Mette looked aghast. "You mean I'll still feel like this tonight? I hope the captain understands."

"Milady, believe me, it will be the furthest thing from his mind!" He gave her a quick wink.

Mette took the slight leer in fun. She hadn't run a dockside tavern for years not to know what was on the mind of men seeing their wives after a long separation. What still took some getting used to was the deference she received as Captain Foxe's wife. She knew in her head he had an important position with the Company, but a lifetime as a commoner was still ingrained in her heart.

As soon as the ship tied up to the pier, Captain James climbed the battens and boarded the _Queen Charlotte_. Captain Bjornsen hurried to the entry port to greet him. "Hallo Thomas, what news? And where is Captain Foxe? His wife and family have arrived to join him."

Captain James had taken the time to dress in his best frock coat and silk shirt and socks. The shoes were salt stained but the buckles were polished to a high gloss. It gave off the appearance more of a prosperous _burgomeister_ than a ship's captain.

"Thank God you're here! We were worried that you wouldn't make it this season. We lost one ship on the voyage here and are short on some items, mostly tools and gunpowder. Captain Foxe will be expecting you to deliver any extra food stuffs at the Bay settlement."

Mette pushed forward, dismayed at the news of the lost ship and the absence of her husband. "Captain James, do you remember me? I'm Captain Foxe's wife, Mette."

Thomas bowed, "I remember you well ma'am, though you seem to have changed somewhat. How soon is the little one due?"

Mette was taken aback by Captain James' personal question. "Not for some time yet." She scowled at the impertinence.

"No offense meant ma'am. It's just that I assumed you'd still want to voyage on to the Bay and meet the captain there. I was worried that the voyage might be too late in your confinement. Captain Bjornsen will have to leave soon to be able to get there and back before the ice closes the passage."

"Oh! I hadn't considered that." Her anxiety was evident when she asked, "How long will that voyage take?"

"This time of year, about four to six weeks, depending on the winds. The trip there should be fine; it's just the return that might see some problems with ice." He noticed the children, for the first time, huddled around the hatch nearby. "Gather up the children. I'll go ahead and find a cabin you can stay in until the ship is ready to sail. You must be exhausted from the voyage here." He turned back to Bjornsen. "We can talk later of the news from Copenhagen. Just one quick question, what news on the war? We've heard some strange tales from the few fishermen that have stopped over here."

"The war's over and done with. Gustavus sent some armored ships that shelled Copenhagen and King Christian promptly surrendered. The old Union of Kalmar has been resurrected with Christian still on the Danish throne. I'll find you after we finish unloading the cargo." Captain Thomas James gave a quick nod and then hurried down the side to locate quarters for Mette and her children.

Christianburg's meeting house did double duty as the port's lone tavern and inn. The second story was more of a large dormer and extended over the first floor. It was built along the lines of a blockhouse, which no one hoped it would ever have to serve as. Captain Bjornsen located Thomas there without any trouble. The first person he'd stopped and asked for the captain's whereabouts had told him bluntly, "Where else would he be? The sun's up."

When he entered, Captain James was seated at a corner table, a jug of rum and a half full glass in front of him. He wasn't drunk, but Bjornsen could smell the rum faintly. "Have a seat, old friend!" Thomas James kicked the chair across from him out. "Tell me more of what's happening back home while I'm stuck here coddling these lubbers."

"Well, as I said the war's begun and done. The Swedes sent some iron clad ships from Magdeburg that shot the hell out of Hamburg and then started to do the same to Copenhagen. King Christian must have sobered up fast, because he surrendered before they could do much damage. Your *old friend,* Bundgaard, finally went too far and the king had him thrown in the dungeon, awaiting execution for malfeasance. He's still a lucky rogue. The bombardment blew his cell up, but in the confusion he got away. There's a price on his head, but no one seems to know where he's gotten off to. My bet is he shipped out somewhere far, far away, with all his ill-gotten gains."

He took a sip of the rum and nodded his appreciation. "The Company's advertising about the gold strike and is getting swamped with people wanting to get rich quick. Those Abrabanel brothers sure have the suckers fooled. I've got thirty of them on this ship and there will be a fleet in the fall with probably two hundred more. I've got a letter for whoever's in charge here that authorizes building a steel mill at the site Captain Foxe recommended on the southeast coast." He took another swig from the jug and sighed. "That's some of the best rum I've had in ages. Where did you get it?"

Captain James held up his glass, examining the contents. "We've had some Dutchmen raiding shipping on the Banks. The fishermen come here with their catches now, rather than risk taking them to Plymouth or New Amsterdam." He pointed at the rum jug. "We got that from a Basque fisherman that had traded south before he reached the Banks. Haven't seen him since that one time. I guess the Dutchmen got him. We worry that they may decide to raid us soon. We helped an abandoned English settlement they burned out last winter. There shouldn't be a problem starting that new settlement. The fishermen are already complaining that the trip here is too long. We're doing all right for workers here if those coming this fall are the only ones we have to send off for that new settlement. It's the Hudson Bay group that's short manpower and supplies. I don't know if anyone told you, but we lost the *Hamburg* on the voyage here. There was a violent storm and we know they lost at least their bonaventure mast before we lost sight of them. What happened after they were lost to sight, only God knows now. In a way, that's how I got stuck here. Sir Thomas Roe was supposed to administer one site and Captain Foxe the other. I hope the Company sends someone soon to take over here. Running farmers and miners is not my idea of a future. Give me the open sea and new lands any day." He sat there brooding, and then added. "I should let Madam Foxe know what happened to the *Hamburg*. She did lose her future daughter-in-law on the ship." He took another long drink of rum.

Bjornsen sized up James' condition and quickly volunteered, "I'll let Mette know. I'm heading that way any ways." He pushed back the crude chair and ducked out the door before Captain James could argue.

The next morning dawned grey and overcast. Bjornsen trudged up the hill to the fort to pay his respects to the commander, Captain Andersen.

He turned toward the bay to check the rigging and trim on the *Queen Charlotte*. The unloading was done and the ship was riding high aft. He'd have to shift some of the grain to the aft hold to balance the trim before he sailed. Peering into the light fog, Bjornsen spotted a dark shape looming close by the *Queen*. As he watched two more shapes coalesced into armed ships. He raced up the rest of the way to the fort shouting, "Man the cannons. The Dutch are in the harbor!" *It appeared that the new site would need a fort sooner than anyone had thought. If they beat off this attack!*

CHAPTER 9

September 1634, Le Havre

E bb tide left the waters of the Le Havre harbor strewn with garbage, city sewage, and animal bodies. The moonless night hid the sight from casual observers. It also gave shelter to any nefarious schemes along the water front. Most captains chose to anchor just off the docks to foil rats, both four legged and two legged versions. The *Maastricht Prince* was no exception. Her captain had unloaded a cargo of Danish cheese when they docked earlier in the day. The outbound wine cargo wouldn't be delivered until the next afternoon. Below deck, Gammel Bundgaard lay quietly locked in the sail locker. He'd been worked nearly to death in the hold earlier. It was four weeks since he'd been shanghaied in Copenhagen, in retaliation for scamming the captain of the *Maastricht Prince* on an earlier voyage. He'd existed on stale bread and green water and was at the end of his strength. The ship's next stop was in the West Indies. If he couldn't escape tonight, he wouldn't make the next port.

It had been over an hour since he'd been locked up and there had been no hint of a sentry stationed nearby. He pulled out the short knife he'd stolen three days earlier, when the cook wasn't looking, as Gammel had cleaned up the pots from the evening meal. The sail locker was dark as a tomb, so he felt his way to the spot on the door where he'd been carving away the lock's keeper. It was all or nothing tonight, but the work was slow. If he broke the blade, he was a dead man. Patiently, he carved slivers out where the bolts were set in the frame. He'd hidden his work using a paste of bread crumbs to hide the holes from a casual inspection. Overhead, muffled steps could be heard but he continued carving. Anyone hearing his scratching would undoubtedly mistake it for rats searching for access to the bread locker nearby. Shortly after the nearby cathedral bells rang for the start of matins service, he felt clear wood at the bottom of the last bolt. He paused and took off his shirt. It would have to serve as a muffle if the wood snapped. He jammed the tip of the knife into the wood just below the bottom of the keeper and then slowly started to lever the bolt out. He held his breath as he strained against the blade. If the blade broke now, there was no hope. A muffled crack sounded and then he fell back onto the pile of sails. The bolt had come free and the keeper hung loose. He could see a sliver of less darkness where the door had swung in. He held his breath, straining to hear any reaction from the watch on deck.

After what seemed an eternity, he took off his shoes and wrapped them in his shirt. He left the arms loose to tie around his neck. He stuffed the knife in his waistband. He'd have to swim and he would need both arms free. He swung the door open and felt his way along the passageway to the ladder leading to the main deck. The crew's quarters were on the next deck up, and he'd have to pass through a short section of the area to reach the final ladder. He strained to hear any movement, but the day's unloading had left everyone tired. Snores were echoing as he stepped up from the lower deck. He walked with a purpose, as if he belonged. Anyone waking would assume he was going to the head to relieve himself. When he reached the coaming, he paused and tied the shirt sleeves across his chest. There was one sailor keeping a watch on deck for any thieves that might try to board. He stood along the ship's waist on the port side, staring at the taverns along the docks. Nefarious actions onboard were the furthest thing from his mind.

So much for night vision. Gammel almost chuckled at the laxness. He spotted a belaying pin nearby and paused to consider his options. He could try to knock out the watchman. The crew had been paid earlier in the day and the sailor should have some money on him. It would come in handy but caution won out in the end. If someone heard the noise now, he was doomed. There would be other opportunities ashore to fill a purse. After all, he had his trusty knife. He waited until he was sure the sailor was not going to turn around and then padded in his stockinged feet to the starboard rail near the anchor chain. Sliding over the railing, he slowly worked his way down the side, holding on to the chain until he was completely in the water. It was pleasantly warm but stunk like a midden. He quietly swam around the prow of the ship and then waited a few moments for a large cloud to pass in front of the sliver of moon that lit up the water near the ship. Ten minutes later, he reached the nearest dock, crawled up the slime covered stone steps and collapsed in exhaustion.

A raucous argument woke Bundgaard from his stupor. Night still covered the harbor, but the torches outside the taverns were guttering low. A drunken, solitary sailor was resisting his mates' urgings to return to their ship. "I've still money in my pouch and there are still whores needing attention. It was a long voyage from the Indies and my pistol still has shots to fire. Go on! I'll be there by first light." He pushed away and staggered off toward the taverns where the torches shown the brightest. Bundgaard pushed himself up and surveyed his appearance. Slime stained his pants, but the shirt and shoes still clung wetly to his back and chest. Sizing up the opportunity that had presented itself so obligingly close, he donned shirt and shoes and followed his intended victim. An hour later, Bundgaard emerged from a dark alley, in a clean set of slightly oversize clothes, and a leather pouch at his waist, that clinked from the coins within. He slid his clean knife into his belt. The body back in the alley slowly cooled in the night air. He paused to assess his situation. He was free from the Dutchman, but was nearly penniless in a foreign country. He would need better clothes and more money if he was to get his revenge on those that had sold him into captivity and return to a station in life he deserved. He would also need influence and there was only one place in France where he had access to that: Paris. *Time to sharpen up my old skills that helped finance me earlier in life.* He made sure the knife was well hidden up his sleeve and set out on his quest.

Gammel wandered the port for the rest of the night, searching for more victims to fill his pouch. After his third successful mugging, he was feeling inordinately pleased with himself. The old skills hadn't even been rusty. A pimp yielded a full pouch and a better fitting set of clothes. A quick stab with the knife to the base of the skull and there wasn't even any blood to clean up. Disposing of the bodies had been child's play. The alleys of Le Havre were unlit and strewn with garbage. Now that he had escaped the ship, he needed to leave, before his crimes caught up with him. Revenge was next on his list of important things to do. He found an inn that was open early. He entered and ordered the first decent meal he'd had in weeks. While he sat there, enjoying the eggs and fresh bread with butter, he considered his options. He still was known to some in Paris as a loyal agent. If he approached them correctly, he might be able to secure a commission as an agent in the New World. That would give him his opening to exact his revenge. A copper *sou* secured the location and times for the next Paris bound barge from the inn keeper.

♦ ♦ ♦

Paris was still speculating on the recent defeats of the French army by Gustavus Adolphus and whether they might soon see Swedish troops in the city, when Bundgaard finally arrived in the city. Two quick muggings secured sufficient capital to cover the bribes needed to reach one of Etienne Servien's clerks. His claim to have recent news on how matters stood in Copenhagen finally convinced the clerk it might be worth his job to schedule an appointment for him on Servien's calendar. The meeting was set for the following Thursday. In the interim, Bundgaard spent his time studying the guards surrounding the *Palais Royale* and gleaning any rumors on affairs in New France. What he found out about the guards suggested a tactic he might take in his negotiations if his plan worked. As far as New France was concerned, most cultured Parisians thought it was the ass end of nowhere and only fools and desperate men would think about going there without a royal commission. That suited his plans even better. He looked forward to the interview with anticipation.

When Thursday arrived, Bundgaard arrived early and presented himself to the guard at the main entrance to the *Palais Royale* "Fister Gammel Bundgaard to see Etienne Servien. I have an appointment."

The guard studied the arrival. Gammel was conservatively dressed and appeared to be some type of merchant or senior clerk. The letter he provided matched the name and was for the current time. He motioned to someone just inside the door. "Go fetch one of *Monsieur* Servien's clerks to escort this gentleman to his appointment." The doorman scurried off to find a clerk. The guard turned back to Bundgaard. "He should be just a few moments. Please accept my apology for any inconvenience, but in these restless times, the cardinal requires that all visitors be personally escorted throughout the *Palais.*"

Bundgaard nodded. "A wise precaution." He surveyed the placement of the guards around the grounds. "By the by, who is your Captain and

72

what is your name? I would like to commend your attention to guarding the *Palais* to him.*"*

The guard assumed an even stiffer posture and replied quickly, "My captain is Antoine Bracy. My name is Sergeant Boiteau." He saluted. Any further conversation was interrupted as the doorman returned with the escort. The guard passed Bundgaard through the door and wished him well on his meeting.

Once inside, the escort introduced himself, "I am Paul Leval, *Monsieur* Servien's clerk. He has someone with him at the moment but should be finished shortly. We will wait for him in the antechamber outside his suite. Does *Monsieur* require anything before the meeting?"

Bundgaard considered a glass of wine to steady his nerves but demurred. It wouldn't be wise to show up for the most important meeting of his life with even the faintest hint of liquor on his breath. As they walked down the corridor, there was evidence everywhere that the building was still under construction. Odors of paint and fresh cut wood hung heavy on the air. Workmen stepped aside to let them pass a load of tile being delivered for a bath. They reached a set of double doors guarded by a Cardinal's guardsman. Leval opened the door and motioned for Bundgaard to precede him in. "We can wait here until the guard sends for you."

A muffled conversation outside the door warned that Servien's meeting had concluded. A moment later, Etienne Servien opened the door and surveyed the waiting visitor. His memory wasn't faulty. He'd never seen this man before, but he did have the correct password. He made sure Leval took a seat as added protection, even though he also had a guardsman stationed behind the painting. He preferred using this room for meeting questionable visitors because of that safety feature. Bundgaard remained standing, conscious that no seat had been offered. Servien frowned and then proceeded with an icy demeanor, "I understand you have *valuable* information on the situation in Denmark. So tell me, what is Christian up to that requires you to come personally to Paris to tell me?"

Gammel Bundgaard realized his fate hung on a thread. He'd gotten his appointment with Servien, but it was apparent that his information better be meaningful or this meeting would be quite short. He took a step toward the windows and motioned toward the scene outside. "I came here as a fugitive from King Christian because of my support of France." *They can't check my story quickly, so make the best of it.* "I worked with Giscard de Villereal to supply the French fleet at Lübeck. When King Christian discovered that, I was condemned and thrown into prison to await execution. I escaped when Admiral Simpson bombarded the city and a shell explosion opened my cell."

Servien interrupted, "*We* appreciate your efforts to support our fleet, but that is hardly important in the larger scheme of things. As far as Giscard de Villereal is concerned, we have heard nothing from him since before Simpson's attack. What can you tell us about Christian's current affairs?"

Bundgaard realized he'd just heard something important but it took a moment for it to percolate to a conscious thought. *He hasn't heard about the Hudson's Bay expedition!* "What I've just said was merely to establish my bona fides. Did Villereal ever pass on my reports on the expedition King Christian was sending to the New World? I passed it to him before Simpson attacked and he said he would send it to you immediately."

Servien sat bolt upright at the disclosure. "What did you say? *Christian* sponsored the invasion on New France's territory? What exactly do you know about this?"

The bait was truly set. Now all I have to do was reel in the mark! Bundgaard merely raised an eyebrow before asking, "And what is this information worth to you?"

Servien smiled. This was familiar ground, the dance for the reward. "What do you seek, money? I can pay well if you truly know what is transpiring across the sea and in the king's councils."

This was the opening that Bundgaard was waiting for. "I seek a position in the New World to assist in defeating this plot. These people helped Christian destroy my life. A commission in the Guards in New France is my price."

Servien studied Bundgaard closely. Revenge was a good motive, if it didn't consume the person. Would Bundgaard be able to follow orders, or would he go off on his own path? Past experience indicated that the problem ones usually became impatient quickly. As the pause continued, Bundgaard remain composed and patient. Servien decided to take a risk. "Very well, you shall have one, the rank depending on the value of your news."

Bundgaard felt a thrill at the news, but stifled any outward sign. He gave a slight nod of acceptance and then started to recite his prepared story. "The expedition sailed in March with four ships bound for Newfoundland and then on to Hudson's Bay. They call themselves the Hudson's Bay Company and are led by Sir Thomas Roe, an English diplomat to King Christian's court. The ships are led by Luke Foxe, another Englishman, who sailed previously for King Charles. As they were preparing for this expedition, Charles refused to help them, so they turned to Christian of Denmark for sponsorship and funding. Their stated goal is to prospect for gold in the New World. I suspect they have plans for much more, but they were quite closed-mouthed on that subject. Just before I left, they had sent word back that they had found gold on Newfoundland's north coast and started a widespread rumor that was attracting scores of potential colonists. A second, reinforcement fleet was sent with additional settlers and shiploads of machinery, and a third is scheduled for this fall. They should have close to five hundred settlers there before the end of the year. They have surplus cannons and guns that Christian sold them from his own stores." *No reason to say that I was the one who arranged that sale!* "I suspect they have large plans around Hudson's Bay. Captain Foxe let slip they would need foodstuffs to sustain them until they could get the mines started so they could pay to import more food. They had miners on the first ships that were free with information after they were drunk. They said they were going to Hudson's Bay to hunt for gold, but they sounded like they had some sort of map to its location. There also were hints that Grantville was somehow tied into the enterprise, but that connection was very tenuous." *I hope I didn't overplay the Grantville connection. I can't prove it, but the French are worked up enough by them that they should believe it based on their fears alone.* "That's the gist of what I know for sure. I have suspicions on more, but I only report facts, not guesses."

When he didn't continue, Servien motioned for Leval and whispered instructions quietly in his ear. Leval nodded a few times and then hurried out of the room. Servien sat quietly, absent mindedly twisting the end of his moustache, and considered the information Bundgaard had revealed. It served to confirm some rumors other agents had reported about Christian's abandonment of the alliance. What troubled more than anything were the hints on the extent of the plans for the New World. If they truly were settling in Newfoundland, it could mean current plans for an expedition there needed to be expedited before they could get firmly entrenched. Control of the Cabot Strait, and access to New France was in danger. The group bound for Hudson's Bay would have to be rooted out, but they weren't the immediate problem. They needed a secure supply route from Newfoundland. Champlain would need to scout them before anything of substance could be sent. The current troubles in France precluded sending any significant number of troops, but ships and guns were another matter. Champlain would have to recruit native allies to fill out his ranks of scouts and fighters. Outdated arquebuses would serve as weapons for them. Bundgaard's slight cough brought his attention back to his visitor.

"Your tale is interesting but contains nothing new. However, someone of your proven devotion to duty does provide an opportunity for an important post. I will need someone in the New World who is familiar with our new enemies and can assist Governor Champlain in his upcoming campaigns. You would serve as a sergeant of the cardinal's Guard and assist the Governor where needed. Monsieur Leval is drawing up your commission and will have it, and a set of instructions we were already planning to send to the Governor, ready when you leave. You will sail from Le Havre as soon as you can. Is that satisfactory?"

Bundgaard was stunned by the swiftness of Servien's decision. A captaincy had been his hope, but a commission was a commission and he knew someone who might be able to *improve* what eventually was delivered to Champlain. "You have my thanks, *monsieur*. I will do my best to merit your trust." He bowed, trying to hide the gleam in his eyes at the turn of events.

Servien motioned for him to take Leval's vacated seat. He then took some time and expanded on his intentions for the mission and provided information that Champlain would need as far as intentions for military operations in the west. These intentions would not be written down, in case something untoward happened to the ship. Natives were to be armed and sent out to remove any intruders on French soil. Servien did not mention the problems that were already plaguing sea trade with New France, nor did he mention the naval ships that were eventually to pay the Newfoundland settlements a visit. A knock on the door interrupted the briefing. Leval had returned with the commission, a pouch, and a sealed package. Servien handed them to Bundgaard and admonished him, "Remember, you work for the cardinal. If you discover anything that needs his attention, don't hesitate to report it to me. Failure to complete this mission will not be tolerated. Leval will provide funds to pay your expenses for the voyage before you leave. Champlain will pay your wages from the *Compagnie* funds he has in New France." Servien rose and opened the door. Bundgaard followed Leval out into the hall.

As Bundgaard's and Leval's footsteps receded down the hall, the cardinal's picture swung aside and Cardinal Richelieu stepped out of the listening port. "So Etienne, what do you think of the rascal? Is he to be believed?"

"I believe so, Your Grace. He had some new information, but he corroborated many tidbits I had recently received. He may be a rascal, but now he's *our* rascal and will serve as a good source on anything Champlain may try to hide from us. If he can help defeat the Danes, all well and good. If not, we lose little. I thought it might be a good idea to speed up our expedition to Newfoundland so I sent orders along that Rene use him to scout the settlements."

The cardinal paused and took a scented kerchief from his sleeve to counteract the breeze that wafted up from the street below. "I fear you're right. When Rene reports back, it will have to be the Navy only. I need all the troops to remain nearby. The Army's recent setback is encouraging too many potential intrigues, without further weakening our defenses." Richelieu looked out the window, surveying the streets of Paris, as if he expected to see crowds storming the *Palais* at any moment.

It had cost three silver *sous* in bribes to obtain the needed name and address. Ducking his head to clear the cracked beam in the ceiling, Gammel Bundgaard finally met the best forger in Paris. "I have a job for you, François. I need the first page of this commission revised to reflect what's written here." He passed across the table the first page of his royal commission to the cardinal's guard and his proposed revisions. Francois le Plume studied the parchment closely, checking for water marks and the color of the ink. He then read the notes, his eyebrow rising at the final request.

"I can do it, but it will cost."

"How much?"

"Twenty *livres,* in gold, half now and the balance when it's finished."

"That's robbery!"

"No, robbery gets you a long spell in prison. This will be death if it's discovered. *Yours and mine.* Is this really worth that chance?"

Bundgaard snapped back, "There will be little chance that the change will be discovered if the job is done well. The only way this leaves my possession is if I'm dead. Changing the rank from sergeant to lieutenant and appointing me to head the guards in New France that are responsible for native forces is imperative. Since it will take almost a year to question it, and the cardinal does not take easily to having his decisions questioned, I can afford the slight risk."

"Very well. Give me the ten *livres* and leave the papers here. Come back in three days and it will be done. Normally, I'd have it tomorrow, but I'll need to clean the parchment of ink. The water mark is too hard to forge, and since I have an original, I'll work from that." He scooped up the papers and gold and left Bundgaard standing alone in the room. Bundgaard swung around and just missed braining himself on the broken beam as he hastened out the door.

CHAPTER 10

September 1634, Fort Hamburg,
south end James Bay

Captain Foxe listened to the conversations among the settlers as the last few stragglers entered the common room. His gaze wandered to the back wall. It was still unchinked with mud. It let in light, but soon it would let in the winter winds if it wasn't finished. Another problem that needs attention that no one seemed to notice. There were concerns being voiced about why the meeting had been called, but no one seemed to be worried. *I hope they realize by the time I'm done that they do need to worry.* He took his dagger and rapped on the table for attention. The room immediately went silent. The twelve men and six women that had been able to spare time to attend waited expectantly for him to speak. John Barrow and Heinrich Reinhardt stood, leaning against the back wall. They knew what was coming and were prepared for any emergency. Hopefully, they wouldn't need the saps concealed in their baggy trousers.

"I know everyone is pressed for time, so I'll keep this simple and straight to the point. We may have a serious food shortage this winter. With our late arrival, the growing season will not be enough to let the crops mature for a good harvest."

"And it took you *this long* to figure that out?" Everyone broke out laughing. Even Luke had to admit the heckler was right.

"I know what's being said and you're right. I'm a sailor who's trying to be a farmer and not doing a very good job at it. But I'm trying and learning. My mistake was spending too long in Christianburg, trying to overcome the problems the *Hamburg's* loss caused."

"Captain Foxe," Berndt Larson struggled to his feet. He was the oldest farmer in Ft. Hamburg, and was the farmers' unofficial spokesman. "Your problem isn't a matter of too little time here. This land and its weather ain't worth shit for raising food crops! Oh, we can probably raise gardens to supplement our fishing and hunting, but even if we had started in the spring, we still couldn't raise enough food to send back for cash. We might be able to raise sheep and cows, but they'll need better shelters than we have right now. Hell, *we* need better shelters," he said pointing to the back wall. John started to fidget with the sap, wondering where this would end. "We might have better houses if we hadn't spread ourselves so thin working on extra houses for settlers that aren't even here yet. Winter's coming on and we're not prepared."

Luke stood up and walked around the table. "You're right. Come spring, we'll have to start sending people further south to find better farm country. In the meantime, we have to make some hard decisions. If the supply ship doesn't arrive in the next two weeks, we're going to have to send people back to Christianburg on the *København* to reduce the mouths we have to feed. All of you have families and are my first choice for the trip. You'll be brought back on the first ship returning after the ice breaks. There should be housing for you in Christianburg and at least enough food that you won't starve." Everyone started to protest, but Luke held up a hand for silence. The protests faded, but the looks of protest remained.

"I also plan on sending a group south to the gold field to start surveying for the mining that's planned for next summer. I made arrangements with the chief there at the treaty meeting. He'll supply them with food and shelter, in exchange for trade goods. There will only be a small party that remains here, to look after the fort and livestock. We only have the four heating stoves. All the others were lost with the *Hamburg*. Even if the crops had been good, we would still face the prospect of freezing if we all stay. My fondest hope was that we wouldn't face starvation this year, but I wouldn't deserve to lead you if I didn't face the realities of our situation." He hung his head, waiting for the protests to resume.

After a long moment of silence he looked up. Heads were nodding in agreement. Larson broke the silence. "Captain, we've been expecting this for the last two weeks. No one likes the thought of that long, cold voyage back, but it's better than starving. I speak for us all when I say we'll be ready when you give the word."

Pride filled Luke's heart. This was truly his settlement and its people would eventually persevere. One question remained. "Who will be the ones to stay? I will accept your recommendation, but bear in mind; they will need to be able to speak some Cree."

Larson answered quickly. "That would be the Sorrensen brothers and Max Brauner and his wife. They're the best with the animals and Max and Anna both speak enough Cree to get by. Anna's friends with most of the Cree women and knows a little doctoring too."

The group Larson had identified stood up and voiced their willingness to stay. Luke stepped over and shook their hands adding his gratitude to the mix. Jens Sorrensen added one caveat, "Just remember your promise to return in the early spring, Captain Otherwise you get to plant *all* the cabbages!" Luke's mournful face when cabbages were mentioned brought a round of laughter to the somber group.

Smoke rose from the log and wattle cabins clustered around the shelter of the fort's palisade walls. Finished boards were still in short supply, so the settlers had to settle for a rough exterior appearance. Gardens had been planted on the open land south of the fort, where a spring provided a year round supply of water. Luke walked through the cabbage patch, surveying the heads for frost damage. It was going to be a long, boring winter of nothing but cabbage, onions, and kraut for vegetables for those who remained. Next year they would plant a wider variety of vegetables, but the short growing season left them by their late arrival had not left many options. The worry now was would they have enough foodstuffs to last the winter even for a reduced population. The cabbage heads were just about ready for picking, but a few days more growth would really help the yield. It had almost gotten below freezing during the night and he was worried the plants might have been damaged. As he finished surveying the lowest lying patch, he was relieved to note it had escaped a killing frost. Luke shook his head in wonder. *If my wife could see me now! Reduced to a farmer. Mette would tell me the humility and dirty hands would do me good. From worrying about gales, to worrying about frost.* He gave a silent grunt. *But the crops are important. If we're to eat this winter, and stave off scurvy, we* have *to have these crops. It's only a matter of time though, before we do get a freeze.*

As he turned back toward the fort, Luke absent mindedly picked at the occasional weed the children had missed. They had done a good job clearing them. Their small fingers and feet limited the damage to the crops, as long as they remembered not to start playing!

At least he had good news for now. The cloudy weather and southerly wind promised at least a few more growing days. If they could harvest the cabbages, the smaller settlement should be able to get through winter without the threat of scurvy. The time had come to start the loading for those going back to Christianburg. At least they wouldn't have to build housing next year. The few that remained would be able to get the early crops in while the ships in Christianburg waited for the ice to clear from the passage. He reached the open gates of the fort. Well, he couldn't put off the inevitable any longer. He'd promised that he would see off the exploring party that was heading south to blaze a route to the nickel and gold fields. Hopefully, they would be safe. Mette would never forgive him if something happened to Svend, but the boy was growing up to be a man and he was one of the best for this job.

When Luke reached the parade ground, Reinhardt already had his party assembled, checking their packs. Chief Longspear was trying to talk to his son, but Karima had Joseph's undivided attention as only a newlywed could. Svend stood off to the side, making sure that his drawing pad and supplies were safely secured in their watertight pouch, while he watched his friends' dilemma. His work case, with the survey tools, was already loaded on one of the two pack horses. There had been a number of heated discussions whether the expedition should go by land or water. It was finally settled that the small number couldn't portage the trade goods, so they were taking the only two pack horses available.

The discussion between Luther, Joseph, and Karima was getting interesting as Svend continued to pack. Luke was aware that Svend was happy his friend had found someone. Last night, Joseph had still been half-heartedly trying to get Svend interested in one of his cousins, but Svend had said he didn't feel that it was right. Luke suspected he still cherished a faint hope that Agnes would show up, but he no longer objected when someone disagreed. Meanwhile, the chief finally gave up and just gave Joseph a swift swat on the shoulder and walked off, smiling. Karima kept whispering to Joseph, who just kept nodding. When Svend broke into a big grin, Luke realized Karima was reminding Joseph that he better watch his injuries that were still healing and return in one piece. She didn't want to lose a husband this soon. They were two that would remain for the winter, no matter the food situation. They would be responsible for watching over the houses outside the fort. Joseph would return once the party was beyond his tribe's allies range. A few of the exploration party, including Svend, planned to overwinter further south; near the locations they planned to mine. Their biggest concern was making friendly contact with the tribes in the area and having some sort of shelter that could withstand the northern winter.

Luke stepped up behind Svend and stood there with his hands on his hips, watching the preparations. When Svend sensed him and turned around, Luke said in a quiet voice, "Son, you've really grown this year. Your mother would hardly recognize you! If this trip goes as planned, you may be leading your own party next year. Learn from Reinhardt and be careful." They stood silent for a moment, and then Luke broke down and gave Svend a massive hug, trying to hide the tears that were forming.

Svend let out a yelp as the hug pressed the striker on his rifle into his back. As he tried to rub the injured area, he happened to glance over his father's shoulder toward the anchorage. Off to the northeast, a smudge of white was visible on the far horizon. He let out a whoop and raced for the fire step on the palisade wall, grabbing the lookout's telescope from the box that had been placed there just for this type of emergency. As he focused on the horizon, everyone nearby stopped work to find out what the commotion was about. "Sail ho! It's a fleet!" Svend called out. "I don't recognize any of the ships, but they appear to be Dutch or French rigged."

Luke took his time climbing the ramp, as befitted his age and rank. "How many can you make out?"

"At least three, though there may be a fourth just coming up over the horizon."

Luke was startled. That was more ships than the Company had planned to send. He yelled back, over his shoulder, "Sound the alarm!" Out on the parade ground, the drummer started to beat out a rolling tattoo to warn the settlement.

John Barrow heard the drumroll and ran up from the beach. As soon as he was within earshot, Luke yelled down to him, "Prepare the ship for battle, but don't run out the guns. They may not expect you to be armed. Hopefully they may close the range enough that our popguns can inflict some damage. Stay anchored and set out springs fore and aft to aim the guns." John waved back to show he understood and charged back to the beach.

Chief Longspear tapped Luke on the shoulder. "What should my people do? Are we in danger?" His eyes were again seeing the scene of death and destruction Captain Thomas James had described during his visit.

Luke looked at the ships again and then snapped the telescope shut. "If these are the Dutchmen, they may or may not be enemies. If they're French, we're all in deep trouble. You don't come this far with four ships for just a friendly visit. Head for the far end of the island with your people and wait. If you hear gunfire, take your canoes and go upstream to the camp near the rapids. If these are enemies, they can't sail their ships that far. Your canoes can out distance any ship's boats if they do pursue you." The chief nodded and gathered Joseph and Karima to him to spread the warning.

The fort's settlers huddled in a group, the men to the front, trying to look brave for their families. Luke stepped forward and motioned for silence. "We don't know what's coming. I've told the Cree to head to the far end of the island and I want our women and children to join them. If this is an armed fleet, we will all abandon the fort and hide out. Take all the food you can carry. As I told the chief, gunfire will be the signal to flee."

Svend interrupted him before he could continue. "Captain, I think you need to see this. There are four ships." There was a strange look on his face.

Luke motioned for Svend to pass him the telescope. He studied the ships intently. Svend was right, there were four ships. They were close enough that he could make out some details. Two were smaller fluyts, Dutch or Baltic in design and one was definitely French. They sat low in the water, like they were loaded with cargoes or armaments. The fourth was a large, four masted ship, with a strange set to her masts and sails. She rode higher in the water, possibly carrying soldiers. He handed the telescope back to Svend. "What do you make of the larger ship? She appears to be higher in the water. Can you make out anything about her? My eyes just can't handle that small of details anymore."

Svend took the glass and studied the ship. He started fidgeting as he tried to get the telescope to focus better. "Father, I think I may recognize the hull of the larger ship."

Luke noticed the odd phrasing. *Why just the hull?*

Svend was grinning from ear to ear. "I'm positive. It's the *Hamburg!* I'd recognize that aftercastle anywhere. She's been rerigged. The masts are freshly painted and the sails are all newer, but it's definitely the *Hamburg.*" He passed the glass back to Luke.

"That's not possible. She's lost!" Luke tried to focus on the ship, but Svend was pounding him on the back too hard for him to hold a steady view on the ship. "Go get my larger telescope," Luke ordered, as much to save his back as to get a better view of the arrivals. Svend raced down the ramp, rifle banging his back as he ran. In a few minutes, he reappeared, at a slower pace, carrying the captain's large telescope. He handed it to Luke, the anticipation beaming in his eyes.

By this time, most of the settlement had heard Svend's view of the arrivals, and the news was spreading fast that the *Hamburg* had survived. As the crowd gathered at the foot of the ramp, questions were called out, asking for confirmation. Luke finally relented and passed the glass back to Svend. His eyes definitely were getting worse. Svend took one more, long look and then passed the telescope on to the other settlers that had gathered for a glimpse. Many had friends who had sailed on the *Hamburg,* and they wanted assurance that the miracle really had occurred. Luke turned to Svend, "You never lost hope while all the rest of us did. I hope your Agnes is safe. It would be a shame if, after all this time, your faith wasn't rewarded."

"Father, I must confess, even I was beginning to lose hope," Svend began, but Luke interrupted.

"I understand. Now, go unpack and get ready to meet them. The expedition down south is on hold." He studied Svend's rough traveling clothes for a second. "You'll want to change into something more appropriate when you welcome Agnes to her new home." Svend's eyes widened as his father's words sank in. With a whoop he raced down the ramp to the log cabin he shared with Luke. "And send someone to the Cree to tell them they don't need to evacuate." He noticed a man at the back of the crowd head for the Cree village. Reinhardt had heard the request over the clamor of the crowd and gone to tell the chief the good news.

Luke picked up his telescope to study the incoming ships. They were near enough now to be able to pick out individuals. A group on the fore castle of the *Hamburg* caught his eye. He counted the group carefully. The taller figure had blonde hair and was surrounded by red headed children. His jaw dropped. It wasn't possible! How had Mette and the children ended up on the *Hamburg?* He snapped the telescope shut and turned around. Down below on the parade ground, the settlers were going wild with their celebration. The Cree who had come to wish the travelers well on their expedition were still standing around, shaking their heads, wondering what madness had gripped their friends. Joseph was trying to explain, while fending off celebrants who seemed intent on pounding his back, unmindful of his still tender injuries. Karima stepped in and finally stood guard at his back. Her looks alone were enough to stop three people who approached too closely. Luke walked slowly down the ramp into the crowd. As the settlement's leader, there were still jobs that needed to be done before the ships anchored. He motioned for Joseph and Karima to follow him down to the beach.

As he walked, Luke considered what the *Hamburg's* rescue meant for the settlement. The supply fleet was supposed to carry the foodstuffs they needed to last out the winter, before the *Hamburg's* passengers were added to the mix. Hopefully, Captain James had adjusted cargoes and settlers to reflect the changing needs before the ships left Christianburg. In any case, all his carefully made plans would have to be changed again. The ships would need to be offloaded quickly so they could return to Christianburg while the route was still relatively ice free. Housing would have to compete with the harvest, but both would have to be done before the snows started to fly. That would necessitate holding the returning ships while their crews helped with the construction. The knife edge for a possible disaster had just gotten sharper. His thoughts were interrupted by a rising discussion between Joseph and Karima. He stopped and called back for someone to ready the longboat and then turned to the youngsters.

Joseph was laughing and couldn't stop. He motioned for Karima to explain to Luke. "It seems that Joseph will have to find someone else for one of his cousins to marry. Now that the settlement's most eligible bachelor is getting married, there are going to be a lot of jealous girls around here this winter as the pecking order shakes out. He's really glad now that he's going south." She paused, carefully considering her next comment. "I guess I'll have to go south with the group now. It wouldn't do to have Svend as the only married man with his wife along. I'm sure Mette would agree."

Her wink and smile as she took Joseph's arm and headed toward the waiting boat left Luke speechless. Having Mette arrive now had *never* even entered his plans! Surely she and Agnes had spent lots of time together, getting to know each other better. Hopefully they had gotten along well, for Svend's sake. It would never do for the betrothal to be called off after all that had transpired. Luke took a deep breath. Take one crisis at a time. He called to John Barrow to prepare to shove off.

Luke had intended that just one boat meet the fleet, but as he neared the *Hamburg,* a small flotilla of ship's boats and canoes spread out behind him. Everyone in the settlement who could find a boat or canoe was going out to meet the ships. At least they were letting him be the first to board! As they reached the *Hamburg's* side, the repairs from the storm damage became obvious. A long stretch of the midship's railing had been replaced. The masts and sails were new. They had a vague semblance to a Dutch cut, which explained the different appearance than he remembered. The passengers thronged the side, waving frantically at missed loved ones and friends. Svend jumped up and started waving frantically to someone up in the lower rigging. Luke immediately recognized Agnes Roe, Svend's fiancée. Before he could caution him to not rock the boat, Luke was repeating the same dangerous maneuver. He had spotted his wife Mette, standing by the entry port. She didn't wave back, but instead used them to support a very pregnant belly. She smiled at Luke's reaction as he realized just what he was seeing. *This was going to be a very interesting reunion!*

CHAPTER 11

The boat bumped alongside, and Luke immediately sprang to reach the battens and rope railing. Svend barely let him get a firm hold and start up before he joined him, almost knocking them both off into the cold water below. Luke secured a better hold and leaned back to chide Svend. "Take your time! I don't think they would appreciate it if we drowned as soon as they got here. They've been waiting a long time for this moment. Let's at least meet them with dry clothes on!" Luke laughed and then hurried up the remaining battens to his wife. As he breasted the coaming, he saw Mette's children gathered behind her, giving Mette sufficient room to greet him. Agnes stood to one side, hopping up and down in anticipation. He quickly pulled himself up and swept Mette into his arms. Without a single word, he kissed her with all the pent-up emotions stored up from the long separation.

Behind them, Svend climbed through the entry port and gazed, dumbfounded, at Agnes. All the fears and lost dreams vanished as he took a faltering step toward her. She stood hesitantly, not sure what the separation had meant for them. It had been almost seven months since they had been separated by the storm. A lot could have changed since then. Her answer was a crushing embrace and kiss. In the background, the ship's crew raised a huzzah for the reunited couples. Oblivious to the turmoil around them,

Svend whispered to Agnes, "I never gave up hope you had survived. Everyone else said you were dead and I should move on with my life. I love you so much; I can't even put it in words." Agnes pulled his head back with both hands and kissed him harder than before. She had the answer she had been longing for.

John Barrow quietly approached Luke and waited until the family reunion had settled down. "Sir, I hate to break up this reunion, but the other captains need to know what they should do. I assume they should anchor near the dock, but I think you should hear from them, what they have for cargoes, before you decide the order of unloading." Luke nodded and turned toward the aftercastle. Sir Thomas Roe stood near the port side ladder leading to the aftercastle, watching the boats cluster around the *Hamburg*. Seeing Sir Thomas, a wave of relief swept over Luke. Sir Thomas was one of the main investors in the Company and had been chosen to lead the efforts in the New World. Now he could transfer to Sir Thomas some of the problems that had been causing him such stress and anguish.

John gently held his forearm before he could walk aft. "I do have one bit of bad news. Sir Thomas told me that Captain Rheinwald was killed during the storm. He says he urgently needs to speak with you. Much has transpired that we're not aware of, including some visitors." He nodded toward the Dutch ship off the *Hamburg's* port quarter.

Luke finally *looked* at the other ships that had arrived with the *Hamburg* and realized there were peculiarities about all the arriving ships. "Very well, John, let's go speak with our leader." The two strolled aft and Luke embraced Sir Thomas with a heartfelt relief.

Sir Thomas broke the embrace with an enthusiastic wave of his arm, taking in the activities and structures on shore. "I must congratulate you on the progress you've made in the short time you've been here. You hardly seem to have missed us." The broad smile forestalled any thought by Luke that Sir Thomas might be disappointed with his efforts.

"We have been busy. We got off to a good start with the local tribe and they've been very helpful." He paused, choked with emotion, "You have been missed, dreadfully. Your arrival couldn't have been timed better. I hope you still have the foodstuffs we loaded back in Copenhagen. We weren't able to get an adequate crop in to feed everyone here through the winter. We were planning to send a large portion of the settlers back to Christianburg to survive the winter. Another group was packing up to head south and start prospecting and surveying for the mining operations. The Cree there have agreed to support them through this winter in exchange for the trade goods we promised them."

Sir Thomas looked forward, where Svend and Agnes stood, conversing *closely*. "I take it he still wants to marry her? She's done nothing but talk to your wife the whole voyage about him."

Luke's features took on a wistful expression. "I think those two may have one of those marriages that all people dream about, but seldom have. He never gave up hope that she would arrive. He's an important member of the group heading south. We probably should plan on a wedding before he departs."

"I think you might want to include her in that group. She's planned on being an explorer's wife. She's been working with the scouts we had on board and has developed into a very capable shooter." Sir Thomas pointed toward his cabin. "But enough of young love. You and I have business to discuss. I know your mate is itching to get the ships anchored and start unloading." The two men entered the day cabin and got down to business.

It was clear that Sir Thomas had appropriated the captain's cabin as an office. The sideboard was stocked with vintage drinks well beyond the means of a ship's captain. Luke willingly accepted a brandy when Sir Thomas offered. The two men sat down across the small table covered with maps. Sir Thomas indicated the Dutch ship just visible out the cabin windows. "No doubt, you're wondering what happened after we lost contact in the storm. I happened to be on deck, speaking with Captain Rheinwald, when the bonaventure mast gave way. He was a brave man, God rest his soul. Almost before the mast struck the deck, he'd mustered the crew and passengers aft to clear away the wreckage. The shrouds had wrapped themselves around the butt of the mast and were holding the mast so that the mast, spars, and sails trailed over the ship's side. Before he could even get the axes distributed, the tension on the running rigging carried away the mizzen and main masts as well. That was when Rheinwald was injured. He was buried under the wreckage of the mainsail, alongside the remains of the midship's railing. We could hear him underneath the sail and cordage, but couldn't reach him. That was when Agnes grabbed a sailor's knife and wormed her way through the ropes to try to cut him free. She sawed at the ropes, all the while the crew was trying to chop away the parts that were trailing in the water. The ship was threatening to broach from the anchoring debris, but the crew kept at it. We all owe our lives to the mate, who kept the whipstaff manned and barely managed to keep us running with the wind. Agnes managed to drag Rheinwald out just before the crew cut the remaining rope and sent the wreckage overboard. Rheinwald's chest had been crushed, but he lived five days before he finally died. All during that time, he tried to guide the crew on repairs. He was a brave man who loved his ship."

Luke's eyes were wide in disbelief. By all rights, the *Hamburg* should have died in the storm. And Agnes! It was even more of a miracle that she survived her crazy stunt. "So who captained the ship through the rest of the storm?"

"The first mate, Johann Strock. He handled the sailing duties, while I helped the carpenter organize work parties to try and repair the rigging damage. The foremast survived the storm and we were trying to shore it up when the second storm struck. The wind was so fierce and came up so fast that the foremast went by the board before we could do anything to try to protect it. Rheinwald tried to have the mast saved, but it was too far overboard to try to hoist it back aboard. The ship ended up completely dismasted and running with the storm. I think that was the final straw that killed Rheinwald. I think he was sure his ship was lost. Strock was able to keep it from broaching by rigging a sea anchor from an old sail. It kept the ship's head into the wind but we were subject to the whims of wind and current after that."

Sir Thomas paused, recalling the terror of the events. After a moment, he gave himself a shake and continued, "We drifted for about a week to the southwest, and then we finally spotted a ship. We fired our guns and she approached us warily. They stood off and sent a boat over under a white flag. She was a Dutch *fregatte*, the *Rotterdam*, and her captain announced in Dutch, as soon as he was on deck, that we were their prize. Strock started to protest a little too vigorously and got laid out with a belaying pin by one of the Dutch sailors for his efforts. Things started to look nasty until I was able to push through the crowd and explain in Dutch who and what we were. Their captain demanded to see our ship's papers to prove what I said. Strock was starting to come around, so I helped him to his feet and the three of us retired to the captain's cabin to retrieve Rheinwald's papers. Before we went below, I told the ship's company to back off and let us handle it. I also suggested to the ship's cook that he break out our last cask of rum for our *visitors*, to show our hospitality for being rescued. It finally seemed to dawn on everyone, that capture or no, we at least wouldn't face dying of starvation or thirst. Thank the Maker that we were on Rheinwald's ship and not yours. Having German papers made it easier to convince Captain de Groot that we weren't Spanish, French, or English allies. He settled down and asked what we needed. I jokingly asked if he had a spare set of masts and sails so we could fix our damage. He stared at me for a minute and then said, deadpan, not here, but back in

New Amsterdam they had some. If I would consent to paying salvage costs, he would tow us back there for repairs. I asked how much *that* would be. He said we'd have to wait until he rendezvoused with his superior to answer that question. It seemed to be a matter of how much in other prize money the time for the tow would cost them. I told him it would have to be done with a letter of credit, whatever the amount, since we were not carrying any specie with us. We hadn't planned on needing funds when we got to our destination in Newfoundland. When I said Newfoundland, his manner chilled again."

"Why are you going? Are you part of the English settlement there?"

"We're a German ship chartered to a Danish company, just as our papers say. We're starting a new settlement there, on the north coast, to mine the coal that's there. We're hoping to avoid any other settlements." I studied his demeanor to try and ascertain why the sudden change in attitude. I almost blurted out, *Is there some problem with the English that I need to know about?* Then I realized this might be a ship from the fleet action in the Channel. If so, they had a very good reason to dislike a lot of people right then. I continued, "We would be most interested in opening trade with the merchants in New Amsterdam. I'm sure we can reach an agreeable accommodation for your assistance." Captain van den Broecke's expression softened at the hint of money, and he nodded and motioned for us to precede him back on deck.

He spoke briefly with Strock as he completed a tour of our ship, ascertaining in detail what repairs we'd made and what remained. At the end, he announced that his ship would pass us a tow cable and at least take us to the rendezvous with the other ship he was sailing with in company.

After he returned to the *Rotterdam,* they passed a tow cable to us. It was an interesting process. First there was a small rope, followed by a heavier line, and then, finally, the actual tow cable. It was as thick as my leg and was secured to the bits on the forecastle deck. They slowly took up the slack. The cable rose from the sea and vibrated like a bow string as we got under way. It was only a few hours before we heard a hail that their consort had been sighted. The other ship was the *Friesland*, another Dutch *fregatte*, captained by Tjaert de Groot. Captain de Groot sent a boat for Strock and me and we all met on the *Friesland*. De Groot was upset that we were not the French supply ship they had been expecting."

"He is a very intense man. He has an intense hatred for the French, because of their treacherous actions off Dunkirk. He's been raiding all along the coast of New France and on the Grand Banks, destroying any French or English settlement he can find and capturing or sinking any French, Spanish, or English ships he can catch. He had the French lieutenant-general, Sir Isaac de Razilly, prisoner with him from an Acadian settlement they had just raided. That man was a real..." A knock on the door interrupted Sir Thomas before he could continue.

John Barrow stuck his head in and asked, "Captain Foxe, what are your orders for the ships? They are ready to proceed upriver and anchor."

Luke looked at Sir Thomas, "Which ship needs to unload first? We need foodstuffs for the winter, but heating stoves are also needed with the cold weather coming."

Sir Thomas paused to consider the options. "I would recommend the Dutchman, the *Amsterdam Prince*. His cargo is strictly food." Luke looked startled, so Sir Thomas explained, "It's part of the story. Let me finish and you'll understand."

Luke nodded and told his first mate, "Start with the *Amsterdam Prince* and the *Hamburg*. The rest can anchor off shore and give their crews shore leave. Any urgently needed cargo on those ships can be lightered ashore until there is a berthing space at the dock. While you're at it, please convey my respects to Chief Longspear and ask if his women could help our ladies prepare a feast of thanksgiving for the safe arrival of the ships. I'm sure there are enough supplies on the *Amsterdam Prince* that this won't be a problem." John grinned from ear to ear and hurried off to see to the preparations.

The two men sat, studying their brandies while the ship prepared to dock. Luke had a chance to study the cabin further. The furnishings were definitely Sir Thomas'. He'd known Johann Strock almost as long as he had known Captain Rheinwald, and neither could have afforded the lush Oriental carpets that covered the deck. Compared to the painted canvas in his cabin, he felt like a very poor relation visiting a rich uncle. His musings were interrupted when Sir Thomas handed him a refilled snifter with two fingers of brandy swirling in the bottom and returned to his tale.

"Where was I? Oh yes, de Razilly. He's the deputy to Champlain and was in charge of the settlement at La Have, in Acadia. It seems the Dutch caught him totally unprepared and leveled the fort after capturing the settlement. They took de Razilly captive for ransom. He made himself so obnoxious that de Groot requested that we hold him on the *Hamburg*. He was afraid one of his men would stick a knife in Isaac after one of his unending insults. De Razilly's verbal abuse seemed to settle down somewhat after he transferred to our ship, but I still found him quite overbearing and unlikeable. He tried to get friendly with Agnes, but she's a good judge of character and had nothing to do with him. Shortly before we docked in New Amsterdam I think he finally pissed someone off because his complexion took on a green cast and he walked funny." Sir Thomas' face assumed almost a cherubic state at the memory.

"During the voyage, I had an opportunity to meet with de Groot and van den Broecke and discuss their plans for the future. It seems they were survivors of the Dutch naval disaster off Dunkirk. They couldn't retire with the remnant of their fleet and were forced to sail north, around Scotland. They made it to New Amsterdam and finished repairs there. Since then, they've been raiding the French and English, causing as much damage as they can. They have some supporters in New Amsterdam, but the leaders are ambivalent about them. They're afraid the raids may bring down French vengeance on the colony. They've taken a number of prizes and had a hard time disposing of them. When I mentioned the need for shipping that we'll have once we get our feet under us and start shipping goods back to Denmark, he de Groot seemed interested."

"We did get a temporary mast raised with a single sail, which helped with steering and reduced the strain the tow put on the *Rotterdam*. In the end, it took the *Rotterdam* almost a week to tow us into New Amsterdam. The *Friesland* parted company with us the day after the rendezvous, in search of the anticipated French supply ship. When we arrived in New Amsterdam, she was already there with her prize. We were met at the dock with a small crowd that had heard about our adventures from de Groot. The Director General, Wouter van Twiller, was the first on board, practically falling over himself, inquiring if there was anything they could do. De Razilly, who was standing near the entry way, took this to mean him and promptly registered his protest with van Twiller about the destruction of La Have and his *kidnapping* by de Groot. He ranted on that unless he was released and returned immediately to New France, there would be serious consequences to New Amsterdam. He also made a big deal that failure to surrender the two brigands, de Groot and van den Broecke, would be viewed as an act of war. After about five minutes along this same vein, he finally ran out of steam and rounded on van Twiller, expecting an immediate answer. I was amused, until I saw the look on van Twiller's face. He stalked over to van den Broecke, who had come aboard to oversee the return of the tow line. He proceeded to ream him out for the unconscionable attack on a civilian establishment. By the time he had finished, he had commanded that de Razilly be freed and that the two captains meet with him to discuss their future in New Amsterdam. I was astounded that something so important could be decided in the heat of the moment. After getting to know van Twiller better and learning more about the politics of New Amsterdam, the incident came more into focus. The colony has been cut off from Holland, and van Twiller is on his own. He's basically a jumped-up clerk and is frightened of responsibility. They have no prospects for reinforcements and, outside of the two *fregatte,* no real military strength to resist an attack by France. Van Twiller is scared of what the Company will do to him once contact is reestablished, and he's trying to straddle the fence while he waits."

"I was able to contract with the shipyard to repair the *Hamburg's* damage. It was an interesting negotiation on the price, since we had no funds on board with which to pay. It took a couple of days, but some of the local fur traders came up with a novel approach to settle the impasse. They agreed to pay for the repairs, and charter *the* Amsterdam Prince *and stock it with provisions,* in exchange for a charter to set up a fur trading company and sites between here and the Western gate of the Iroquois. They've wanted to expand their territory west, but were facing a great deal of difficulties with competition from the French. They think that by bypassing the Hurons and shipping from here, they can tap into the tribes around the western Great Lakes. Since we will still get a small commission on each pelt they ship through here, I signed off for the Company. It solved our problem of repairing the *Hamburg* and getting extra provisions here without costing us any more funds right now. If I'd known about your gold strike in Newfoundland, I might have held out for a higher commission, but that's a *fait accompli."* He shrugged his shoulders in resignation.

Luke considered the implication that the Dutch would be permanent neighbors. "Did you make any commitments on how they would be *treated?* We've spent a great deal of effort to reach an understanding with the Cree on the laws we all will live under."

Sir Thomas was astounded that Luke had managed to reach that level of relations with the Cree. Luke had always struck him as a man who could tell people what to do, but the nuances of diplomacy had seemed to be something beyond his skills. He'd have to find out more on this new revelation. In the meantime, the answer to Luke's question was simple. "They have already agreed that they are under our authorities. They break the law, they pay the penalty. In reality, they're here because they have no place back in New Amsterdam. They were pushing to reach a more peaceful understanding with the tribes so that they could increase their trade in furs. They stepped on too many toes in the process. These traders are here as settlers, not visitors. That seems to be a common problem there since they were cut off from Holland. After a few weeks there, de Groot paid me a visit. It seems that van Twiller released his captive without any ransom and told both de Groot and van den Broecke that it might be time for them to move on. New Amsterdam can't afford to anger the French any more. To say I was surprised is putting it mildly. The colony has almost nothing in the way of defenses. The two *fregatte* pose a serious obstacle to anyone trying to attack them, but van Twiller is scared that an attack will occur while the ships are out on their own raids. I told de Groot we would be more than willing to act as a base for their operations, as long as any prize ships were sold through us as their agents. That would give us a steady supply of ships as the trade back to Denmark expands. This was *before* I knew about your exploits in arranging to acquire the settlements around Cape Breton. That was a brilliant move, by the way. If we have to fend off the French, it gives us the means to blockade the Cabot Straits and throttle any trade going into the interior."

"By the time work on the *Hamburg* was completed, de Groot did say he would at least use us as a northern base and handle all prizes through us. That way he would avoid angering the leaders in New Amsterdam any further. I suspect it will eventually turn into a permanent arrangement. My last words with him were to the affect that, *You're a smart man, Captain. You know what you need to do if you want to continue your game with the French.* He just smiled in acknowledgement. When we finally sailed, the *fregatte* escorted us as far as the Straits. They planned to continue raiding and make one last attempt to work out their status with van Twiller. I expect they'll winter in Newfoundland."

Sir Thomas stretched and leaned back in his chair, his feet hooked on the table's cross bracing. "When I arrived in Christianburg, I found out that Captain Thomas James had already started work on a major port along the southeast coast. It's ideally situated for defense. In the original timeline, it was the site of a major British port and fort. I left him in charge, since he was doing such a good job. I did warn him to watch out for the French. The Spanish are too busy trying to work out their situation with the Netherlands. No one seems to know for sure who's going to end up in charge there. They all agree that a Spanish fleet is unlikely. They were too damaged in the battle off Dunkirk. Captain Thomas James suggested that we try to contact the English in Plymouth. They're facing action with the French, and the enemy of my enemy could be a friend. He isn't sure if they can be flexible enough to try to work with others. I hope to find out when I return there."

Luke was overwhelmed by the news. He'd intended to improve the Company's access to mineral resources, but it sounded like Sir Thomas was looking toward establishing something even bigger. In any case, the actions he had taken seemed to satisfy the largest stockholder in the Company. Sir Thomas' announcement that he was returning to Christianburg didn't leave much time for unloading the boats and getting them back on their way before ice shut down the northern passage. It also left the question open as to the food situation. From what was visible from the decks, it appeared that *more* people would need to be fed. *I just hope he brought along enough for them and the people that are already here. Otherwise, there are going to be a lot of frustrated passengers taking a long voyage right back to Christianburg.*

Luke took a deep breath, "I don't know how to say this *diplomatically,* so I'll just have to lay it out. Sir Thomas, just how much food and how many people are staying from the group you brought? As I said earlier, we were just about to send a group south for the winter and send most of our settlers back to Christianburg for the winter. We were facing possible starvation this winter without additional foodstuffs. That's my fault because we spent too much time doing the surveys for the minerals around Newfoundland." Luke got his confession out and waited for the axe to fall for his failures.

"Captain Foxe, we brought eight Dutch fur traders with us and they are self-sufficient for their supplies. The other settlers include three shepherds to manage the extra sheep we brought with us, three woodworkers, two scouts, me, my cook, Agnes, and your family. We have almost forty tons of fodder and ten tons of foodstuffs. The rest of the cargoes are dry goods for trade or tools. I would hope that could tide you over until spring. The folks in Christianburg agreed that they could spare that much food. They couldn't foresee any disaster that would leave them short. Captain Andersen did request that any of the militia you could spare be sent back to help with the new fort. The chance that the French might visit us has him deeply concerned. I was going to go back to act as the administrator of the Newfoundland sites to make sure the construction goes smoothly. Captain Thomas James is most anxious to return to sea, but he will just have to wait a little longer. The threats from the French make it imperative I return to Copenhagen and lobby the king for military help." The thought of another sea voyage seemed to weigh heavily on Sir Thomas.

He pulled himself together and continued in a lighter vein, "I do hope we can get Agnes married before I have to leave. I'm the only family she has. It's all she's talked about for the last week."

Luke chuckled, "Well it's a good thing you arrived when you did. Another day and she would have had to spend the winter here alone. Svend was about to set out with the survey party when your ships were sighted. I'm sure we can manage one simple wedding before you have to leave. I'm not sure how happy she'll be to find out she'll be married and her new husband will immediately pull up stakes and be gone for another half year."

Sir Thomas suddenly had the look of a henpecked husband. "Don't write her off as far as the expedition. She's continued to practice her shooting, and Joachim and Kurt Hasselman taught her a lot about woods craft. She may surprise a lot of people with what she can do. If Joachim and Kurt go along, I'm sure she will insist on going too, and she'll probably pull more than her weight." Sir Thomas reached inside the desk, drew out a manifest listing for the entire fleet, and tossed it on the table. "Let's finish going through this so we can be ready in time for that feast you ordered." The two men spent the next hour planning where the colony should go after Sir Thomas left.

Svend and Agnes took the opportunity that the confusion on deck provided to slip below to the cabin she shared with Mette. Svend surveyed the tiny cabin and sat down on one of the two swinging cots that occupied most of the usable space. Agnes settled in beside him, holding his hand tightly in her grasp and snuggling against his shoulder. They just sat there for some time, enjoying the quiet and each other's company before Svend asked almost the same question Luke had asked Sir Thomas, "So tell me, what happened since the last time we spoke?"

Agnes wiggled loose and gave him a soft smack on the arm. "You never kept your promise to come back the next day! I was devastated." Svend's jaw dropped. She held her pose for about ten seconds before breaking down in giggles. "I wish you could see your face! It's precious. I suppose I do owe you some explanation of where we've been and what I've done for the last few months, but you owe me your story too!"

"Fair's fair, but you start," Svend managed between stifled chuckles.

"Well, I assume you know we lost our bonaventure mast when we tried to set out a storm anchor?"

"No, but we guessed something like that must have happened. We did the same thing, and it was nip and tuck when the captain did the maneuver."

"When we tried it, the repair on the mast didn't hold and it went by the board. It sounded like the world was coming to an end, so I ran from my cabin to try and catch a last glimpse of your ship. When I got to the main deck all I could see was a pile of ropes and sails and wood piled up on the after castle and hanging over the side. Sailors were running around with axes trying to cut the wreckage loose. Then one of them shouted they'd found the captain. He was tangled in ropes and pinned alongside mangled railing. The wreckage was pounding the ship's side and sliding as the waves struck the ship. I found ropes tied off by the door to keep people from washing overboard. I tied myself off and went up the ladder on the other side."

"Mister Strock was there directing the rescue effort, but no one was small enough to reach through the opening in the wreckage to free Captain Rheinwald. I could hear him moaning each time the ropes tightened. I grabbed a knife from a sailor that was just standing there. Captain Rheinwald had been so nice and treated me like a lady, I couldn't let him suffer. I watched the wreckage and spotted an area near the captain that wasn't moving much. I jumped down the ladder, squirmed through the few ropes, and started to cut the captain loose. After a minute, I finally cut the one that was holding him against the rail, and two sailors were able to pull him out. I worked my way back out and found my uncle standing there with Mister Strock. He started to yell but then just shook his head and walked forward. Mister Strock took me aside and yelled in my ear, over the storm, that I had been a fool to try what I did. He then hugged me and thanked me for freeing his Captain.

"Just then a yell forward gave us a moment's warning that the other masts were giving way too. We ran to the aft railing and watched them fall over the opposite railing from the other wreckage. When the tangled wreckage hit the water, it was like the ship dropped both anchors. We started wallowing in the waves, and Mister Strock was afraid we'd capsize. While he organized the sailors to clear the aft wreckage, Uncle went below and herded all the able-bodied passengers on deck to start on the wreckage along the main deck. The first thing he did was to ensure everyone roped themselves off. The waves were washing over the deck, and anyone who wasn't tied down was lost. First, they started cutting the lines that were threatening to bring down our last mast. That went quickly, but then they went to work casting off the loose rope and sails. By the time the loose items were off, the sailors had finished with the bonaventure mast and sent it off into the sea. They tried to salvage parts of the main and mizzen masts for repairs, but they were hanging over the side, threatening to punch a hole through the hull. They finally gave up and cut those free too."

Svend asked, "And what were you doing during this mess?"

"I was down below, helping the surgeon with the captain. His visible injuries were a broken arm and leg, and cuts all over his body. Those were severe, but survivable. When the surgeon started to check his ribs, he just shook his head. He said there was nothing he could do but make him as comfortable as he could. A lung was punctured and collapsed. Unless a miracle occurred, the lung fever would be his death in a few days or a week. Captain Rheinwald heard him and told him to bind him up tightly. He needed to make sure his ship and passengers were safe. So I helped bind his chest, and four crewmen took him in a canvas sling back to his cabin, where he could pass orders as needed. He improved a little during the next day, but when the next storm hit and we lost our foremast, he seemed to just fade away and died a day later. I was there with a lay preacher when he died. His last words were "see that the passengers get safely to port." Agnes was crying as she clutched Svend to her.

Svend was in turmoil. He was so mad that she had risked her life, but proud that she was so brave. Discretion finally won out and he whispered, "I'm so proud of you, and so glad you're still alive, but how in the world did you get to port with no masts?"

Agnes sniffled and wiped her nose on her sleeve. "We did get a spar up with a small sail that at least let us steer somewhat of a southwest course. Mister Strock said we might make landfall before we ran out of water if we rationed it closely. A few days later, we spotted a sail to the west and fired our guns to attract their attention. It turned out they were Dutch raiders. They took us in tow and stuck us with one of their captives, a French official by the name of de Razilly." She made a very sour face at the mention of the name.

"Was he really that bad?"

"He was terrible. At first, he just shouted and complained about the Dutch, but after a day or so, he started pestering me. Two days before we made port in New Amsterdam, he tried to corner me below decks. He thought I was some weak peasant girl that would throw herself at an aristocrat. When I rebuffed him, he tried to force me. I remembered the training Kurt Hasselman gave me when we were practicing shooting. I kicked de Razilly sharply in his groin and then slammed my knee into his nose when he doubled over in pain. As he was puking all over the deck, I simply walked away, with one last kick in his stomach." She giggled, "He sure walked funny until we docked."

Svend sat there with his mouth hanging open. He finally managed to stammer out, "Remind me *never* to get you that mad at me."

Agnes giggled again, "I should hope not. I have other plans for your assets." She got up and swung her left leg over Svend's knees and caught him, open mouthed, with a long, deep kiss. Kneeling on the cot, facing him, she started to rub against him with all the anticipation the long voyage had pent up. It only took Svend a moment before he responded to her ministrations.

He managed to murmur in her ear, "We aren't married yet. Do you think this is a good idea?"

"You better believe it! Now hold still. I'll do all the work from here." Agnes unbuttoned his shirt and started to play with the thin wisps of chest hair, when the latch of the cabin door rattled. Mette walked in and the two youngsters stood bolt upright, each blushing furiously.

"Ahem…Ahem … and what do we have here?" Mette asked, trying to stifle a grin. "You do realize this is my cabin too? Luke just told me that we have to get ready to go onshore right now. It seems we're to be the guests at a feast that the settlement is preparing to celebrate our timely arrival." Svend was trying to rebutton his shirt, but kept getting the button in the wrong opening. As he hurried out the door, trying to apologize for some imagined transgression, Mette whispered under her breath, "Luke *really* needs to get that wedding scheduled as soon as possible."

Agnes quirked an eyebrow. "I heard that. I'll be ready whenever it can be set."

Mette finally broke down laughing. "I'm sure you are, girl. It's the men-folk we need to get accustomed to the idea. Now get moving! It would not look good if two of the main guests were late for the feast." She passed Agnes a soft, brown riding outfit she'd found in the trunk that had served as Agnes' clothes closet on the voyage. "This should be warm enough for the evening and still set off your figure for Svend. It may also help remind him you are able to handle yourself in the woods."

Agnes was puzzled. "Why would that matter?"

"So he didn't have time to tell you. You must have really kept his attention on other matters." Agnes blushed again while Mette continued, "He's set to leave on a survey expedition that won't return earlier than late next spring. We'll have to convince him and Luke to postpone it for a few days for a wedding and then let you go with him. The two of you have been separated far too long to make you wait that long for wedded bliss."

She gave Agnes a knowing smile. "That's one reason why I came out early." She looked down at her swollen belly. "That, and other important reasons." Agnes giggled and scooped up the outfit and started to change. When she had finished, Mette took her by the shoulders to get her complete attention. "Listen carefully! Here's what you need to do tonight. I'm sure Luke and Svend have completely forgotten...."

CHAPTER 12

When Mette and Agnes arrived at the fort, they ran into John Barrow, carrying his sea chest toward the beach. When John set the chest down to chat and catch his breath, Mette sent Agnes on ahead to find Svend. "I hoped I'd have a chance to thank you, Mr. Barrow, for keeping Luke and Svend safe. I'm certain they were a handful."

"No need for formalities, just call me John. And yes, they both needed tending to frequently. Svend has really blossomed into a fine young gentleman. I wish I could say it was my doing, but he already had good upbringing. He has a stubborn streak that stood him in good stead many times. He never gave up hope for Agnes when everyone else had written off the *Hamburg*. I think they will be a fine couple." He looked wistfully across the field where Svend and Agnes were locked in a tight embrace. "You know, I never had a family. I shipped out when I was just fifteen, and I've been at sea since then. These last few months, teaching Svend the ropes and watching him grow up, have made me regret not having a family."

Mette smiled at the indirect compliment. "When he announced that he wanted to sail with Captain Foxe, I was afraid it might rob him of his youth, but I see now he's made some good friends on this voyage. Thank you." Shouts from the dock area interrupted Mette. Luke's voice carried and it was evident someone hadn't done what they were supposed to do. "I see Luke still can't stand sloppy work. How has he been?"

John suddenly got very somber. "He's been under enormous pressure. He tries to hide it, but I think his stomach is starting to bother him again. I don't know if he's told you, but we were just about to send most of the settlers back to Christianburg because we hadn't enough food here to last the winter. We spent so much time getting the settlement there on a firm footing that we arrived here too late to get much in the way of crops planted in time. He's become just like a farmer, worrying about weeds and frost and varmints! I'm really glad you decided to come early. You're just what he needs to bring some balance back to his life."

Mette gave John a quick hug. "I was so worried that I would be a burden to him. He has enough problems brewing elsewhere that I didn't want to add to them."

"Problems elsewhere? What haven't I heard about?"

"It seems our new found Dutch friends have some problems that may spill over onto us. I'm sure you've heard about the Dutch ships that were raiding the French and English. Even Captain James told us you knew something about them from the settlements you helped. What you might not have heard was that they were the ships that rescued the *Hamburg*. When they got her towed into New Amsterdam, they found themselves in trouble with the authorities. It seems they had ransacked the main French settlement in Acadia and taken its leader for ransom. He was a thoroughly despicable lout, but his threats of French retaliation cowed the Dutch. It seems they're cut off from the home country and are afraid the French would reciprocate by leveling New Amsterdam. The two Dutch *fregatte* reached an understanding with Sir Thomas that they could use our settlement in Newfoundland as their new base and sell their prizes to us. I know Sir Thomas is going to ask Luke to send as many of the soldiers as he can spare back to Newfoundland. It seems there's a new fort being built at the

English fishing village called St. Johns. There was also talk of opening some type of iron or steel foundry there."

John took a deep breath. Things were moving much faster than he cared for. "I had not heard that part of the news. I'm sure Sir Thomas said something to Luke when they spoke aboard ship. I'll keep it to myself until Luke tells me more. In the meantime, I see your husband has finished aboard ship and is heading this way. Maybe we'll have a chance to speak further during the party. Now go see him and make sure he enjoys himself tonight." With a jovial leer, he left Mette speechless and hoisted the chest on his back and headed for the *København*.

As Luke reached Mette he asked, "What were you and John talking about so earnestly?"

"Nothing special, we were just catching up on gossip. Now let's see to getting you ready for the party. I want to see this cabin where we're going to be living!"

The festivities lasted far into the night. A bonfire in the fort's parade ground cast wildly gyrating shadows on the walls from the dancers celebrating the fleet's arrival. A fiddle and a fife alternated between hornpipes and land lubbers' dances, to the delight of settlers and natives alike. Cree drummers took up a counterpoint beat and two of the tribe's dancers gave an impressive rendition of a classic Cree story with a fife accompaniment. Luke sat with Mette and surveyed the crowd. After weeks of worry about the upcoming winter, everyone seemed to be shedding their worries with the dancing. Mette leaned in and tried to whisper in his ear but failed. She finally cupped her hand and almost shouted, "This is the best party I've ever been to, but I had other plans for our reunion. When and where are we bedding down tonight?" The music hit a lull just as she shouted her last question and everyone nearby heard the request.

Gasps and laughs punctuated Luke's nearly choking on the beer he was trying to drink. The band stopped and stared at the commotion centered on Luke. As the pregnant pause continued, Svend casually asked, "That question had occurred to me too, Captain. I know Mister Barrow said he was planning on returning to the *Hamburg* for the time being, but I hadn't given it much thought. I'm sure you and mother would prefer that the children make themselves scarce." Out in the crowd someone bawled out, "I'm sure that's not your only reason, Svend!" Svend reddened, but smiled back good naturedly.

Embarrassed by the banter, Luke realized he'd been so busy worrying about the arrivals he'd completely forgotten John and Svend had been sharing his cabin. Now that Mette had arrived with the children, something would have to be done about those arrangements. As the music resumed, Karima walked over with Joseph. "We can watch the youngsters tonight over at the meeting house, if you want. It's heated and we can find some bedrolls for them. Svend will have to fend for himself." She turned and gave Svend a quick wink.

Before Luke could answer, Svend quickly volunteered, "I'll bunk out onboard tonight too! No need to do anything else before tomorrow." Before a surprised Luke could answer, Mette took his arm and used it to help her stand up. "Now that that's settled, you and I have some unfinished business to discuss." Open mouthed, Luke let himself be led off like a lamb to the slaughter. Karima kicked Svend to get his attention. "I'm sure you have something better to do too." She looked pointedly toward Agnes.

Finally realizing this was the end game certain friends and family members had engineered, he announced, "I think it's time I cleared out my bedding and headed to my bunk. Agnes stood up and volunteered, "I'll help you gather them up to clear out the cabin." She took Svend's arm and hustled off after Luke and Mette. The plan she and Mette had concocted seemed to be working perfectly.

When they reached the cabin, Svend opened the door and walked in. Mette and Luke were locked in a passionate embrace. "Ahem,… and what do we have here?" It took a moment before the embrace ended. When Mette realized what Svend had said, she broke out laughing. Luke was puzzled and finally asked, "What's so funny?"

"It seems I'm to be hoist on my own petard!" Mette explained. "I caught those two in the same situation in my cabin earlier today." Turning to the two interlopers, she asked, "And what brings you here?"

"Well, this is *my cabin too,* and I need to get some things if I'm to sleep on board for the next few days. Agnes came along to help carry." Svend was trying hard to keep a straight face. Mette eyed the pair but said nothing. Luke was oblivious to the by-play.

"Then be about it! Your mother and I have much to, ah discuss."

Agnes said sweetly, "I'm sure you do." Mette smiled broadly and gave an almost imperceptible nod. Svend gathered up his few clothes and handed his drawing supplies to Agnes. Before the door finished closing, Mette and Luke resumed their earlier embrace.

As they reached the fort's gate, Svend stopped and studied the ships at anchor. The *København* was moored out in the bay, while the Dutchman and the *Hamburg* were still tied up at the dock. Before he could say anything, Agnes gave him a nudge toward the *Hamburg*.

"You didn't say *which ship* you would be bunking in! I have a perfectly good cabin with no roommate tonight, nor for the next few nights if I read the signs right. Let's go, lover!"

Svend hitched up the bundle, "Just what I was thinking. Lead on!"

They didn't actually run, but by the time they reached the gangplank they were both out of breath. No one was keeping watch at the entry port.

The crew had been given liberty to attend the party. They hurried up the plank and raced to Agnes' cabin. The loads were dropped and they resumed the festivities that Mette had interrupted earlier in the day.

Over the next two days, John Barrow acted as a watch dog for his captain, protecting his privacy and seeing to the myriad of details that the unloading required. He also had a chance for a long conversation with Sir Thomas about the events that had transpired in New Amsterdam and since then. Sir Thomas' optimism about the colony's future was tempered by the actions of the Dutch *fregatte* and the expected French reactions when they learned more of what was happening in New France. When pressed on the issue, Sir Thomas admitted he was planning on returning to Copenhagen to pursue reinforcements from King Christian. He was skeptical about what might be available, but more settlers could help limit French options. The new settlement and fort at Thomasville were the cornerstone for the near term.

Others in the settlement aided John's effort. Karima and Joseph shepherded Mette's children and showed them the sights around their new home. In all the bustle, no one noticed that Svend and Agnes had also made themselves scarce. On the third day, Captain Foxe rose early and joined John at the dock as the last of the cargo was off loaded.

"You're looking well sir!" John remarked with a smug smile.

"Thank you, John. I feel better than I have in months. Mette's cooking seems to do wonders for me."

"Is that what you call it? My da always said he was getting his ashes raked. While you've been busy getting well fed, we've finished unloading the ships. They should finish wooding and watering by tomorrow. Sir Thomas wants to leave the day after."

"Why wait? If he's leaving with the ships, they need to start as soon as possible. The ice up north won't wait for them."

"Wellll, there's a certain wedding that he wants to attend before leaving, and that's in two days."

Luke's jaw dropped. "In all the excitement, I'd totally forgotten!"

"That's all right, even the bride and groom don't know yet. I suppose I should find the lucky couple soon. Svend's going to need a little time to recover before his wedding night."

"What do you mean, *find*? Are they missing?"

"Oh, I think they believe they're fooling everyone, but Karima saw them heading toward the *Hamburg* after the party. I made sure the aft cabins were given some privacy, but sounds do travel! It's been quiet this morning, so my spy tells me. I'll go over there just as soon as they tarp off this load. They need to get the news so they can prepare."

Luke shook his head in amazement. "It seems my wife and my best friend are conspiring behind my back to make sure I don't forget my duties. Well, two can play at that game. Has Sir Thomas informed you of our decision?"

John suddenly got a sinking feeling in his stomach. Whenever the captain used that tone, the shoe was about to fall. "What decision?"

"That you will be returning with him to Christianburg on the *København*. You'll be her new captain." John was stunned, but Luke continued. "I'm staying here with the family. I've come to realize I'm not getting any younger, and, with the baby due, Mette needs me around. We're keeping the smaller of the Dutch prizes here over the winter. She's stoutly built and we can haul her up on the beach to avoid the ice. We have just enough time to build a ramp for that. We need the *København's* capacity for shipping goods back to Copenhagen. It's costing too much to keep her here, just in

116

case. Sir Thomas will sail with you and will act as owner on board. You'll command, but heed his advice. He performed well when Rheinwald died and will have to give Captain James directions for the future. We're both worried about what the French may do when they learn of our expansion into territory they claim. He already has the new steel furnace started at Thomasville, and we will have to defend that site. It's much more exposed than we are here so I'm sending the soldiers we brought along. Relations with the Cree are going well and the volunteers can handle any internal problems we may face.

"But enough of this. I have specific orders from *my captain,* that I have a wedding to pull together. Mette told me that I'll be sleeping aboard if I don't get Svend and Agnes married before you sail. Sir Thomas would be quite upset if he sails and they aren't married." Luke looked around, searching for someone, "I need to find Karima and Joseph. I understand she's already got most of the preparations done, but I need to see about another feast." He shook his head in disbelief, "I hope our new food supplies can stand the onslaught!"

The sun was barely up, but preparations for the wedding were in full swing. Karima and Joseph's cousins were hanging pine branches in the council house to add color and a sweet fragrance to the bare hall. Agnes had spent the night ashore with Mette, getting some last-minute fittings done to her dress and advice from her future mother-in-law.

With pins in her mouth, Mette tried to finish the dress' hem and still talk. "Now pay attention! I'm only going to say this once. Relax and enjoy the proceedings. You only get married once in your life and it's a time for joy. Svend's a good man and I *know* he loves you. There will come a time when things don't go the way you expect, but try and listen and talk. There are few things in the world that can't be solved if both of you listen to each other's feelings. And when all else fails, just put your foot down and tell him what he's going to do! Men sometimes need to be given a firm nudge in the right direction."

Agnes thought for a moment. "You mean like this trip he's planning?"

"Exactly! He may not realize you have to go along, but I'm sure by the end of the day, you should be able to make him see sweet reason. Or by the end of the night at the latest!"

A soft scratching at the door caught Mette's attention. "Come in!"

Svend slipped in, holding a large package behind his back. "How's the bride doing? I brought a groom's present for my intended."

Agnes jumped down from the fitting stool and tried to steal a peak at the package. Svend twisted around and kept the package hidden. "This is just for you. Mother, would you please be so kind as to give me a few minutes with my bride, *alone?*"

"All right, but remember, we have to finish the fitting and the sewing before noon. You can't be late and keep everyone waiting." She shook her head as she closed the door. *To be so young and so in love. I hope it lasts.*

Agnes made a quick grab at the package and Svend let her capture it. "Can I open it?"

"That's why I brought it for you. I wanted to show you the other night, but we seemed to have other, more pressing things to do." Svend became flustered, "I know it's not some rich gift that your uncle might get you, but it's something I did for you when everyone said you were lost."

Agnes carefully untied the strings and unwrapped the package. It was Svend's first drawing portfolio It opened to a well viewed spot. The picture was a profile view of Agnes from her first visit to the *København*. Her mouth dropped open in surprise. "You did this from memory? It's beautiful." She leafed through the portfolio. She paused and studied the whale drawings he done after the storm. "This seems alive. Did you actually see them his close?"

"Yes. I even remarked to father that I did that to show you what happened while we were separated. He said I was foolish, but I just knew in my heart you would see it someday."

Agnes came to the pages where Svend had gotten pigments from the Cree. She gasped in surprise. The colors were so vivid and the details seemed to come alive. "You never told me you were trained as a painter!"

"I wasn't. It just seems to come naturally to me. John Barrow kept after me all during the voyage to record what I saw to try to improve. He's a tough critic and always pushed me to do better."

Agnes gently set the portfolio down and then wrapped her arms around Svend and kissed him with a passion that promised volumes. After a long moment, she broke away and whispered, "This is the best present any bride could hope for."

"But it's such a simple thing. I want to give you the world! Your uncle has so much and all I have for you now is this thing." Svend's entire posture was a picture of distress.

"Do you remember when we first met?"

"Of course! I'll never forget that."

"Well do you remember the dress I was wearing? It was a hand me down. Uncle has had a very difficult time accepting me. I came to live with him shortly after his wife had died and he treated me more like a servant than family. I grew up in a household where I was best described as *poor relations*. The love these pictures show is worth more to me than all the gold my uncle has."

"But it's just things!"

"Things! You call that *things*? You just wait 'til tonight and I'll show you things!" She started to tickle Svend where she'd discovered his weakness on their first night together. She was smaller than him, but pressed her advantage ruthlessly. He fell on the bed with Agnes on top.

"All right! All right! I surrender to your superior judgment! Just stop already."

Sensing an advantage, Agnes decided to press forward, "Now, there is one thing you can do for your new bride."

"Whatever you want!"

"I want to go with you when you leave on the surveying expedition." She crossed her arms as she sat on his chest.

Svend stared at her in disbelief. That was the last request he'd expected. He'd assumed she'd want to stay in the fort with his family and wait comfortably for his return. The expedition promised to be cold and uncomfortable under the best of conditions. Nothing that would be suitable for a young bride. But as she sat there glowering at him, he remembered her shooting lessons, the story of her rescue of Captain Rheinwald, and the cryptic comments on how she had *handled* de Razilly. *Maybe I'm the one she'll protect.* He started to smile and then slowly lifted her off and stood up. "If the captain and Heinrich say you can go, I can't think of anyone else I'd rather have along. It will definitely mean the nights won't be as cold!"

Smiling, Agnes gave him a warm embrace. "I don't know about Heinrich, but I'm sure Mette already has the captain firmly in line."

CHAPTER 13

Luke walked the field with Sir Thomas, pointing out the crops they had managed to get planted after they arrived. "We did the best we could, given the lateness of our arrival. We hope to have at least some vegetables for this winter, but they'll be small, at best. I tried to manage the plantings, but the farmers have informed me in no uncertain terms, that this area cannot support enough agriculture to sustain a large population. The soil is too poor and the season is just not long enough. If we're to stay here, we will have to import foodstuffs to prevent scurvy and starvation."

Sir Thomas kicked at a stray rock the children had overlooked in their attentions. "I can see that now. Just one more reason to try and expand our territory southward. In the meantime, your idea to start steel production is working."

Luke considered the statement. "I hope you're right. Those *fregatte* that you spoke of worry me on that score. I knew when I went to Cape Breton that we might antagonize the French by taking over land they claimed. If they should choose to make an issue of it, blood could flow. Going south from here could irritate them too. Do we want to go in that direction?"

"We don't really have a choice *not* to. When I was in New Amsterdam, the Dutch were extremely concerned about French intentions. The French have claimed all the lands north of the Spanish territories. Claiming and *holding* are two different things. The Dutch are probably going to throw out the *fregatte,* because they are afraid they might draw French attention. We are inevitably going to draw French attention. Having two frigates based in our new port of Thomasville could result in control of the Cabot Strait. As you know, the Kirke brothers conquered all of New France with a lot less just a few years ago. If Captain Andersen gets the fortifications at Thomasville finished before the French arrive, we have a very good chance of winning. That's the reason why the soldiers that are going back with me are so important. You yourself said relations here are good and you don't need them. The French won't come here without first conquering New-foundland. I'll be returning to Copenhagen to solicit additional arms and cannons to strengthen our defenses. The prospect of the new steel pro-duction may sway Christian into favorably considering our request. If we get the new arms, hopefully we'll prove to be too tough a nut to crack and the French will leave us alone." Sir Thomas spotted a rabbit watching them from the low brush just beyond the field. He made to pick up a rock to chuck at the beast, but Luke stopped him.

"Leave him be. He and I have an understanding. He doesn't eat while I'm around and I don't embarrass myself trying to get him. So far it's work-ing out for both parties." The rabbit wiggled his nose and loped off before Sir Thomas could reply.

Hearing a scuffle, the two men turned around and found Mette watch-ing them. "So I see my husband has been showing you his farm. I can't say it makes me confident on our future meals." She laughed to ease Luke's angst. "I came to round up the two fathers for the wedding. It's time, and you need to get dressed properly." She took one man on each arm and let them assist her back to the fort's gate.

122

On the roof of the council house, a sailor perched, straining to catch the words of the wedding ceremony inside. Suddenly, he straightened and began to madly wave his cap. It was a signal to the ships at anchor to ring their ships' bells. The crowd gathered outside started to cheer. A moment later the door swung open and the blushing bride, with her husband on her arm, stepped outside to meet their friends. The fort's cannon fired a blank round in salute. The crowd held back for a moment and then gathered the newlyweds on their shoulders and carried them to the waiting musicians.

Svend and Agnes were gently set down and a space gradually opened for them. The two pipers played a soft, English love song and Svend took Agnes in his arms. He managed a slow, clumsy dance that John Barrow had taught him the day before. When it was over they kissed long and warmly. As they broke, the crowd cheered again and the musicians and Cree drummers broke into a hornpipe. Everyone found a partner and started to dance. Svend turned to Agnes and tried to whisper in her ear, but the celebration drowned him out completely. Agnes took him by the hand and eeled her way through the crowd with him in tow.

As they reached a relatively quieter spot she asked, "What was it you were trying to ask?"

"Should we try to go somewhere a little quieter so we can talk?" They both chuckled at the similarity of their thoughts. Agnes pointed to the heavily laden tables. "Let's grab a bite of food while we have a chance. I have a feeling we won't have too many later." They filtered through the crowd and, after a load of back slaps and quick kisses, reached the serving tables.

Mette and Karima stood there, fending off anyone trying to steal a quick snack. Karima noticed them first. "Ah, here is the lovely couple. They shall have the first bite of the feast!" She handed them two wooden platters heaped high with roast pork, carrots and spiced apples. "Go find a quiet

spot and finish quickly. You won't have a chance for the rest of the day."
She gave them a wink and pointed toward Joseph, who was holding a tent
flap back nearby. "We'll give you at least twenty minutes before we tell
anyone where you went."

Thirty minutes later, Svend and Agnes emerged, straightening their out-
fits and munching on the remnants of their meals, beaming with happiness.
Svend leaned over to Joseph and whispered, "Thanks for the time."

"Don't thank me until you see what everyone has in store for you." He
gave Mette, who was standing guard at the food table, a nod.

Mette loudly announced that food was being served and if you wanted
something, get it quick. The well-wishers swamped the table and the feast
began. As soon as a small group was finished, they found Svend and Agnes
and brought them back to the dance area, and the celebration continued.

Off to the side, Luke, Mette, Sir Thomas, and Luther stood with plates
in hand, surveying the festivities. Sir Thomas shook his head in wonder.
"I've been to the king's wedding and the Moghul of India's coronation,
and I've never seen people celebrate with so much joy and energy."

Chief Longspear thought for a moment. "Don't you remember the stories of the prodigal son and the lost lamb?" Sir Thomas looked puzzled.
"Your niece was the lost lamb and has been found and returned. Svend is
the prodigal son who's returned to his family. Everyone knows of their
love and their faith and has many reasons to celebrate. Many here were
facing hunger or a long, perilous journey until you arrived with food. In
this land, death is often no more than a scratch away. When faced with
dangers and sorrow, why shouldn't joy be just as intense when it's time
comes?" He left the three standing there, stunned at his insight, and turned
to join the dancers.

Sir Thomas looked at Luke in surprise. "I think I was just taught a valuable lesson on life. People in Europe may call them heathens, but I think

you made the wisest decision to have them as friends and equals." Luke just nodded agreement and then led Mette to the dance.

The sun had set many hours before, but a small group still mingled around the fires, talking and eating. Agnes leaned over to Svend and whispered, "Have you had a chance to talk to Heinrich yet? He's still here, over by your father."

"No, but now's as good a time as any. Wish me luck."

"No. I'm going with you. Your mother says it's harder for a man to turn down a pretty face."

"So, you've been talking with mother about this?"

"Why not? Good planning always pays off in the long run," she giggled and then pulled him along.

Svend wondered at the plans that seemed to be sweeping him along. *Somehow, I think this is already a done deal. Heinrich just doesn't know it yet.*

Two days later, two groups prepared to leave on their journeys. At the tide, Sir Thomas and the ships that were returning to Christianburg weighed anchor to set sail from James Bay. Before he left, Sir Thomas asked to see the pictures Svend had drawn during the voyage. He specifically asked for five Svend had drawn of the local wildlife. Sir Thomas wouldn't say why he wanted them, just that they were important for the settlement. Svend was surprised at the request but readily acquiesced. Still life drawings of a beaver, polar bear, whale, loon, and cod were carefully wrapped in an oilskin and stowed away with Sir Thomas' baggage. At the crude dock, the settlers waved farewell to recent friends and the soldiers that were returning with Sir Thomas. The ships sailed serenely down the river. As they reached the mouth of the river, a sudden snow squall quickly hid the ships from view. The weather was definitely changing and the crowd quickly dispersed to their jobs. A small party gathered at the fort's gate to send off the survey expedition that was to head south. Two Dutch fur traders also prepared to depart with the expedition. No one was there to see them off.

Svend walked to the fort with the Hasselman brothers. Luke had decided they would be added to the expedition. Their experience as *jaegers* might prove useful if things went wrong. Joachim grabbed Svend's arm and pointed to a pair of figures emerging from his cabin. "Would you look at them!"

Agnes was shouldering a frame backpack, almost as large as she was. She was dressed just like Karima, in a buckskin tunic and beaded leggings. Karima helped her adjust the pack and then hoisted her own up. Agnes also had a rifle sized to her stature. Svend turned to Kurt. "Did you cut down that beautiful rifle of yours and give it to her?"

Kurt was surprised Svend even remembered that he had an extra rifle. "No, her uncle had that made up special for her when we were in New Amsterdam. Whatever you do, don't let her hear you criticizing it. She can shoot the eye out of a squirrel at fifty paces. She has some of the new bullets for it and a mold to make more. Sir Thomas described the bullets to the gun maker so she could load it faster. When the master saw what the bullets could do, he made the rifle and mold for free. It's extremely light and reloads twice as fast as a rifle with normal bullets." He chuckled as Agnes stumbled under the pack. "I just hope that pack doesn't drag her under when we're crossing a stream."

Svend nodded agreement. "I'll check it and make sure she's only packed what's absolutely essential." They quickened their pace to catch up with the two women. They caught up with the pair just as they reached Chief Longspear and his son.

Chief Longspear quickly huddled with Joseph and Karima. "I don't know how you convinced the captain to let women along on this venture son, but I wish you both a safe and swift journey. Nearby, the conversation was repeated almost verbatim between Heinrich and Svend and Agnes. Mette stood by, holding Luke by the arm and occasionally whispering something in his good ear. Luke finally stepped forward to give a farewell speech.

"As our friends and families prepare to depart on this adventure, I would like to remind them that they represent our hopes and dreams for the future. They are our representatives to the clans to the south and will have to depend on good relations with them to survive. Heinrich is in charge and has my and Chief Longspear's instructions on what has been promised to our friends in the south. Search well for the metals we seek, and travel safely. God speed you to your destination."

Mette wept softly and clung to Luke's arm. The group of twelve made quiet goodbyes and then hoisted their packs and headed to the waiting canoes.

As they boarded, Agnes asked Joseph, "Why are we taking the river west, if our destination is south?"

"The river bends to the south and we will portage the canoes to other rivers to speed the journey."

Agnes looked dubiously at the canoes and the size of the packs. Trade goods filled one of the five canoes almost to overflowing. Maybe staying home would have been a better idea, but the die was cast and she'd pull her weight.

CHAPTER 14

September 1634, Copenhagen

S ummer was definitely giving way to a blustery, rainy fall as the Danish capital tried to decide whether the broadsides trumpeting gold strikes in the New World were truly real. King Christian had reviewed the preliminary mining report from the Company and knew that the gold strikes were real, just not as easily reached as the rumors were sounding. It left the king in a dilemma. Once word reached French ears, whether the tale was real or not, there would be a response.

The man across the table would be responsible for meeting that response. As the Minister of War, Captain-Admiral Aage Overgaard was still new to his position. He was just being informed by Christian what the king had gotten the country involved in. "Your Majesty, I agree that the New World adventure gives us a good chance to expand Danish interests in the future. I'm confused though, on what's been promised if France strikes back at the settlements. Do we go to war, which seems quite risky to me, or does the Company have to handle it alone?"

"No, obviously we can't go to war with France. Gustav Adolf is trying to reach a settlement with them and—"

He broke off, looking exceedingly sour. Given that Denmark had recently been forced to surrender to the USE in the Baltic War and had been frog-marched into the Union of Kalmar, Christian was in no position to aggravate Gustav Adolf by starting a war with France that would interfere with the USE emperor's own plans. Gustav Adolf wanted to settle the conflict with France so he could turn his full attention to the east.

"But the Danish crown has no official involvement with the Company," he continued. "So long as we keep it that way, we should be on solid ground. Your job is to find a way to improve our defenses in the New World without giving a *casus belli* to the French. I would suggest that our new lands in the North Sea islands be a starting point. The French have no involvement with them. In the future that now will not happen, the English would have had their main naval base there. What would you suggest?"

"Your Majesty, we have a surplus of twelve pounders in the arsenal that we could transfer to the Company. How many would you want to give them?"

"Don't give them, sell them! If you give them, they'll take all you have. Sell them for what it would cost to replace them. That way, they'll appreciate what they get and we can use the funds for other purposes. The rest of the cannons can be sent to Scapa Flow to arm a fort there. Send enough workmen, troops and supplies to build the fort at Scapa Flow."

Aage could see the king's frustration level building. A flash of inspiration struck. "Your Majesty, this might be an ideal chance to use the submarine. It's limited to a very short operating range. We could have it carried there aboard a tender and it could serve as part of the harbor defense. The French would have no idea how to prepare against it and it would provide a short-term defense until the fort is ready. Best of all, it is not and never has been part of the Danish navy. It's the personal property of the Crown."

The king visibly brightened. "Which means I could officially lease it to the Company and what they do with it later is their affair. Splendid idea!"

The *Scheherazade,* as it had become known, was one of the king's pet projects, but no one in the Navy had been willing to find a use for it. It had finally been finished with a small steam engine, which made it operational. It could attach two spar torpedoes to an enemy vessel and then back off about fifty feet before discharging them, giving it some protection against the explosion. It could submerge far enough that only the breathing tube and a periscope stuck up above the surface. Its biggest drawback was that it could only hold enough fuel for about an hour's operation before it had to retire to its tender ship.

"Very good, Aage! And send some of the Prince's small craft with it. No need to send large warships until the port facilities can hold them, and it saves the Treasury the cost of paying for extra sailors. The warships can stay laid up here until the base is ready."

The king took a long draught from his flagon and then beamed like a school boy who'd just fooled his teacher

Captain Commodore Hans Jeppesen stared at the motley collection of ships he'd been commanded to shepherd to the Orkney Islands. He still wasn't sure who he'd angered, or whether he'd just been unlucky, but this was not an assignment that promised fame. As the younger son of a minor noble from Norway, his influence at court was minimal. Perhaps that was the reason for this not-so-plum assignment. No one wanted to deal with that bizarre vessel now being carried in a cradle on the deck of the *Princess Sophie,* so the assignment went to someone who was of no consequence. If he failed, no great loss to the navy.

A flash caught his attention. The sun had made an appearance from behind the clouds that covered most of the sky, and the *Scheherazade*'s copper clad hull was bright whenever the sun shone upon it. Jeppesen realized that could be a problem under certain circumstances, but there was no point in worrying about it at the moment.

Just like his assignment, he'd heard that no one wanted to command the submersible, but they'd found a young, ambitious volunteer in the end. Lieutenant Mortensen was assigned to captain the submersible when it was detached from the tender. He was an eager, zealous officer with no patron, who was too proud of his command to appreciate the career disadvantages it posed—not to mention that he'd had to resign from the Danish navy in order to take a commission from the Company.

The three gunboats assigned with it, from the Copenhagen harbor defense, were also commanded by junior officers who'd accepted Company commissions. The ships' sailing qualities would pose problems if they encountered foul weather. Thankfully, the rest of the ships under his command were crewed with seasoned officers. The troop ship, the vessels carrying the settlers, and the three galleons carrying the cannon and building supplies were already weighing anchor off in the distance. He could count on them to maintain station during the voyage. The only real warship he commanded was his ship, the *Aalborg*, and it only mounted a ten-gun broadside.

He turned to his first officer. "Signal the fleet to get under way. You have the deck, *Fister* Johannsen. I'll be in my cabin if you need me."

CHAPTER 15

Late October 1634, Christianburg

Sir Thomas stood at the dock with Captain James, discussing last minute details for his mission to the English at Plymouth Plantation. "I know I can count on your discretion to deal with these Puritans. You say you know Captain Standish, so try and get some type of commitment from them to stand together if the French should attack. If all else fails, at least establish a trading pact so that we can exchange goods and news."

Captain James studied the small brig he was sailing on. "I don't *say* I know Miles, I've worked with him previously. If there is anyone there that might be willing to see reason, it's him. As for the rest, I will do my best."

"That's all anyone can ask, Thomas. Good luck and God speed." They shook hands and Captain James strode up the plank to the waiting ship. Behind him, Sir Thomas muttered beneath his breath. "*I just hope you don't rile them up more than they already are. If I wasn't needed so badly here, and you needed so badly anywhere else, I'd have sent you back to Denmark and gone in your place.*"

Captain Andersen waited nearby. Karl had arrived just that morning from Thomasville in summons to a note dispatched by Sir Thomas by boat immediately after he arrived in Christianburg. Sir Thomas turned away from the departing brig, "So tell me, Captain, how goes the construction at Thomasville?" Karl's smile spoke volumes of the successes they had accomplished in the short time he'd been there.

November 1634, Christianburg

The small trading brig hadn't even finished tying down from its return voyage when Captain James dropped down to the dock. Sir Thomas was there to meet him and find out how the mission to the English had gone. From the captain's demeanor it didn't appear promising.

"Those sanctimonious bastards! It was like a Greek chorus. Every time I brought up the subject of the French and their intentions, all they could say was, *The Good Lord will protect us!* If I *ever* hear that phrase again it will be too soon."

"I assume things didn't go as well as you hoped?" Sir Thomas had reservations about the mission even before Captain James had left, but had kept those thoughts to himself. His previous experience with the Puritans in England had raised serious doubts about their flexibility in dealing with uncertain conditions. Captain James had claimed he could work with them. It seemed his previous contacts within the Puritan community had not been as good as he thought.

"Oh, the trading side went fine. As far as military matters, they plan to put their trust in God to spare them from the heathen French! Captain Standish was 'away on military matters' and I had to deal with the religious leaders. They'll have nothing to do with us now, but trade for items they can't make or buy elsewhere. We're a convenient evil to be held at arm's length."

Sir Thomas was mildly surprised. It sounded like the mission had succeeded. In all his years as a diplomat, he'd never met with complete success on the first try. People needed time to get used to new situations. They'd have to make sure the traders that followed up were briefed on how to act.

This had interesting possibilities for the future. "It sounds like you did your best. Let's go get a beer and you can tell me the details. I have to leave for Copenhagen with the tide tomorrow and you can fill me in on the brig's sterling sailing qualities." They both smiled at the jest. The brig's sole passenger cabin made a coffin look spacious.

CHAPTER 16

November 1634, Thomasville's Harbor

Commodore Hans Jeppesen surveyed his small fleet of ships as they neared the entrance to Thomasville's harbor. The crossing from the Orkneys to Newfoundland had been difficult but fast, even by normal late fall weather standards. Four days out from Scapa Flow, they'd encountered gale force winds from the east. The storm had stayed south of them and driven them westward under plain canvas. The *Princess Sophie* had had a particularly rough time, since the submarine it carried on its deck made it ungainly.

The worst, though, was the loss of the other brig they had chartered in Aalborg. On the tenth morning, it simply wasn't there anymore. Over a hundred sailors and passengers were lost. While it wasn't uncommon to lose ships during the fall gales, losing a ship under one's command still hurt. On a better note, the foodstuffs had survived the trip and should be enough to see the settlers through until the early spring supply ships arrived. The hills above the harbor had a dusting of snow, but the harbor area itself was still ice free.

Hans turned to his first officer. "See that priority is given to unloading the lumber and canvas so that construction on the shelters can commence at once. I'll be going ashore to let the Company know about their *new settlers*. I hope they don't scream too loudly."

"You have *how* many passengers?" Captain Karl Andersen was trying to comprehend the amount of crap that had just been dropped on him. He'd been placed in charge of Thomasville primarily to oversee the construction of the steel works, docks, and fortifications. No one had envisioned almost six hundred new settlers arriving right at the start of the winter season. Long range plans had allowed for maybe three or four hundred a year over the next five years. It was sheer luck that the portable sawmill had been sent back from Ft. Hamburg for the winter.

"As I said, about six hundred. Your Company officials back in Denmark had suggested that they be split up between here and the coal mines in Cape Breton. They left it to your discretion how many should stay here. We do have food with us to last the winter, as long as strict rationing is enforced. We will stay as long as you need us to help build the shelters. I also have some presents from the king for you. We have ten new cannon and a submarine."

Karl was confused by the offer. "What is a *submarine,* and what does it do?"

"It's something the king designed for underwater naval defense. It can travel submerged and attack a ship with underwater charges. You're the lucky recipient because no one else wants it. They're all afraid that it might sink itself and its own crew. Or at the least, their careers. Personally, I think it might have some uses for your defensive needs, now that I've seen your harbor."

Hans pointed to the object of discussion. It had been lifted off the deck of the *Princess Sophie* and was now lying off the docks, tied up to its tender. "It doesn't have a lot of range. It's tender, The *Princess Sophie,* supplies its fuel and munitions and can carry it on longer voyages. Her captain is young and inexperienced, but he did volunteer, as did all of his men. If you have any other ships that it can work with, it might be a very effective weapon. Or it will be a widow maker."

Karl studied the Commodore's expression, trying to determine how much he'd just heard was fact and how much wasn't. The earnest pose argued in favor of fact. "We have two Dutch *fregatte* that occasionally call here. It's kind of a loose arrangement. They have Dutch letters of marque that permit them to raid the French, English, and Spaniards, and we act as prize agents for them. Nothing formal, and they come and go as they please. Usually you can find one of them here. We expect at least the *Rotterdam* back in any day now. Pickings are slim once the winter weather sets in."

Hans nodded acknowledgment but refrained from commenting, so Karl continued. "As far as your question about how many people we can take, I'll have to consult with the new iron master. He's the one in charge of building our new steel furnace, and he'll have a lot better notion of how many bodies he can use. I suspect he'll be quite ecstatic to hear he has more workers. I'm not sure how ecstatic I'll be, trying to find them some type of shelter."

◆ ◆ ◆

"Well *Fister* Claussen, one stop down and one to go." Commodore Jeppesen lowered his telescope. "It will almost seem lonely without our submarine and those merchantmen. We should make Cape Breton by Sunday. We'll have to spend more time there to help them build their shelters. As I understand, their lack of workers is hampering their production something fierce. They won't have any extra workers to build the shelters and they don't have a sawmill like Thomasville's. Captain Andersen made our lives a lot simpler by volunteering to complete the shelters at Thomasville, though I'm not sure the merchantmen he drafted would agree."

The first mate grinned, "The look on Nielsen's face when Andersen said he'd not provision any ship that sailed before he approved was priceless! I thought the old fart was going to have an apoplectic stroke. I counted six sputters before he finally got out his objections. Even I learned some new words then. And there was Andersen, quietly sitting back and waiting until he wound down, then softly saying 'I take it you agree then, Captain? Or should I inform my quartermaster we have extra supplies for everyone else?'"

Hans smiled at the memory, "But did you notice? After that, the rest just fell into line."

A hail from the lookout aloft interrupted the conversation. "Sail off the port bow! She appears to be a fishing boat."

"Lay her alongside, *Fister* Claussen. I think some fresh cod would make an excellent meal this evening. I'll have my steward prepare it and the officers can dine with me. We'll go over plans for the rest of our adventure then."

CHAPTER 17

Mid-November 1634, between James Bay and Lake Superior

"You're sure you know where you're taking us, Joseph? I'd hate to have to carry these canoes back over that last stretch of trail." Svend pointed to the low pass they had just descended. There was a stream up ahead, but the banks were steep and rocky with no visible means to descend to the water, which was leaving white trails around the numerous rocks that jutted up above the surface...

"I told you, I was here once, when I was young. The stream takes a sharp turn about a mile beyond those trees. There's a small waterfall and the water's calmer after that. There's also a trail down to the water where we can launch safely."

Karima gave him a questioning stare, "I remember hearing that line before, just before we had to back track for a day. Are you *really* sure?"

"I'll clean up after the meal tonight if I'm wrong!"

"So what! It's your night, anyways." Karima assumed a contrived pout that no one believed and caused the rest of the party to break into laughter. That broke the tension and everyone hoisted their loads and headed on downhill. Fifteen minutes later, the promised landing was reached. The stream was skimmed over with ice in the calm shallows, but the main channel was still open water.

As Svend and Joseph set their canoe down on the gravel shore, Karima and Agnes unshouldered their packs and centered them in the canoe. All but Svend quickly climbed in. He grabbed the rear of the canoe and shoved off into the stream, following the lead canoe. He slipped aboard, dripping from the short push in the water. With an ease grown swift with practice, Karima and Agnes pulled out the paddles and passed them out before the current managed to turn them broadside. Joseph pushed off from a snag that threatened to upset the canoe. With short, practiced strokes they started to paddle. The Dutch fur traders followed closely behind.

Their long journey was almost over, and they had managed to avoid the worst of the snow. They had started with five canoes, but now had six. Two distant cousins of Joseph had joined them at the first village they stopped at. The cousins had previously agreed to join the expedition during the summer council meeting. They were interested in learning from the Danes and wanted to start a trapping business to buy the new items the Danes had showcased to the council. They had constantly pestered Joseph and Svend during the portages about what they were planning to do. Along the way, Svend had made updates to the maps Luke had brought from Grantville and made color drawings of the wildlife they encountered. The cousins wanted to know why he was drawing animals and making the funny marks. Luke explained as best he could about what maps were used for, but the concept was beyond the cousins. Luke showed them on the current map about where they were and how far it was to where Joseph thought the village they were seeking was located. They measured the distance with their hands and then looked about, expecting to see the village. The concept of a map *representing* something was foreign to them. For them, you simply traveled to where you needed to go, because it had always been there and you knew the route. Luke finally had to admit defeat and gave up. They would get there when they got there. The current proved swift enough that only an occasional stroke was needed by the lead paddler to hold the middle of the small river. The two cousins were still constantly calling out from their canoe, "Are we there yet?"

As she sat and watched the trees slide past, Agnes quizzed Joseph on what to expect when they finally arrived at their destination. She had trusted that Svend would have ensured they were provided for, but details were more satisfying. "So Joseph, tell me, what exactly are we going to do for shelter? The ground is frozen and the snow is staying on the ground longer after each snowfall. I do hope you're not intending to simply camp out until spring."

Joseph was puzzled by the question. "Well, we won't have houses like you're used to. My people usually build a very simple shelter and stay very close during the winter. Your Captain Foxe made an arrangement with Chief Keme to construct chimneys and platforms before the weather turned too cold. They had our new council house to use as a guide. We will still have to build the basic huts we will be using. There will be one hut for the couples and one for the single men." He stopped talking and started paddling to hide his grin.

Agnes took a deep breath, "You mean to tell me I have to share a cabin all winter? I just got married! I had plans for spending a long winter getting to know Svend better. I know Karima had similar plans for you."

Svend tapped her on her shoulder with his paddle. "I warned you that this was not for the faint of heart and you insisted on coming along." He started to chuckle until Karima used her paddle to give him a good whack on the top of his head.

"You'll just have to do better! Otherwise, you and Joseph will be joining the other men in their cabin. *Maybe* we'll allow monthly visits, if it suits us."

Both girls tried to leer, but their effort failed. Svend did raise his arms in surrender and called out to Joseph, "I think we need to talk to the others when we get there. There has to be some solution that works out for everyone. I have no intention of sleeping alone for the entire winter."

Just before the early evening sunset, they rounded a bend in the river and their destination was spread out along the inside curve of the river. The bank there was slightly higher and promised protection against spring time floods. There were about three dozen Cree winter houses with smoke rising through openings in the middle of their roofs. Off to the side were the promised platforms with stone chimneys. Surprisingly, piles of split logs lay off to the side. Svend studied the scene, etching it into his mind for a future drawing. Joseph let out a yell to attract attention and make sure they were received as friends. This far south, there were sporadic attacks from Huron to the east, seeking women and furs.

A small crowd quickly gathered to greet the visitors. Clad in rough finished furs, the crowd seemed to completely ignore the snow that had begun to fall. Chief Keme stepped forward and greeted Joseph in an embrace as he stepped from the canoe. "We had begun to wonder if something had happened to you. We expected to see you almost a moon ago."

Joseph pointed toward Svend and Agnes. "My brother's wife, who we had feared was lost at sea, arrived just as we were preparing to depart. We had many feasts and a wedding for them before we could finally leave. The women insisted they accompany us and our chiefs agreed." Joseph pulled the chief aside and whispered, "I think *their wives* actually made the decision, but who am I to say? Just don't say that aloud in front of the women, they can both shoot a running deer at fifty yards." A brief, shared chuckle of husbands, and a slap on the back settled the question.

Keme pointed toward a small clearing, "Come, I will show you the cabin floors and chimneys we agreed to build. I hope they meet your wishes. We spent many hours building them. The trade goods we were promised, you do have them?" Hopeful expectation was evident in his request. His position as chief would be seriously damaged if the promised goods weren't available.

Joseph pointed to the canoe heaped with boxes and packs. "They are there. Just as my father and Captain Foxe promised." They reached the platforms and the craftsmanship was immediately evident. They were built with a stone foundation and split log floors. The chimneys were stone and mud, exactly like the one at the council house at Ft. Hamburg. "They are excellent, Chief! I am very satisfied with the work. As soon as we unload and get our tents set up for the night, I will have the agreed upon goods brought to you. We will work on finishing the cabins in the morning." A yell from one of the Hasselman brothers required Joseph's attention and he made his departure.

The new tents were quickly erected and bedding settled in for the night. Around the evening cook fire, Chief Keme showed his people the tools they had labored so hard for. The expedition watched the celebration with the weariness of travelers finishing a long journey. Joachim pointed toward the excited crowd with a piece of deer meat on his knife. "Svend, I think we've made a good impression on these people."

"I do too. Now we just need to show them we really mean it." Svend replied in solemn agreement, "The chief has summoned the other leaders in the area so we can make our request for land known."

Later that night, Joseph sat staring at the fire sending sparks up the flue of the nearby chimney, and going back over the day's events. The villagers had been ecstatic about the new tools and cloth they had received. But were the changes that were coming going to be worth the cost to their way of life?

Feeling the warmth from the fire and thinking back on what the doctor had done for him after the bear attack, there had to be a middle ground. He just had to be sure to keep that in mind when dealing with the Danes.

At a minimum, they had to provide the medicines and education to his people for them to thrive and make their new way in the future.

CHAPTER 18

December 1634, Sudbury area

Two weeks of daily snowfalls had left the Cree's winter camp site with a foot-deep blanket of snow. The Dutch fur traders had left to make their rounds of the outlying camps, to let the Cree know that beaver pelts could be traded for Dutch trade goods. The survey party had used the enforced down time to recover from the journey and meet with the tribal leaders. All of the clans that controlled the area that the Company was interested in wintered near the site. That was the main reason Luke had been so eager to have the expedition locate there. Having the chance to get to know the white men better and discuss a treaty in their own village seemed the best way for everyone to reach the best arrangement. At the last council session, Svend and Joseph had presented the Company's proposal for developing the minerals in the region. It had been a long session, trying to explain why they were seeking the metals and how they would have to be mined. At one point, Svend had resorted to drawing pictures of the mining operations. That brainstorm resulted in a flurry of questions, some of which were quite probing and a few that resulted in good natured laughter when the answer was finally conveyed. Tonight's council meeting would be the Cree's answer to the proposal.

145

Svend donned his best shirt and buckskin pants and reached for his bearskin coat. After he finished fastening the coat's buttons, Agnes handed him his felt hat and then studied the figure he cut, "You look just fine! Quit fidgeting!" Svend started to protest that he wasn't fidgeting but Agnes cut him short. "Your eyes always start to dart back and forth when you're nervous. How do you expect to convince the council if they pick up on that trait?"

"I do not dart my eyes!"

"Dearest husband, you do when you're nervous. Take my word on it. Now take a deep breath and relax. Joseph assured me in the strictest secrecy that the council will accept your proposal." Svend's eyes lit up, along with a broad smile. "With a few stipulations that Joseph added." The smile turned to a stare.

"And just what might those be?"

"Small items you simply forgot to mention." Agnes' smile dimpled her cheeks. "Mostly things dealing with education and medicine. Joseph insisted that the Company provide protection against diseases they aren't immune to. The education is to insure they can bridge the differences between us and function as equal partners as quickly as possible."

Svend let out a deep sigh. He hadn't realized he'd been holding his breath, waiting for a disaster. He felt like smacking his head for his own forgetfulness. He and Joseph had discussed this so often, he'd simply assumed it would be included. "If that's all we need to add, I should be back early."

Svend went out the cabin door and found Joseph waiting patiently for him by the council hut. As he approached, Joseph asked, "Are you all right? You look a little flustered."

"Nothing's wrong. Just learning more about the marriage process."

Joseph laughed and slapped him on the back. "Keep working at it! Maybe in twenty or thirty years you'll start to figure it out."

"So says the man with less than a year under his belt himself."

"It helps to be a fast learner! Now let's get inside and get down to serious business." He held the door flap open for Svend to enter first.

Inside, the five clan leaders were seated around the central fire, chewing on dried deer meat and chatting quietly. Joseph and Svend walked over and seated themselves across from the chiefs. Svend executed a seated bow and began the session.

"I would like to thank the chiefs for considering our proposal and returning with their answer so promptly. What are your thoughts on this matter?" Svend sat back and politely waited for the reply.

Chief Keme rose and faced the two visitors. "You have shown my people that you keep your word and can provide many things that will make our lives better. You have also been forthright and told us what would have happened to our people in the future that will no longer happen. We still have reservations about what your mining operations are searching for, but we do understand what you are promising for payment. We have spoken with Joseph about his travels in your land and he has suggested some additional items we need to discuss before we agree." Chief Keme paused to let Svend digest what he had said.

Svend nodded and added, "My brother has spoken of your concerns and I must apologize. My people have a saying; *Sometimes you stare so hard you can't see the forest for the trees.* I think I have been guilty of that. I assume you're referring to the education and medical issues you've discussed with Joseph. I've worked so long on this effort; I forgot to mention them because I knew they would be included. Please, expand on what you feel needs to be added. If it's within my power, I will try to accommodate your needs." Svend silently thanked Agnes for her warning earlier. Negotiating with the clan chiefs should be simple from here out.

The chiefs smiled. Negotiating with this youngster should be simple from here on out. Chief Keme continued, "We desire to have a school set up here so that our children can study during the winter. We also want a doctor, like you have at Ft. Hamburg, to treat our sick and injured. It would be best if he could travel from clan to clan during the warm weather and stay here during the winters. In all else we agree. The promised payment seems reasonable and we will provide workers to help, as long as we have sufficient food supplies."

Svend looked to Joseph, who maintained a straight face and managed to nod his agreement. "Done! I will draw up the treaty and have it ready for the council to ratify by tomorrow. Thank you! This should be the start of a long friendship."

Chief Keme remained standing. "As friends, we do have one other concern, our enemies."

Svend looked to Joseph, who shrugged in surprise at the announcement. "What is this concern?" Svend finally asked.

"There have been reports of Huron raiding parties to the east. You have said you intend to search there for some of the metals you seek. We cannot let our friends go into danger without warning. Will you help us defeat these enemies if they should appear?"

Svend paused, wishing Reinhardt had attended this meeting. Military matters were more his specialty. Even advice from one of the Hasselman brothers would have been welcome. Not wanting to insult the chief, Svend made a snap decision, "We will welcome your help and we will provide every effort to defend our friends. I will include a provision in the treaty for this also." *I just hope I don't live to regret this in the future.* The entire group sat down, and Chief Keme motioned for the celebratory meal to be brought in.

CHAPTER 19

Winter 1634-1635, Newfoundland

Karl Andersen waited patiently in front of the fire, warming his hands, for the doctor to finish his examination in the adjacent bedroom. Murmurs through the door warned him that the doctor was wrapping up his exam. As the door opened, the ship's doctor, who had remained after the rescue fleet departed, gave some final instructions to the anxious wife kneeling bedside beside her husband. "Make sure you keep him warm. I will send a jar of sauerkraut as soon as I get back to my office. Make sure he eats the entire jar within the four twenty-four hours." He shut the door and walked over to the fire.

"So, what is it doctor? Some new type of plague?" With the departure of Sir Thomas Roe, Karl was the senior Company official at Thomasville, responsible for the health and safety of all the settlers and militia. The patient, James Wilson, was one of his sergeants.

"No, not a new plague. It's something I've seen too many times in my naval career. It's scurvy."

"Scurvy? How did that show up? I thought that was strictly something you got on long sea voyages. James has been here since we first landed here." Karl's attitude appeared to question the doctor's competence.

"Captain, it's very simple. We're trying to live on fish and bread and not much else. We're not getting the right kinds of food. In fact, our diet is very similar to a ship on a long voyage. I'm sure we'll start seeing more of this in those men that are doing the more rigorous work. There is a small store of sauerkraut that came in the last supply shipment. I want special attention paid to anyone that complains of sore gums. I'll put those people on the sauerkraut right away to try to stave off having too many patients. With any luck, we'll get those promised supplies before this becomes an epidemic." He picked up his case and headed back out into the snow storm that was swirling outside.

King Christian kept his word and two galleons arrived a week later with the promised provisions. Doctor Nielsen looked at the last two jars of sauerkraut sitting on the shelf in his office and let out a sigh of relief. *I don't care how necessary it is, I still can't stomach the taste of sauerkraut!*

Temporary tarp tents sheltered the supplies after they were offloaded. A new warehouse was started to house them, since all available space was occupied by refugees. Work was slow going due to the cold and snow that sapped the strength of the scurvy-weakened workers. The building was finally finished just before Christmas. It was decided that the actual transfer of the supplies would wait until after a Christmas party could be held to celebrate the timely arrival of the supplies to give proper thanks for the deliverance of the refugees who had survived the perils of storm and sea.

Storm clouds to the west promised another round of rain in the morning. Captain Roussard studied the figure in the approaching boat with mild disgust. Gammel Bundgaard was one of those men who always managed to turn up around influential men who needed questionable tasks per-formed in relative secrecy. Etienne Servien's orders to assist him in his scouting mission of the Danish settlements had been vaguely worded and Bundgaard had pushed that authority to the limit. The two ships assigned to the mission were close to the new port that was being called Thomasville. A passing Danish fishing boat captain had provided surprisingly detailed information on the settlements the Danes had established. The gold guil-der and the hint of trading goods had made him very loquacious. It seemed that a food shortage was threatening the settlement, and the imaginary food cargo that Bundgaard had hinted at would be greatly appreciated. Rene's ruminations were interrupted by the arrival of Gammel on deck.

"Monsieur Bundgaard, follow me to my cabin. I'm sure a glass of schnapps will take the chill of the boat ride away." Gammel simply nodded, as his teeth were chattering too much for him to say anything. Once below deck, Gammel shed his boat cape and took the offered glass readily.

After the schnapps had the desired warming effect, Rene inquired, "What brings you out on an afternoon like this? It must be something ter-ribly important."

Bundgaard couldn't suppress his sarcasm, "No, I just felt I needed some exercise for my health! Of course it's important. We reach Thomasville within the day. I've decided only one of the ships will actually make for the port. Since the Dutch *fregatte* already know that you're Dutch, the *Petite Amalie* will remain hove to southwest of the port, out of sight. I'm trans-ferring to your ship for the scouting mission. We'll sail into port and give our men shore leave. If anyone asks about our cargo, you'll say we're con-tracted for New Amsterdam and were driven off course by the storms. Since all we have are clothing and trade goods for the Indians, that should satisfy any nosy officials." He shivered from the drenching he'd gotten in the boat. "Do you have a cabin where I can dry off and change?"

Rene led him to the first mate's cabin. There was a spare set of hammock hooks near the ceiling. "You can bunk in here. Jacques usually has the night watch. You should be comfortable here until we reach port in the morning. I assume you've informed Captain Torcqville that he should head for the rendezvous point if you don't return?"

"Yes, and if *we* aren't there by the following night, he's to sail for New France and advise the Governor General of the developments." Bundgaard gathered up the bundle he'd brought with him and then shut the cabin door.

Their arrival was greeted by a small crowd at the docks. Karl arrived at the dock as the lines were being tossed to waiting hands to secure the ship. Karl cupped his hands and yelled, "Which ship and what's your cargo?"

Rene stood at the portside rail with a speaking trumpet. "*Der Alter Bruder,* from Rotterdam, bound for New Amsterdam with cloth and trade goods. We were driven off course by the storms and need water and shore leave, if that's possible."

Karl waved for them to come ashore. When the gangplank was in place, Rene approached Karl to confirm the approval to land. Karl cut the request short, "Of course you're welcome. We may be short on food, but we have plenty of water. There's a spring just up that hill where you can get water that will make you forget wine." He laughed and pointed up one of the two streets that wandered up the hill. "Just don't use the shallow well over there. That's where they water the work animals."

Rene nodded and waved for the seaman that were standing by the rail to start swinging casks over the side for filling. They had just emptied them before approaching the harbor, to give their story for needing to make port more plausible. If they'd been refused, both ships would have had to make for New France to take on water. If things worked out, Bundgaard would rendezvous with the *Petite Amalie,* and *Der Alter Bruder* could return to France with the intelligence needed to mount France's response to the Danish invasion.

Karl gently guided Rene away from his seamen. "Captain, just between the two of us, do you have any foodstuffs or tools that you would be interested in selling? I can make it worth your while."

Rene laughed, "Sir, you are persistent, but no, I have nothing to sell. I'm chartered to a factor in New Amsterdam, and he is very insistent that his cargo, *his entire cargo,* be delivered. The penalties for failure are very unpleasant. But since he pays well and we understand each other, it works for me. I appreciate your offer." Seeing the nearby tavern, Rene was about to offer to buy Karl a drink, when he noticed Gammel casually strolling in the same direction. A shout from the first mate caught his attention and he apologized to Karl. "I must see to the watering. We want to be able to sail with the tide." He hurried up the gangplank, chivying two of the sailors to watch how they rigged the water cask for lowering.

In the tavern, Bundgaard sought out a table away from the candlelight. He had recognized Karl Andersen from his days in Copenhagen. The last thing he wanted was to try and explain his presence here to someone in authority. Pulling his cap low across his forehead, he called for the barmaid to bring him a beer. When the older gal brought the beer, she demanded payment. "I've had too many sailors try to get a free drink on the house in my day!" Gammel quickly shot back, "And I'll bet that makes for *a lot* of free beers!" She stopped dead in her tracks as the jest sank in and then retorted, "And most of them looked as scruffy as you!" Everyone in the bar broke out in jeers and laughs, with Bundgaard laughing the hardest. He raised the stein to her and took a long draught.

Setting the stein down, Gammel slouched back against the wall and concentrated on the conversations around him. He'd learned at an early age that you could glean more tidbits by listening than questioning. It also raised fewer questions in return. He was here to learn about the local weaknesses, and a tavern at night was the best spot to learn them.

Over the next hour, the crowd turned over as workers at the coke plant came off shift and stopped to have a quick one before heading home for a meal. It quickly became evident that there was some type of food shortage. Conversations centered on the new food warehouse that was being built to store the relief supplies they had just received and the expected arrival of the coal boats from Cape Breton. One loquacious fellow demanded to know why the food warehouse had to be built so close to the coke plant. His table mate smacked him on the head and reminded him, it was just temporary. When the spring came, the new general store would have a room for the food. Afterwards, the warehouse would be used for the new coke plant and steel mill.

A plan started to form as Gammel heard the remarks about the warehouse. It solidified when he spotted a cup with matchsticks customers could use to light their pipes. Captain Rene had told him the watering effort should occupy no more than an hour or two, so he needed to make his preparations quickly. He rose and stepped to the bar to ask the barkeep where the jakes were. The barkeep turned and pointed out back. As he was turned, Gammel palmed a handful of matchsticks. He went out the back door and looked around. Aboard ship, he could see the sailors hoisting the next to last cask aboard from the dock. A pungent odor caught his attention.

The smell of fresh cut wood guided him to the new warehouse. It sat on blocks, above ground and it was unguarded. A pile of shavings and sawdust had spread underneath the corner where the remaining lumber was stacked. Checking to make sure no one saw him, Gammel bent over and felt the kindling. Underneath the building it was dry! Checking back frequently toward the light from the tavern as he worked, he scraped together a pile of shavings and inserted most of the matchsticks under the pile. He rose and sauntered back to the ship.

Rene met him at the gangplank. "Did you find out what you need to know?"

"Of course. How soon can we set sail?"

"We're ready now. Someone needs to find the three men who decided to take some extended shore leave."

"I'll go. I saw them at the tavern when I was there." Gammel jogged down the gangplank and headed straight for the tavern.

When he entered, the three sailors were in an argument with two of the locals. Before a fight could break out, Gammel grabbed two of the sailors by their shoulders and spun them towards the door. "The captain said you had to come back now. Something about grab your drawers and drop the whores. These two are the worst I've ever seen you pick." The third sailor stood there staring at the two men he'd been arguing with. One local turned to the other, and, totally deadpan, remarked, "You know Thorson, even your wife says that!" Gammel quickly led the three sailors out, while inside, the remaining patrons broke out in a gale of laughter.

Outside, Gammel made a few quiet threats to the three that they better report on board *now,* or they would be left. "I have a quick errand to do, so you better step lively. As the three staggered toward the ship, Gammel casually checked the area and then sauntered over to the warehouse. Kneeling down, he quickly struck a match and shoved it under the pile of shavings he'd left. Flames quickly danced throughout the pile and started toward the larger pile under the shed. Nonchalantly, Gammel walked to the waiting ship. As he passed Rene he remarked, "I think you might want to shove off smartly. I think things are going to get hot here very quickly."

The next morning, two ships left the rendezvous southwest of Thomasville. One bound for France and the other for Quebec.

CHAPTER 20

January, 1635, Quebec

F our days later, the *Petite Amalie* dropped anchor in the St. Lawrence off Quebec. A small crowd of Frenchmen and Hurons greeted the ship with cheers and musket shots. She was a very welcome sight. The winter already held the city tight in its grasp and the river was verging on freezing over. Captain Torcqville was frantic to unload and try to force a path back downstream before it became impassable. Everyone nearby, whether they wanted to or not, were dragooned into carrying sacks and bundles from the ship's hold to one of the nearby storage sheds. The pelts for shipment back to France were quickly loaded. The squad of soldiers who had accompanied Gammel was led away to an empty barracks nearby. The troops normally housed there had either died during the past year or were working on a new blockhouse to the west of the city.

Lieutenant Gammel Bundgaard ignored the unloading and grabbed the first white man who looked like he lived in town. "Where do I find *Monsieur* Champlain? I have orders to report to him on my arrival." He waved his dispatch pouch to emphasize his importance.

The man pointed toward a larger wooden fort up the hill about a hundred yards away. "If he's in town, you'll find him at Fort Saint Louis. If he's not in, wait there. It means he's probably out at one of the Indian

157

camps meeting with their chiefs. Those meetings don't usually last long. Snow's going to start soon so he'll definitely be back before nightfall." The man pulled away and hurried off to the nearby tavern.

Bundgaard approached the fort, pausing to study the structure before entering. It was a simple wooden building facing the *Palais Royale* and doubled as the *Compagnie* offices and Champlain's residence. As he stood there, the snow that had been threatening all morning started to fall as fine flakes. A soldier stood guard at the entrance to keep out unwanted visitors. *Definitely not the Palais Royale! Not even the equal of my residence in Copenhagen. This presents an interesting* opportunity. The guard was beginning to study the stranger standing and staring at the Governor General's house in the snow, so Bundgaard hailed him and showed him his commission. "I just arrived on the ship with orders to report to the Governor General. Is he here?"

"No No, *Monsieur,* he is not. I expect him back before dinner." He stepped back and swung the door open. "Will you wait in the sitting room until he returns? I can have a servant lay a fire in the fireplace for you."

"*Merci!*" Bundgaard entered the room and checked it out. It was sparsely furnished, with locally made wooden chairs and a large table that had made the journey from France. The only window was small and opposite the fireplace. A small alcove offered concealed shelter from anyone trying to look in, or trying to shoot someone near the fireplace. "Thank you, this will do fine. A fire would be welcome to drive out the cold." He pulled a chair near the fireplace alcove and settled down to wait.

As the smell from the kitchen of roast venison was starting to make Gammel's mouth water, Samuel de Champlain, Governor General of New France swept in from the snow storm that was strengthening outside. He was accompanied by three *coureurs de bois,* dressed in furs and looking like small snow-covered bears. The woods runners headed straight to the kitchen, calling out to Samuel's adopted Montagnais daughters. "Faith, Hope, Charity! Is that your famous venison stew we smell? Your father promised there would be enough for us." Giggles from the kitchen indicated the question was heard frequently from these visitors.

Champlain stomped the snow from his boots before going back to the kitchen. He paused as he spotted Bundgaard rising from his seat by the fire. "The sentry mentioned you had arrived on the ship today. Your name, *Monsieur?*"

Bundgaard executed a precise court bow. "Lieutenant Gammel Bundgaard, of the cardinal's Guard, with dispatches for Governor Champlain and additional verbal instructions from Etienne Servien. At your service Governor."

Champlain stepped in and closed the door behind him. "I assume the verbal orders are confidential?" Bundgaard nodded and passed him the dispatch pouch. Champlain broke the seal open and began reading the orders. His countenance became grimmer and grimmer as he read the orders from Cardinal Richelieu. He finished and dropped the papers on the table. "Are you familiar with what's in here?"

"*Monsieur* Servien briefed me before giving his additional instructions. He told me to answer any questions you had."

"So what were the orders he gave you?" Champlain glared at him, trying to discern the truth. He'd dealt with many men like Bundgaard and few were ever as honest as they tried to appear.

Bundgaard never paused for the answer. He'd had the whole trip across the Atlantic to perfect his story. The only possible problem was that he had not actually read what Servien had written. If the written orders mentioned a Sergeant Bundgaard, then *Lieutenant* Bundgaard had a great deal of explaining to do. The only answer he'd come up with for that question was that the cardinal had promoted him just before he departed, due to the services he had rendered to the Crown. It would take at least three months for any questions in that regard to be answered, and he planned to be long gone if that was the case. Or for the party *asking* the question to be gone.

"I was instructed to assist Your Excellency with matters along the western borders. I have some familiarity with the parties that have settled there. *Monsieur* Servien left it to your discretion to direct me on how you wanted those actions to proceed. His main direction, from the cardinal, was that all the interlopers were to be expelled, by deadly force if necessary, with their buildings and possessions to be preserved for future French settlers and businesses. We made a stop in Newfoundland on our way here, along with another ship. That ship is on its way back to France with information necessary for removing the soldiers and ships that are based there. When they are through with that task, the soldiers will continue here to reinforce you and finish any removal work for the western trespassers. In the meantime, I am expected to use whatever troops and allies you have to start that process. It was hoped the extra troops would be unnecessary and could be used to simply strengthen your positions here in the north. There was some discussion on other expeditions against the English and Dutch, but I was not privy to those plans." Gammel stopped and waited for Champlain's response. Champlain showed no signs of anger or disbelief. Evidently, the orders had not mentioned his rank. He stifled a sigh of relief, since Champlain clearly was a man of considerable perception and experience.

"You're to assist me in the west." He tapped the papers against the table top. "You might as well understand now, you've been handed a nigh on impossible task. I have a sum total of twenty eight soldiers here, as of last sick call, and another thirty spread across the rest of New France, plus whatever you may have brought with you. My allies, the Huron, Algonquians, and their allied tribes, are hard pressed by the Iroquois and have only a handful of warriors to spare. I will give you what I can, but your first task will be, by the very nature of our shortages in men, to scout out what is happening in the west. I will authorize funds for the capture of any white men they can catch and return with alive. You will go to the *sault* and *detroit* and start forts there to protect the passage to the fur trade territories to the far west. It's too cold to start out right now, but word can be sent west by messenger for the tribes to scout during the trapping season. You'll leave in mid-February and should reach *detroit* as the first trappers are returning with their pelts. I'll send reinforcements as they become available. In the meantime, I should be able to find a house here to billet you in."

One of the adopted daughters stuck her head in the door to announce that dinner was ready. *On the other hand, being close to the Governor may have its benefits!* Samuel ushered Gammel to the kitchen at the rear of the living quarters.

CHAPTER 21

January 1635, Copenhagen

The late morning was crisp but clear. The snowstorm of the previous two days had left nearly a foot of snow in its passing. The king had sent his own carriage to collect Sir Thomas and the Abrabanel brothers. As Sir Thomas watched the empty streets slowly pass by, snow flying from the iron bound wheels, he pondered the implications of the summons. Based on the wording of the invitation, the king had evidently received some type of urgent communication from the New World. Since no new ships had docked during the storm, the message had to have arrived from Aalborg by radio. *We definitely need to advise our people at the radio station to warn us when these types of messages arrive. Even if they can't read the encrypted message, we need to know* when *they arrive. Knowing that a surprise is coming allows one to prepare.* He broke out of his reverie as the carriage unexpectedly pulled up in front of the king's brewery. *Must be running short of beer at home! I hope there's at least a stove here to keep the meeting room warm.* The three men pulled their cloaks closer and stepped out into the cold morning air.

Inside, the brewery was delightfully warm, with a fragrant odor of malt and hops on the air. Chancellor Scheel met them at the door and personally escorted them to an upstairs room where the king was sampling a new batch of beer. "Excellent! That research from Grantville was worth it.

Those up-timers do know something about brewing after all. I want a full batch brewed for my personal cellar as soon as possible." The brew master bowed his head and quickly shooed his assistants out of the room to make way for the important guests.

The king noticed the new arrivals and waved them in. Stoneware steins were already filled and on the table for the visitors. Sir Thomas sat down and pulled his toward him. *It's way too early for this, but I suppose I can nurse it for a while. I don't want to offend the king by making him drink alone.* He took a sip, and then took a deep drink. "This is good, Your Majesty! Give your brew master my compliments. I'd appreciate a keg if there's one to spare from that next batch."

Reuben and Saul took their cue from Sir Thomas, with the same pleasant results. Examining the contents of the stein, Reuben inquired, "This has a very smooth flavor. What has he done differently?"

The king beamed, able to show off his knowledge. "It seems the up-timers filtered the water and the beer a number of times in the brewing process. They claim to take out impurities that way. They say the beer holds better over time also. I doubt I'll ever verify that. It doesn't seem to last!" Everyone laughed and then settled down to business.

King Christian held up a sheet of paper. "No doubt you've already deduced that I've received word about the colonies. What you probably don't know is from where." He looked at the Company officers and their faces confirmed his statement. "One of my agents in France reports that Cardinal Richelieu plans to send ships out to scout our defenses in Newfoundland, with the intent to drive the settlers out. I think he's due for a shock when he learns how many people are there already. It's up to us now, to make sure they have what they need to fend off any attacks. At the same time, I need to continue the stance that it's the Company, and not the Crown, that is sponsoring this effort. I'm not in a position to take on France directly.

"I also received a report from Commodore Jeppesen concerning the settlers he transported to the New World. He has them unloaded and in shelters at Thomasville and Cape Breton. He also requested that additional food be sent, if it hasn't been already. Supplies of items to prevent scurvy were highest on his list of needs. He also suggests that medical personnel be sent. It seems Captain Foxe needs them at Ft. Hamburg to help the natives.

"Captain Foxe's request is the other main reason why I invited you here, though. In his treaties with the natives, they specifically requested that they be provided medical assistance to prevent the spread of 'European' diseases. Captain Foxe endorses this request and adds that he thinks it will be beneficial in the long run for developing the resources there. The tribes have indicated they are willing to work with him in mining the metals, but their living conditions are very tenuous. If there should be plagues, like happened in the Grantville future, they would not be strong enough to feed themselves, help protect the lands and still mine the metals. He pleads that his promises to the natives be honored. What are your thoughts?"

Saul was pleased that the king had finally seen the advantage of the medical program he'd been advocating. "I have word back from Grantville that they are also in favor of this idea. They propose sending a team of four medical workers and a chief nurse. The Company will pay for this effort.

"Their approval does contain one stipulation however, that a radio network be started to maintain contact for these workers." He cleared his throat. "Which will be paid for out of the Danish treasury, not the Company's."

Chancellor Scheel nearly blew the head on his beer into Sir Thomas' lap as he sputtered, "That's preposterous! We can't afford that; and besides, we can't get the parts to build it!" He looked to the king for support. What he saw stopped him dead.

King Christian was in something of a trance, considering the future the proposal made possible. After a minute, he finally broke free and answered, "I think they've got us again. If we can get communications across the Atlantic, we gain a tremendous military advantage over the French. We can warn the settlements when and where to expect attacks, if our spies are even half-way competent. If they're willing to move us to near the front of the line of those waiting for this new technology, I don't see how we can refuse."

The king was still chuckling as he said, "I agree to their stipulation. The Chancellor will send an agreement to Grantville as you asked, for radio and medical aid. It will be paid for with royal funds for the radio work and with Company funds for the medical team. Now, is there anything else?"

CHAPTER 22

January 1635, Paris

Captain Roussard wrapped his cape even tighter as the small lugger approached the city dock. Working directly for the cardinal did have its advantages. Last trip he'd had to make his way from Le Havre to Paris as best he could. This time, chartered boats up the Seine directly to Paris made the winter trip at least bearable and much quicker. It was only a few blocks from the *Quay des Tuileries* to the cardinal's palace. As the boat scraped against the stone landing, Rene tipped the boatman and then stepped onto the quay. A city guard reluctantly stepped away from a fire to challenge the arrival, but quickly headed back when Rene showed him his pass from the cardinal. A short five-minute walk saw Rene inside the *Palais*, waiting for his superior, Etienne Servien.

When the waiting room door opened, he was surprised that the cardinal himself stepped in. "I understand that you have a report on your visit to Newfoundland. Etienne told me you were expected. He's away on business and your news cannot await his return." The cardinal seated himself by the fire and settled down with the small cat he'd been carrying inside his cassock sleeve. "So tell me, what transpired during your reconnaissance?"

Rene took out the notes he had prepared. He wanted to be sure he didn't miss anything of importance. Bundgaard had written down everything that occurred during his scouting trip into the new settlement.

So he said, anyway. With that man, the only thing one could be sure of was that he would cast himself in the best light.

Rene began his report by saying. "As directed, our two ships sailed to Newfoundland to ascertain where and to what extent the Danes had settled and, if we could, attack and drive them out. We were surprised to find a number of well established, fortified sites in both Newfoundland and on the Cape Breton peninsula. In addition, the two Dutch *fregatte* that had been reported have now transferred their operations base to that area and seem to be working with the Danes. We discovered one merchant ship anchored in Thomasville harbor that was previously French flagged. The Danes had bought it and were converting it to carry coal. *Monsieur* Bundgaard recommended that I carry him into the port to reconnoiter and find out more information. Since my ship was known as Dutch, it would be safer than using the ship he had sailed in, with its evident French lines."

As Rene related his story of the visit to Thomasville, Cardinal Richelieu mentally reviewed the few naval assets that could be spared. Ships were available, but the men and funds to supply them were not. It sounded like there had been a recent influx of Danish settlers and that immediate action was needed or they would get so well entrenched that only a major expedition could dislodge them. Bundgaard was deserving of recognition for his initiative in destroying the food supply for the main settlement. If an attack could be launched before they were resupplied, the intruders might be too weak to offer any effective resistance. There were two frigates at Le Havre, but only one was fitted out with cannons at this time. The fact that the other was *en flute* would allow it to serve as an additional troop ship. Without most of its cannons, there would be sufficient space below decks to carry a regiment. A brig or two could serve to carry the balance of troops and any supplies they would need. If orders were dispatched to the Armory immediately, sufficient Cardinal rifles could be issued to the entire force. Against a motley collection of farmers and hired mercenaries, that size force should be more than sufficient to remove the intruders.

Rene's narrative intruded on the cardinal's musings:

"That's all that I can positively state about the situation in Newfoundland. The rest is rumors and suppositions from *Monsieur* Bundgaard's foray into Thomasville. According to his report, the Danes have suborned the few French fishermen in Cape Breton to move to the north coast and set up a mining operation. There are also wild rumors of gold being discovered on the north coast of Newfoundland. He heard stories of it, but no one had actually seen anyone with gold. The most disturbing reports were about the settlement in James Bay. They are calling it Ft. Hamburg and an Englishman, Sir Thomas Roe, is supposedly in charge. They have concluded some type of treaty with the Cree and plan to move south to open mines there. Again, Your Eminence, I must say these are *not* verified. That's the gist of what we learned."

Rene stood there, twisting his cap and waiting for the cardinal's reaction. They had been far too weak to do anything about removing the intruders and failure to accomplish the cardinal's orders was fraught with danger. The fire that Bundgaard had set had been visible as they cleared the harbor, but that was the only direct action they had been able to take. Hopefully, it was sufficient to meet the cardinal's orders.

Cardinal Richelieu considered Rene's report. The man had been very precise in stating what was observed fact, what was rumor, and what was conjecture. It was rare to find such a quality in one's agents. "Rene, that is an excellent report. I want you to repeat that to some officers I will have brought here later this week. They will undoubtedly have more military questions to ask you about what you saw. Servien should have returned by then, too. I will have a room set aside for you nearby. If you need anything in the meantime, let one of my servants know." To emphasize his opinion of the value of Rene's report, the small bag he dropped on the table gave the soft ring of gold. Rene scooped up the purse and stuffed it in his coat, unopened. To have done otherwise would have been an insult to the cardinal's generosity.

"Thank you, Your Eminence. Your generosity is greatly appreciated."

"You've proven your worth, Rene. I'm sure Servien will have more work for you in the future. You may leave." A short wave of the hand confirmed that the meeting was over. The small cat on his lap decided the wave meant it was time for more back rubbing and meowed plaintively.

Etienne Servien sat to one side, recording minutes of the meeting for the cardinal. Two French naval captains, a colonel of infantry, and two merchant captains stood very stiff and formal, digesting the orders they were being given by the cardinal. "Captain Duval, you will be in charge of this expedition to remove the Danes. You are sailing under my orders, not the Crown's. You will start with the settlements along the Newfoundland coast. Make sure that you find them all! If you have to sail around the entire coast, do so. There must not be one foreigner left to challenge our rule of North America. Once that is done, clean out everyone who is involved at the coal mine on the north coast of Cape Breton. That includes any French fishing boats. If they want to work for the Danes, let them be treated like them. I don't want a massacre, if it can be helped, but I want them gone.

"Two frigates and a regiment of infantry with the new rifles should be more than sufficient to remove these invaders. As for the settlement around James Bay, Colonel Rousseau, you will disembark your troops in Quebec after they complete these missions and turn them over to Governor General Champlain. I will give you separate orders to present to him on dealing with the invaders at James Bay. Do not destroy the buildings and mines, if you can help it, when you remove the invaders. I intend to send French colonists to those sites to solidify our hold on those territories. Do you have any questions?"

"Your Eminence, what of the reported Dutch *fregatte*? Do you have any specific directions concerning them?" As the junior Naval Captain, Jacques Le Clercq had ample reasons to be concerned. His ship, the *Dauphin,* would only be carrying its main deck armament. Traveling *en flute* allowed more space for transporting troops, but left him vulnerable in case of a sea engagement.

"According to the reports, only one ship is in port at a time. Disembark the soldiers immediately upon your arrival. Even with only your main deck guns, you will outnumber the Dutch. I hope I've not chosen the wrong officers." Richelieu's stare promised a short career for the wrong answer.

Captain Duval assumed an even stiffer stance, if that was possible. "No, Your Eminence! I'd not had time to brief Captain Le Clercq, since he only arrived a short time before this meeting. We will be more than enough to handle any Dutchman we encounter." He glanced at his fellow captain. Le Clercq wisely held his tongue and simply nodded agreement.

"Very well. Etienne, please see that they have written copies of my orders before they leave. Send a copy to the clerks at the Minister of Marine also, so there are no misunderstandings." He turned to the merchant captain, "I want no delays on your part from loading the cargo. This flotilla must sail no later than two days after your return to Le Havre. You may go." Richelieu picked up a folder and started reading. Servien ushered the four officers out and guided them to his nearby office to pick up their written orders and those for Champlain.

As he tucked the documents in his pouch, Captain Duval paused and asked one last question. "*Monsieur* Servien, just so that I am clear on what the cardinal said. No massacres unless we can't avoid them, correct?"

"You heard perfectly. We don't want to start a war. If challenged, though, you are there at the behest of the *Compagnie Cente Associaes,* not the Crown. When you see Governor General Champlain, please make it clear that we expect that he will handle those invaders to his west. Whether they survive his attentions is immaterial. They *must* be eliminated." Servien handed over one more set of sealed orders. "Here is one more packet for you to deliver in Quebec. I have an agent there, named Bundgaard. Make sure he receives this packet, and he only! These spell out how he is to proceed in the west."

CHAPTER 23

February 1635, Newfoundland

"Take a break, no need to get overheated in this cold! We'll get this last cannon mounted after lunch." A few stray snowflakes were falling from the nearly clear sky. It was so cold the few flakes were all that could be squeezed out of the stray clouds floating in from the ocean. Karl Andersen waved to the two boys standing nearby to bring over the hot cider for the workers. The cold weather was slowing work, but the lost time due to illness had been kept to a minimum by the simple expedient of insuring the men didn't sweat and then get cold. The warm fluids had also helped. Karl stepped over to the gun embrasure and took in the view of Thomasville's harbor below. This last battery on the hill high above the harbor entrance had been difficult in the extreme, but it guaranteed any attacker would face plunging shot if they tried to force an entrance into the harbor. The twelve pounders could reach the far shore with their elevation. Combined with the water-level batteries on both sides of the harbor entrance, Thomasville was shaping up to be a tough nut to crack for any attacker. The next step would be to erect palisades and bastions with firing steps behind the batteries to make sure any force that attacked didn't land troops up the coast and seize the works from the rear.

Good planning had ensured that the holes for the palisade walls had been dug before the cold weather had frozen the ground. Fires on top of the dug spoil, combined with cinders from the steel works, would be loose enough so that the backfill could be packed down after the logs were in place and stiffen the wall. They'd have the palisades up in the next few weeks, as long as the food supplies held up. They were going through the extra food that the king had sent faster than planned. Working hard in cold weather, workers needed more food to stay healthy. Luckily, the fire in the new food warehouse hadn't happened a week later. They had just started to transfer the supplies from the temporary storage tents into the warehouse when that fire had occurred. A few barrels of flour had been scorched, but nothing had been lost. Some folks were convinced that it had been set, but why anyone would destroy the food at the start of a long winter was a mystery. Karl harbored some doubts about the Dutchmen who had been in port at the time, but there was nothing to substantiate his suspicions.

Karl was pleased with the progress. The extra workers meant that the work on the steel works hadn't stopped just to improve the defenses. When spring arrived, they could improve the fortifications with proper ditches in front, protected powder magazines, and overhead cover in case of exploding shells. It was amazing what one remembered from working on fortifications and depending on them to keep one safe. While he'd never been trained as an engineer, over twenty years as a mercenary had taught him a lot about fortifications. It helped to be working with a site that had natural strengths to start with. The hills at the harbor's entrance meant any attacking ship could not effectively fire at batteries placed there. The large, deep water harbor could hold many ships. Right now, the two *fregatte* were anchored at the navy's dock, along with the submersible and its tender. The *fregatte* were taking on supplies for their first raiding expedition of the season. They would probably be gone about four to six weeks each. The spring supply ships for New France were expected soon. Keeping those ships from resupplying Quebec was their paramount mission. The prize money was what kept them at that mission.

From the hill, Karl could just barely make out the copper tower that rose from the middle of the submersible. The tender blocked all view of it from the harbor entrance. The strange, copper-clad ship was tied alongside the tender, and anyone wanting to board had to cross over on the tender and then descend a ladder to the submersible's rounded deck. Unless an attacker knew beforehand that the submersible was there, it would come as a nasty surprise.

Over the past two weeks, the submersible's captain, Oskar Mortensen, had been running the ship through its paces, trying to learn how to use his command. By and large, the vessel seemed to function properly, but it had a number of vulnerabilities and limitations. One time, Mortensen had made the mistake of trying to sneak along the shoreline during the falling tide and had gotten stuck on a mud bar. As the tide finished falling, its copper covered hull had been exposed. One of the workers had remarked that it looked like an upside down copper wind vane with its propeller on the rear. That night, the ship's crew took a lot of good natured ribbing at the tavern after they finally got free with the high tide. Nothing seemed to discourage the cocky attitude they were developing, though. If they were anywhere near as good as they thought they were, any attacker was due for a surprise.

The first hint of spring was in the air as the militia drilled on the open ground near the new steel furnace. The blast furnace was starting to take shape and loomed above the drilling troops. The troops liked the site because, during the winter, all the workers coming and going had kept the snow packed down and easier to march in. Today, the troops were divided into squads based on their abilities. The green militiamen were the largest group, their military ardor driven by the rumors that the French might be paying a visit soon. There were just enough arquebuses to equip any of the settlers who showed the least skill in shooting. They were going through the drill for loading and shooting at a line of man-sized targets thirty yards away. The volleys hit about three targets each try. Karl had let the sergeants handle this chore. They chewed the shooters out, as sergeants throughout history had done, even though the results were actually quite good. Arquebuses were notoriously inaccurate over twenty feet. When the militia was done, they would proceed to resume work on the fill for the new docks. The coal boats from Cape Breton would then be able to unload into carts on the wooden railed tracks that would take their cargo directly to the coking ovens north of the growing town. It had been decided that the steel works would be there to keep the smoke away from the growing town as much as possible.

Food supplies had been getting short, especially the cabbages that helped prevent scurvy, but the first supply ship had arrived four days before and was still unloading at the docks. The only other sailing ship in the harbor was the tender for the submersible. The *fregatte* were expected back any day now. They had already been gone five weeks.

Captain Duval carefully studied the charts spread out on his cabin desk. It had been cloudy the past three days and no course sightings had been possible. By his best reckoning, they should be within a day's sailing time of the settlement at Thomasville. The voyage had been relatively uneventful but had taken a toll on the troops they were transporting. Sickness had broken out three days after leaving Le Havre, and fevers had killed ten outright, and another dozen were stricken with the lung fever. The *Besançon's* doctor said this was a *flu* that the people in Grantville had brought with them. In any case, those who had died were still just as dead as if it were a common fever. The warmer weather seemed to be helping, with no new cases in the past three days. Losses had been expected during the voyage, but no commander liked to lose men before the battle.

It had been decided earlier that the small fleet would approach the coast north of Thomasville, sail south during the night, and attack at dawn. The early morning light should make it difficult to sight their sails in the gray dawn. It would also limit the time the Dutch *fregatte* could coordinate with any shore defenses. With any luck, they could enter the harbor before the Dutch even knew they were there. His orders were specific. The Dutch were to be treated as pirates, with no quarter given. That would help cow the local militia and improve the chances of a bloodless landing. Duval called for his lieutenant, "Signal the other ships to send their captains. We need to discuss the plan for tomorrow's attack. We'll do it over dinner."

As dusk was approaching from the west, a signal broke out from the semaphore on the hill top battery above Thomasville. *Three unknown sails to the northeast.* The lookout at the harbor's battery immediately sent a runner to Captain Andersen.

He interrupted the family at their supper. Before he could finish his report, another runner arrived. "Sir, the lookout now reports four sail sails to the northeast. What are your orders?"

Karl pondered the news. It could be the Dutch with two prizes, but they should be returning from the south. He made up his mind to err on the side of caution. "Notify Captain Mortensen that we may have some business for him. Have him report here immediately. Then notify the batteries that they are to prepare to receive an attack. The hilltop battery will not fire unless I send specific orders to do so. We'll keep them as a surprise, in case we need one. I'll wait on the militia, until we know for certain our visitors are up to no good. No sense interrupting dinners. It's going to be a long enough night as it is."

The runners gave a very sketchy salute and bolted out toward the navy dock and the batteries at the harbor entrance and the hilltop. Karl turned to his wife. "I hope I'm just starting at ghosts, but this feels like it might be what we feared. Please go to the church and ask the pastor to prepare for patients. Stop by the doctor's on your way and let him know too. I'm sorry I got you into this." He kissed her and tried to pat her on her head.

She glared at him. "Karl Andersen, you are no more responsible for this than I am. I agreed to come along and have always known I was a soldier's wife. This is just the first time I haven't had to wait at home, wondering about your fate. Now go do your job, and I'll do mine!" She gave him a quick hug and a peck on the cheek and hurried off to do her errands.

Ten minutes later another signal came from the hill. *Sails are hostile, possibly two armed warships.*

Aboard the *Besançon,* Captain Duval was beside himself. A cloud bank had hidden the approaching coast from view. His last dead reckoning calculation indicated he should be about thirty miles further north than he was. The setting sun had broken through the clouds and spotlighted his upper sails in a golden shaft of light. They were certain to have been sighted if the Danes were keeping any type of proper watch. So now they would have to approach the harbor during the night and try to achieve at least some measure of surprise.

If the *fregatte* were in port, they would have to attack immediately. The odds were too even with his one frigate traveling *en flute* to allow the Dutchmen to prepare for an attack. If the *fregatte* were absent, he would simply scout the harbor, out of range of any cannons, and then attack as the situation warranted. The defenders would be forced to remain at their stations all night to fend off the threat of an attack. They would get little sleep. A tired enemy was halfway to defeat already. Based on the updated charts Captain Roussard had supplied, the full moon should allow for a safe approach since the harbor entrance was plainly visible. In a calm voice, he passed his orders to his officers, "Set all plain sail, we're half way down the lion's throat already. The sooner started, the sooner finished."

Captain Mortensen reported to Karl twenty minutes after the first report of the sighting had arrived. He was dressed in his leather coat and was wearing his signature hat, a peaked hat that someone had fashioned after a World War I submariner's hat in a movie. Oskar looked like he needed a shave, but the straggling blonde whiskers were an affectation he sported to look older than he was. He came to full attention and saluted after he entered Karl's parlor. "Reporting as ordered, Sir! The runner said we might have some business finally?" His enthusiasm was brimming over.

Karl restrained himself from smiling at the serious young officer. He was about to send him in harm's way in an untried vessel. Enthusiasm was about the only shield Oskar had. "Sit down, Captain. We need to develop a strategy to meet this threat."

He pulled out a chair by the table and then sat down opposite him. "Is your ship ready for action? And can you operate at night? It looks like we may have some Frenchmen coming to pay us a visit." He paused to let that sink in. "The reports indicate possibly two frigates and two merchantmen. My guess is they're carrying troops and supplies in the merchantmen."

Oskar didn't even pause before he responded. "My submarine is fully operational and can have its torpedoes loaded in an hour. Yes, we can operate at night—in some ways, it's an advantage—as long as there's some illumination. Which we'll have tonight, because the skies are clear and there's a three-quarters moon. What do you want me to do, attack the frigates?"

"No, the first thing I need you to do is take care of the two merchantmen."

Oskar's surprise was evident. "Why them? I would have thought the warships should be my primary target."

Karl leaned forward, with the best grandfatherly look he could muster. He didn't want to discourage Oskar, but he needed him to understand and follow the orders he was about to give. "Son, the batteries should be able to ward off any bombardment the frigates can deliver. They can bombard us 'til doomsday for all I care. The *fregatte* should be back soon and then they can deal with the frigates. Ships, by themselves, can't capture us. Troops, on the other hand, are a different matter. We probably have more men under arms, but the French should be much better trained and equipped. They *can* capture the port, if we let them get a foothold on shore.

I need you to win the battle by sinking or disabling them before they can land troops." He studied Oskar, trying to determine if honor or duty would win out.

Duty was the victor. "What you say makes sense. I'll go prepare my ship to sortie. If you're right, the troopships should remain offshore while the frigates try to soften up our defenses. With a little luck, they may never even know what hit them." The wolfish grin was what Karl had been hoping for. "After we've finished with the merchantmen, I'll return to the tender and reload, and then you can tell me where we can serve you best after that."

Karl simply nodded, and then Oskar executed another precision salute and left. Karl sat there for a few more minutes, reviewing his strategy.

I pray to God that young man knows what he's doing. Our future is riding on that contraption of his.

CHAPTER 24

Duval's two frigates quietly worked their way toward the harbor entrance. He'd left the troop ship and the supply ship two miles north of the harbor with orders to await further orders. If the *fregatte* were not in port he would send a boat with orders to start landing troops and supplies two hours after he started to bombard the fortifications. That should concentrate the defenders' attention on him and clear the way for an unopposed landing. Once the troops and supplies were landed from the merchantmen, he would send his second frigate to land the additional reinforcements she was carrying. The weather was cooperating with broken cloud cover that should hide the landing from watchers and an almost calm wind that would make rowing the landing boats easier. The risk from breakers was negligible, given how the seas were running. A restrained call from aloft quickly caught his attention. "Full harbor in sight. Water level batteries on each side of the harbor entrance. Possibly another battery near the docks."

Duval stood, holding his breath. *What about the fregatte? Were they there?* After a pause that seemed to last a lifetime, the lookout continued, "Only a small coaster tied up at a far dock. No Dutch *fregatte* in sight."

Duval pounded his fist in his palm. They had them! There was no need to wait until dawn. They could finish the landings tonight and the port should be captured within a day.

"*Monsieur* Giscard, lower the boat and send it to the landing party. Tell them it's to be two hours from the sound of our bombardment and they can land. Clear the decks for action, *quietly*. We will commence firing on the entrance batteries as soon as we are ready." *Nothing can stop us now!*

The exercises were paying off. The crew was going through their assignments with a minimum of wasted movement. Oskar mentally walked through the steps to prepare for battle, since this was to be their first actual fight. Better to take a few moments and make sure nothing was overlooked. In an exercise, missing something was an embarrassment. Now it could mean lives lost needlessly.

The two torpedoes had been loaded and secured in their tubes. In battle, one of them would be extended, and when the submarine drove it into a ship, the barbed harpoons sticking out in front would attach the torpedo to the hull of the ship. That was the theory, at least. But they'd tested that operation many times against wooden hulls and found that if they were driven in by the steam engine the harpoons held five times out of six. By using the manual crankshaft, they only held about half the time. Whichever way, if they failed to hold, they would just try again.

The torpedo would then be released from the spar, and the *Scheherazade* would back away from the target. From experience, they'd learned that they could retreat about fifty feet before the mechanical trigger cord became too difficult to pull. The cord would be pulled and the torpedo would detonate. In theory, the submarine should be safely out of range, but that had yet to be tried with a live torpedo on a live target.

The crew filed below as they finished their respective tasks. Oskar was the only one left standing on the curved deck. Under foot, a repetitious throb indicated that the flash boiler had steam up and the submarine was ready to sail. Oskar checked once more to make sure the deck was clear and then proceeded to cast off the lines holding the submarine to the tender. He turned toward the tender's stern and called out, "Casting off! I have the conn!"

A muffled answer came quickly, "You have command! Good luck and good hunting!" A cheer went up from the sailors lining the tender's starboard rail.

Oskar climbed the short adder ladder to the *Scheherazade's* cylindrical conning tower. The harbor entrance was just visible in the patchy moonlight. He yelled down the hatch, "Ahead one third, course east by northeast, prepare to submerge!" He took one last look around and then slid down the ladder inside the conning tower into the submersible. As soon as the hatch was dogged tight behind him, the ship slowly submerged until only the top of the conning tower, snorkel, and periscope were visible.

The full moon had broken through the evening's overcast and lit the harbor in a soft radiance. Oskar flipped his hat around and then peered through the periscope. Off to the east, two white ghosts coalesced into two warships approaching the harbor entrance as he dialed in the focus. "Interesting. I wonder where their *other* two ships have gotten off to. Captain Andersen was right. They probably split them off to land the troops. If I had to guess, I'd say they were probably on the northern shore. The frigates haven't had enough time to sail south and come back up the coast. What little wind we have tonight is from the north. Two merchantmen would be even slower."

He turned to his helmsman, "Steer to the east/northeast. We'll pass inshore, between the frigates and the shore. We don't have a lot of time for fancy maneuvers, and they aren't likely to spot us in the dark. At least the periscope and snorkel are painted black and should be hard to spot. We have to make sure we don't show off our hull. Even in this low light, the copper should reflect enough to be spotted by a sharp lookout."

The next fifteen minutes were tense as the submarine picked its way clear between the shore and the approaching ships. Oskar continually made minute course corrections that started to irk the helmsman. When the final order to turn north was given the helmsman muttered under his breath, "About bloody time." Oskar ignored the comment and smiled. *At least they're more worried about my nattering than they are about the French. If I do my job right, this should work.*

He called aft to his engineer, *"Fister* Tonnesen, what's the status on our fuel?"

The engineer stuck his head through the hatch to the engine room. "We've enough fuel to operate for another hour at the current speed. I'll still have enough steam left at that point to return to the tender. I might stretch our hunting time another twenty minutes if I hook up the manual crank for the return trip."

"Very well. If we don't sight something within the next thirty minutes we'll return to the harbor." Oskar hated the idea of returning to the harbor with both torpedoes still in their tubes, but this was perhaps the greatest limitation of the submarine: it had a very short operating range.

Oskar froze as a flash of light was visible to the northwest. He focused on the location and was soon rewarded with another flash. In a soft voice he informed the helmsman, "Come left five degrees. I think we have a target."

Five minutes later, a scene unfolded before him. Two merchantmen were transferring cargo and men into longboats to land about three miles north of the harbor entrance. The spot was screened from the battery on the heights by an intervening rock formation, but the ships showed enough light from their lanterns to make them perfect targets for the submersible.

Oskar described the situation to the crew as they prepared to launch an attack. "We'll approach from the seaward side. There's just enough chop that they may not ever see what hits them."

The *Scheherazade* spent the next five minutes trying to maneuver into the optimum attack position.

Aboard the *Madrigal,* the lookouts were focused toward the south, trying to catch the sound of the initial bombardment that was to be the signal to send the longboats ashore. The boats were loaded and maintaining station with their respective ships. Captain Lefebvre paced the afterdeck impatiently, anxious to unload his cargo and retire from the vicinity of any potential combat. The king and Cardinal Richelieu were notorious for not paying for battle damage, and the ship was his livelihood. He glanced toward the open sea, wishing that he could put more sea room between his ship and possible cannon fire from shore. Even though Captain Duval had assured him and Captain Dupre that there wasn't the least chance of them encountering gunfire, he was a cautious man. The night was now bright from the full moon, and the waves were making only about a foot-high chop. As he stared out, he noticed a flash low on the water, about thirty yards out. He strained to make sure that the *fregatte* hadn't returned, but there were no accompanying shadows to be seen. He rubbed his eyes and looked again. There was a burst of bubbles in the area. *Probably just a whale or some dolphins.* He was distracted by the sound of cannon fire to the south. Captain Duval had opened fire on the harbor batteries. He picked up the nearby speaking trumpet and called out, "To hell with the two hour wait!

Nobody's on the beach. Head for shore. We'll start early and get this done before dawn."

◆ ◆ ◆

The *Scheherazade* began its charge on the *Madrigal*. In the poor lighting provided only by the moon, Oskar wasn't worried that anyone aboard the enemy ship would spot the submarine's periscope, snorkel, and conning tower. He wasn't even too worried that they'd spot the exhaust from the engine that came out of a pipe just behind the conning tower. So, they could use the steam engine to drive in the harpoons on the torpedo's head. In daytime, they'd have had to make their final approach using the manual crankshaft with the engine throttled down. That lowered the chance of making a successful strike because even with the whole crew making a tremendous effort, human muscles simply couldn't drive the *Scheherazade* very fast, and the harpoons might fail to attach to the target.

A solid *thunk* and an abrupt lurch announced that the torpedo had struck its target.

But had the harpoons attached it to the hull of the French ship? Oskar couldn't tell from what little he could see through the periscope. All they could do was release the torpedo from the spar, back away, and hope for the best.

Hurriedly, Oskar slid down the ladder into the main compartment of the submarine and took the release cord in his hands. One powerful yank freed the torpedo.

"Reverse," he said. Moments later, the *Scheherazade* began moving backward—slowly, but it only needed to retreat fifty feet or so.

From the complete lack of tension on the release cord, Oskar could tell that the torpedo had, indeed, attached itself to the target's hull. Quickly, he pulled the cord all the way back to the submarine, where a plug near the end of it snugged the cord tight. There would be some water leakage but not much.

He then took the trigger cord in hand. Everything involved in this process was mechanical, not electrical. With the technology they had, trying to use electricity in salt water wasn't possible.

Fifty feet. He watched the cord as it slid through his hands—slowly, slid through his hands, so he had no trouble following the colored markers indicating the length it had gone. The submarine was not moving quickly.

The fifty-foot mark came into view and, with no further ado, he gave the trigger cord a powerful yank.

The concussion from the explosion arrived at the same time as the sound of it. The *Scheherazade* was slammed backward, sideways, and upward. For a moment, the bow of the submarine even surfaced a few inches before sliding back beneath the waves.

The shock was quite a bit worse than Oskar had expected. As it turned out, fifty feet wasn't as safe a distance as they'd thought it would be.

Still, as he quickly looked around, he didn't see that any critical damage had been done, either to the ship or the crew. The worst seemed to be that Seaman Bendt Møller was grimacing with pain and holding his left wrist. It might be broken or sprained.

But there was nothing they could do for Møller right now. Treating his injury would have to wait until they returned to the tender. They only had a very limited amount of time left to conduct operations, and they still had one spar torpedo left. Oskar wanted to use it.

He scrambled back into the conning tower and peered through the periscope. It took him a few seconds to bring the French ship into view.

It was already showing signs of settling by the stern. He could make out men hurrying about on deck, like an anthill kicked over by a small boy, trying to lower the remaining boats. The cargoes hanging in the netting were forgotten in the rush to save themselves.

He swiveled the periscope and spotted several longboats frantically rowing for the beach. They were full of troops. They would undoubtedly try to unload quickly and return for survivors. They should be mostly successful in that effort, since the French ship was not sinking quickly. But they wouldn't be able to salvage any of the gunpowder and firearms on board the ship, and none of any heavier ordnance that might be aboard.

Good enough. Most—almost all, perhaps—of the French soldiers who'd been aboard that ship would make it to shore. But with no cannons and a shortage of gunpowder, there wasn't much they could do against the Danish fortifications.

Oskar swiveled the periscope again, trying to find the remaining French ships. That took a while, since the visibility was poor.

He spotted the two frigates first. Both of them were lying perhaps a hundred yards to the southwest, just off the shoreline, firing on the Danish fort and the fieldworks before it.

The water level battery's return fire was sporadic. The hilltop fort was not firing at all Captain Andersen had said he would not return fire so long as the frigates didn't do much damage to the fort—which, apparently, they weren't. He wanted to save all his ammunition for later, for use against French ground forces launching an assault.

Oskar searched for the second merchantman, which would be his target. When he found it, he hissed his displeasure. The French troop ship was a half mile or so further down the coast than the frigates, and two hundred yards further out to sea.

Just barely within the *Scheherazade's* remaining range—maybe—but the risk would simply be too great. Given the fuel they had left, the submarine would have to pass close to the frigates; they couldn't circle around them. It was not likely the frigates would spot them, in moonlight, but they might. And if they opened fire—the range would be no more than fifty yards.

The *Scheherazade* was never meant to withstand even light cannon fire. A single cannonball striking them, even when submerged, was almost certain to breach the hull.

So be it. They'd done what they could. Hopefully, the reduction they'd caused in the fighting capacity of the French troops would be enough.

"We're returning to the *Princess Sophie*," he announced to the crew. The announcement was followed by the needed directions.

Once they were a few hundred yards from the frigates, Oskar brought the *Scheherazade* to the surface. Even if they were spotted now, they were effectively out of range. The submarine could make better speed on the surface than submerged; not much, but every bit helped. More importantly, Oskar wanted the better visibility he'd have from the conning tower instead of peering through the periscope.

He'd have to bear off far enough from shore to avoid the sandbar that they'd gotten stuck on during the recent exercise. God help them if they did get stuck now. No one could come to their rescue, not with two enemy frigates close by. The crew would have no choice but to abandon ship and swim for shore—in northern waters, in February. None of them would probably make it.

Aboard the French frigate *Dauphin,* Captain Le Clercq studied the effect his guns were having on the enemy's battery. Even with only moonlight, it was evident the battery was suffering little damage.

He wasn't surprised. As they'd expected all along, the fort would have to be taken by ground troops. They'd launch the assault in the morning.

As the morning sun rose over the eastern waters, a lookout on the *Besancon* spotted a longboat rowing for the ship. As it neared, it was evident something was seriously wrong Most of the rowers' clothing was in disarray and the two officers at the stern were bandaged, one of them heavily Captain Duval was summoned and reached the side rail just as Captain Lefebvre struggled onto the deck.

"What in God's name happened to you?" Duval was stunned at the sight of the captain he had sent to oversee the landings.

"I have the misfortune to report that the *Madrigal* was severely damaged. It's still afloat, more-or-less, but the hull has been badly breached. It's drifting out of control and will soon be stranded on shore. It will take months to make it seaworthy again, if it can be done at all with the equipment and materials here."

"What happened?"

Lefebvre shrugged. "We don't really know. A huge explosion struck us after nightfall which tore a great rent in our side. We saw no ships about prior to the blasts, nor were any seen afterward. I suspect that somehow the Danes were able to slip saboteurs aboard who set explosives with some sort of timed fuse."

Duval took a deep, somewhat shaky breath. "And the troops aboard?"

"Most of the soldiers were able to land safely because they were in the first wave of boats we loaded. A few drowned when they tried to swim ashore. This time of year…" He shrugged. Even good swimmers couldn't last long in waters this cold.

"How much use they will be is debatable," he continued. "We lost all the artillery and most of the ammunition in the explosion. Some of the soldiers didn't salvage their firearms, either, so they're effectively disarmed unless we can capture some weapons."

Lefebvre staggered forward and collapsed into Duval's arms.

Duval yelled for the ship's doctor to be summoned. He passed Lefebvre to a seaman nearby and then checked on the boat that had brought the news. The seamen were lying exhausted, with their oars in tangled clumps. Pointing to the boat he ordered the deck watch to their assistance. The doctor arrived and examined Lefebvre.

"He's suffered a concussion and appears to have a number of minor wounds. He should recover with bed rest. Take him and the rest of those men below," he said, pointing to the men that were being helped aboard. "With your permission, Captain, I'll see to my patients."

Duval stared at the disaster that had just boarded and simply nodded. It seemed that the action that had started so well during the night had taken a dramatic turn for the worst. A sharp cannon volley from high above his ship wrenched his attention toward the northern heights. A cloud of gun smoke was billowing out from the crest of the hill. It was evident the Danes had another surprise for him. As he watched, the volley of cannonballs was just visible, descending on his ships. The first volley sailed over the *Besançon* and landed short of the *Dauphin*.

The splashes of the misses roused him from his musings They needed to make new plans, and until they'd done so, remaining here was pointless and ran the risk of taking damage.

"All hands on deck! Prepare to make sail. We're heading back out to sea!"

It took almost ten minutes to set the sails and get under way. By the time the two frigates were out of range, the *Besançon* had taken five hits to her hull and lost her main topmast. The *Dauphin* was somewhat luckier. She only suffered two hits to her hull, but those hits had wrecked one of her remaining cannons. She now had only nine guns left to defend herself in a fight. The two frigates anchored about a mile offshore from the wreck at the landing site. Smoke wisps still curled into the breeze from the wreck of the *Madrigal*.

Captain Lefebvre insisted on hobbling up the ladder from the surgeon's bay to survey his ship in daylight. The *Madrigal* had drifted onto submerged rocks or a sandbar. She had settled on an even keel, but her sails had burnt away when the debris from the explosion had scattered in her rigging. The masts were still there, but with the standing rigging gone, the sea would make short work of them, snapping them off as the wreck rolled with the waves.

Lefebvre stood there, his expression bleak. "She was a good ship. Why did this have to happen?" He looked to Duval but there was no answer. "You said we wouldn't be in danger. Now I have nothing. What will you do now?"

Duval gave a Gallic shrug because he had no idea what he would do next. His forces had suffered a defeat, but the majority of the ground troops were still available, between those already ashore, those on the other brig, the *Aceline,* and those aboard the *Dauphin*. They'd be shorter than planned when it came to artillery, true. But if need be, the nine remaining cannons on the *Dauphin* could be unloaded and mounted on make-shift artillery carriages. Colonel Mansour still had enough soldiers to mount an amphibious operation. Once ashore, no militia should be able to stand against trained soldiers armed with Cardinal muskets.

He turned back to Lefebvre, a plan forming in his mind. One important piece of information still eluded him, though. "Captain Lefebvre, when you first came on board, you said you suspected that someone had boarded the two ships and planted explosives. What led you to that conclusion?"

"I'm positive that no ship inflicted the damage. It had to be the work of saboteurs. What else could it have been?"

That was Duval's own great fear—except he knew this wouldn't have been the work of saboteurs who somehow gained access to the *Madrigal.* He had several friends who'd been stationed aboard ships in the Bay of Lübeck during the final stages of the Baltic War, and had heard their tales of the mysterious destruction of several Danish vessels. The work had been done, they said, by Americans—*frogmen,* they were called—who had equipment that enabled them to swim underwater for some distance and place mines on the bottom of ships. The explosives would then be set off by a timing device.

Duval had not been advised by the *Minister de Marine* that he could expect to face such forces here, but that was the only logical explanation of what happened here.

Not much was known about the capabilities of the American frogmen. But it seemed unlikely they could operate very far from shore, especially in waters this cold.

"We will anchor further offshore to launch our next attack," he said, "and keep guard boats on duty, patrolling the waters. That should prevent a re-occurrence of the disaster that struck here. Thank you for your information. You did the best you could." Duval turned away to issue orders for the next assault on Thomasville.

As he turned away, Lefebvre muttered under his breath, "Thanks for nothing, you pompous ass! I'm the one who lost my ship. I wish your Cardinal was here to risk his fortune, like I had to." He spit on the deck and limped off below.

CHAPTER 25

The view from the hilltop battery provided a panoramic view of the coastline bending away to the north and the two French frigates hove to about a mile off shore. With his telescope, Karl could make out that the French appeared to be preparing for another landing. *What* they would land was the question. Unless the French commander planned to use sailors against his militia, just landing a few naval guns made no sense. He snapped the telescope shut and beckoned one of the runners over. "Locate Captain Mortensen and respectfully, but firmly, invite him to join me here. If he asks why, tell him we may need to pay the French another visit."

About an hour later, Oskar came trudging up the hill, breathing hard. "Now I remember why I chose a naval career, none of these long marches!"

Karl laughed, "That's exactly what Captain Foxe told me when he inspected the fort at Christianburg." He handed Oskar the telescope. "Take a look at our French friends. They're up to something but I don't know what. The one ship looks strange, but I can't say why."

Oskar took the glass and trained it on the ships. After a moment, he started cursing under his breath. He handed the glass to Karl and started to describe what had set him off.

"If you'll look carefully, you can see she's riding high in the water, compared to the other frigate. You'll also notice her lower gun ports are sealed.

She's sailing *en flute,* as the French call it. They removed all the guns from her lower deck and sealed the gun ports. That way they can cram *a lot* of soldiers in the space they vacated. I'd hoped we'd damaged their invasion force enough with last night's success that they'd break off. But they're not, because they have more troops than we thought they did."

He pointed to the enemy ships in the distance. "If you'll notice on the larger frigate, they're swinging out cannon barrels to bring ashore. They may not be as mobile as field artillery, but they certainly can play havoc with your fortifications in a siege."

Karl studied the ships, hoping to see some tidbit that would refute Oskar's analysis. He turned to the submersible's captain and asked, "Do you have any recommendations? Is your ship ready to resume action again? I really don't want to send my militias up against trained regular army troops."

"The submersible won't be ready today, I'm afraid. Once we got back to the *Princess Sophie* and were able to examine the condition of the *Scheherazade* more closely, we found a number of things that had been damaged from the blast. Nothing major, other than the snorkel being loosened, but it all has to be repaired before we can engage the enemy again. Tomorrow morning, at the earliest. Even then, we'll have to sail most of the way on the surface, to reduce the stress on the snorkel. It would be better to spend another day or two, reinforcing the area around the snorkel's base, but I can see we don't have that much time. If they keep going at their current pace, they should be landing within the next hour. Whatever you do, do not send your troops to the beach and contest the landing! Those ships have enough firepower to shatter any troops they catch. If the militia is routed, you'll never stop the regulars when they attack the batteries."

Karl took a deep breath and looked at the troops awaiting his orders. They had been trained, but they were raw and were armed with a mixed assortment of pikes, arquebuses and the captured Cardinal muskets. Throwing them up against trained regulars was a sure way to lose the fight.

He would hold them back and threaten the landing, but ultimately retreat to the prepared defenses. He asked Oskar quietly, "Can your engineer spare you from the repairs? I may need your expertise again before the day is out."

"Certainly, Sir! I stand ready to help."

Just after noon, the French launched their second assault. The longboats turned and headed toward the beach. Other boats continued to patrol the waters between the frigates and the landing site. When Karl sent a small body of troops toward the beaches, the frigates sailed closer to the shore and started a bombardment. Curiously enough, they didn't just head straight in and anchor as Oskar had expected, but executed a complicated maneuver of circling in, firing their guns and circling back out to open water. They kept repeating this until the militia retreated out of range.

Karl watched as the last frigate turned its stern toward the shore and retreated. "Oskar, is that a common maneuver in this type of situation? For a moment, I thought I was fighting cavalry and they were executing a caracole."

Oskar rubbed his eyes from exhaustion. "I've never heard of it being done this way. Usually a ship will sail in and anchor when there's no enemy artillery to contest the landing. A stable ship offers a better platform for firing. It's almost as if they were afraid of something." A puzzled look crossed his face. After a few moments a thin smile began. "Maybe they *are* afraid of something. I wonder if they do know what happened last night. If no one saw us, they may suspect the merchantmen were sunk with some type of mine. That would explain why the boats are patrolling so heavily inshore. It means we still have a chance against them if we can get the repairs done in time. If you will excuse me, Captain Andersen, I must get back to my ship and expedite the repairs."

Oskar's face practically glowed with the thoughts of future triumphs. Karl waved him on his way.

It was two days before the repairs to the submersible were finally completed. In the meantime, the French had landed and even managed to manhandle two 24 pound cannon barrels to the beach. There the ship's carpenter had fabricated rough field carriages with spare wheels the *Dauphin* had in her supply of spare parts for the troops. The troops had only been able to advance along the shoreline, where the frigates were able to fend off any attacks by the militia. The militia force was large enough to swamp the French regulars if they ever ventured beyond the range of the frigates' guns. The French strategy had devolved to a straight forward envelopment of the water level battery on the north shore. With that position destroyed, the two frigates could enter the harbor on a dark night and bombard the town. Once the town was lost, the hilltop battery could be surrounded and starved into submission.

The French were struggling to drag the two cannons over the last of the broken ground north of the harbor entrance. Captain Duval and Colonel Rousseau watched the efforts from the safety of the *Besancon's* deck. The militia had marksmen positioned higher up the hill to maintain a galling fire on the struggling soldiers. The frigates returned the favor with a steady fusillade of cannon balls. Neither side was inflicting much damage. Captain Duval pointed out the final reassembly of the second cannon to the Colonel. "It shouldn't be long now. We can get the guns close enough by nightfall to destroy the lower battery. It should be dark enough tonight to slip into the harbor and attack the town. After what they did to the *Madrigal,* your men can sack the town for all I care. Just remember, the coke and iron facilities *must not be touched!* The cardinal was adamant about that."

"Don't worry Captain; my sergeants have warned the men many times. The town is theirs, but the plants are to remain safe. I've already told off a squad just for that purpose." A cry from aloft interrupted any further discussion.

"Object in the water on the aft quarter!" The lookout pointed to two shafts that stuck up from the water and were leaving minor bow waves.

Captain Duval hurried aft to see if he could spot what the lookout had seen. As he reached the stern the lookout called again, "Object in the water and it looks to be headed toward our stern!"

Duval looked out, over the taffrail, and tried to see what it was. All he could see—and it took a while to spot them—were a stubby copper-colored cylinder and two pipes sticking up from the water, with a froth of bubbles coming behind them.

"What…?"

The truth dawned on him. He knew from his reading and discussions with other French officers that in the world the Americans came from, they had the capability of building vessels that could operate underwater. "Submarines," they were called, if he remembered right. But he'd always assumed that capability was beyond the reach of his own era.

Apparently not. He turned to the gun crew closest to him and pointed at the oncoming trio of whatever-they-were. "You see them?"

The chief of the crew nodded.

"Fire on them immediately." He moved down to the next gun and gave the same order.

By the time the first gun crew got its cannon realigned, the mysterious objects were much closer to the ship. So close that the gun could barely be depressed far enough to have a chance of hitting it.

But… There was still a chance.

"Fire!" the crew chief bellowed.

The impact as the *Scheherazade* drove in the harpoon was gratifyingly solid. Oskar was quite sure the torpedo was attached to the target. He yanked on the release cord and began pulling it in, while shouting: "Reverse!"

Before the submarine could go back more than a foot or two, however, there was a loud *clang* from above.

"What happened?" demanded Oskar.

The seamen closest to the source of the clang stood up and examined the ceiling of the vessel above.

"Ah… I think the snorkel is gone, Captain. Almost all of it, anyway. We'll start taking on water soon if we don't go closer to the surface."

Snorkel… *gone?* How in the world had that happened?

"Keep reversing!" he ordered, and raced to the conning tower to see what he could through the periscope.

It took him a few seconds to bring the French warship into view, and what he saw froze him in place for a moment. Two—no, three—of the enemy's guns were being trained around to bear on the *Scheherazade*.

One of them fired. Oskar could sense, if not see, the cannonball passing right over the submarine.

He only had seconds. He came out of the conning tower and rushed to the bow. There, he took the trigger cord in hand. It had been unreeling slowly as the *Scheherazade* reversed—oh, so very slowly. The thirty-foot marker was just sliding through his hands.

He wouldn't wait; whatever the risk of being too close. He yanked on the cord.

The *Besançon's* stern heaved up, as if a leviathan had struck it. Duval was thrown off his feet, landing on his hands and knees.

He understood instantly what had happened. The use of spar torpedoes—to quite good affect—by the Danes against the USE's naval forces at Copenhagen was a story well-known by now to most professional naval officers. Just about all of whom—Duval was no exception—considered the weapons foolhardy to the point of being suicidal. But they worked, no one could deny it. In essence, the Danes had figured out a way to deliver the torpedo while underwater instead of approaching visibly across the surface.

But he had no time now to worry about the Danes. His ship had been gravely, perhaps mortally, wounded. He needed to take charge of getting it to safety.

The chaos produced by this blast was far worse inside the *Scheherazade* that it had been when they'd managed to back away the full fifty feet. Then, the worst injury had been Seaman Møller Møller's breaking his wrist. This time, Seaman Jepsen broke his neck when he was hurled against a corner of the steam engine. And Seaman Nygaard was lying unconscious against the curving wall of the submarine. Oskar could only hope his injury wasn't fatal.

But Nygaard would have to wait until later. Oskar had three men left, and a vessel that was on the verge of sinking. Water was now coming in through a leak in one of the torpedo tubes as well as the severed snorkel.

Thankfully, the steam engine was still working—and still faithfully driving the *Scheherazade* in reverse.

Oskar pointed to the simple controls. "Henriksen, put it in forward." He then seized the equally simple controls toward the bow and started bringing the vessel to the surface. Normally, that would have been Nygaard's job.

As he did so, Oskar steered the *Scheherazade* to the left. That was to the north, if he still retained his bearings—which he very well might not, after the pandemonium produced by the blast.

He didn't really care which direction he was going, though, as long as it was away from the French. The accuracy of their gunfire had been startling and unnerving.

While Duval successfully managed to ground the *Besancon* on the beach—the same beach where hundreds of French troops were now assembled, albeit pretty raggedly—the *Dauphin* when went in pursuit of the *Scheherazade*. The *Dauphin* had been close enough to see everything that happened in the brief struggle between the brig and submarine, so they knew the nature of the enemy.

Which was made all the easier, a short time later, when that enemy bobbed up onto the surface.

It was headed toward the harbor, away from the French, but it was moving very slowly. The *Dauphin* would have it within close firing range in less than five minutes.

Captain Le Clercq's vengeance, however, was cut short by a cry from the sailor perched in the crow's nest. *Two sails to the southwest!*

The final outcome was anticlimactic. By the time Captain Le Clercq aboard the *Dauphin* was made aware of the approaching Dutch *fregatte;* all possibility of escape was gone. The *Dauphin* was completely out of action, and with only nine guns left he had no chance of defeating two frigates.

Le Clercq ordered the French flag lowered on his ship. Less than two minutes later, he saw that the *Besancon* was following suit. Duval was no more of a fool than he was.

The *Princess Sophie* had sailed into the harbor when the Dutch were in sight to use her four popgun four pounders to harass the longboats, if necessary, to get as close as possible to the struggling *Scheherazade*. When the French flags came down, Captain Friedrichs hurried on board the *Dauphin* to accept the French surrender. Captain Le Clercq was relieved that the Danes, and not the Dutch, were his captors. The rumors concerning the Dutch treatment of Frenchmen after the Battle of Dunkirk were rampant and ominous.

As Captain Friedrichs accepted Le Clercq's sword, he nodded toward the approaching Dutch ships, "I think you made a wise choice. I just wonder how this will play out."

Le Clercq was startled at the openness of the comment. "Surely you intend to treat us decently! I have surrendered honorably."

"What concern of yours is the division of spoils?"

"So you intend to turn us over to the Dutch?"

It was Friedrich's turn to be puzzled, "Why would we turn you over to the Dutch? I was talking about the prize money for your ships. I'll be a made man if I get the standard captain's rate for the capture. I suppose Captain Andersen will have to settle on what, if anything, the Dutch get."

He looked back at his ship, taking in the incongruity of a four-gun tender capturing two frigates. "I suppose they'll get a full share too. Still, I'll get to write the report that goes back to the Minister. That should help my career." He bowed to Le Clercq and pointed to the waiting longboat. "If you will please accompany me, I will escort you to the town's commander, Captain Andersen. The two of you can work out the arrangements for the surrender of your troops."

Le Clercq winced at the reminder that his surrender also meant the end for Colonel Rousseau's infantry. "It seems that your good fortune is my downfall. I will have to explain in my report to the good Cardinal why our efforts failed. Just so I'm clear in my report, what was that thing that damaged the *Besancon?*"

"That's the *Scheherazade,* our Company's submersible warship. We've leased it from King Christian."

◆ ◆ ◆

Captain Andersen met them at the dock, with Colonel Rousseau already in tow. Karl stepped forward to shake Le Clercq's hand. "You made a gallant effort Captain, but we were prepared. I must say, never in my long career as a soldier did I ever expect to accept the surrender of two frigates to the forces I commanded. Your Colonel Rousseau met me under a white flag as soon as the two Dutch ships arrived. I'm ready to discuss the terms of your surrender." Friedrich made a small motion to Karl. "If you'll excuse me, I believe the captain and I have something to discuss before we begin.

As they stepped aside, August whispered to Karl, "Karl, the French captain let something slip that you should know. I'm not sure whether this is a French expedition or a *Compagnie Cente Associaes* expedition. He said 'the cardinal' not 'the Minister of Marine' when he talked of sending his report on the action."

Karl stood there, rubbing his chin in thought. Finally he replied, "That casts everything in a different light. You were right to warn me. This may leave us with a whole different set of options. If Richelieu forgot to give them a Letter of Marque, we could consider them pirates. The French may be forced to deny them. It could buy us some extra time from any reprisals by Richelieu."

He gave August a pat on the back and returned to the prisoners.

"Captain Le Clercq, just so I understand the situation properly, *whose* orders were you sailing under? The French government or Cardinal Richelieu?" Karl gave him the best drill sergeant stare he could muster.

Le Clercq started to answer, but then paused. If he said the government, it could mean war. On the other hand, if he said Richelieu, it would mean his head. He decided on a middle ground. "I sailed under orders of the *Compagnie Cente Associaes.* They have a French charter to settle this land. I was simply following those orders.

Karl smiled. It was the answer he'd hoped for. King Christian would not have to decide if this was sufficient cause for war. War might still come, but it would be between companies, not countries. And if he was a betting man, he'd put it on the Hudson's Bay folks in a minute.

"Very well, since you are mercenaries, you will be treated as such. Until such time as a ransom is paid, you will work for your food and shelter. We have a small project planned to strengthen our fortifications that needs lots of manpower. The soldiers and sailors will be offered the option to settle here as immigrants, or to ship out to Ilse le Haut, off our southern coast, and cut stone for our new forts. That decision is final."

Le Clercq and Rousseau were stunned. There was little chance Richelieu would pay a ransom for the release of two failed officers. Rousseau recovered first, "I would like to accept your offer of transfer. I believe my services are available as of this meeting. I believe I speak for my men as well." Le Clercq glumly nodded concurrence with the request.

Karl positively beamed. The new recruits would be worked hard and split up to prevent an uprising. Many would still go to cut stone, but they would go as free men, not prisoners. The only question remaining was what to do with the captured frigates.

CHAPTER 26

March 1635, Sudbury area

Svend stood back, open mouthed, at the drama unfolding in the cabin. It was like watching a mouse tell a hawk where to get off. He and Joseph had been trying to convince Heinrich Reinhardt, the expedition's leader, that it was time to break winter camp and start on the precious metals surveying part of their assignment to the east. They had spent what little good weather winter had offered scouting the nickel deposits around the crater to the west. The rest of the time had been spent cooped up in the cabin or counting beaver pelts as they were brought in by trappers. They were bored and so were their wives and they wanted to do *something!* Heinrich had countered that this was no type of weather that Karima and Agnes should go out in. The words were barely out of his mouth when Agnes shoved Svend aside and laid into Heinrich. That was five minutes ago and she was still going strong.

"Heinrich Reinhardt, don't even try to go there! Karima grew up in weather much worse than this. If you think for one minute that I'm going to spend another month cooped up in this cabin when I could be out in the woods with my husband you are sadly mistaken. I am so sick of staring at the same faces and the same walls day in and day out. You know full well Karima and I can hunt and pack out our fair share under any conditions."

As she paused to finally catch her breath in preparation for her next biting comment, Heinrich held up his hands in surrender. "All right, all right already! You've made your point. What I said was stupid."

"You're damn right you were! It took you long enough to finally admit it. And another thing..."

Karima grabbed her arm and cut her off, "Enough. I think he gets the picture. All of us can go, but someone still has to stay here. Those beaver pelts stored out in the shed need someone to watch over them. And there are still trappers out in the woods who expect someone to be here and buy their pelts when they get in."

Heinrich interrupted, "I'll stay here and handle the business end of this work. All I was trying to say was that there have been disturbing rumors of Huron sightings where they shouldn't be. They seem to be a lot further west this season than the Cree normally see them, and they're a lot more hostile. I just don't want to lose anyone if it can be helped."

Svend stepped forward, gently guiding Agnes away from Heinrich. "I understand that. It's the reason why the four of us plan to head out together to begin with. We'll get an advance camp set up for my surveying work and then Joseph and Karima will do a little trapping of their own. We'll need to replace some of our cold weather gear for next year and the pelts are still in prime season. Agnes and I will stay close to our camp. Besides, the Huron don't normally go that far into Cree territory. It would be tantamount to war if they came this far west."

Heinrich shook his head in defeat. He knew they were going, no matter what he said. Better they should go with his blessing. At least then they might pay attention to some of his warnings. "It sounds like you've thought this out. Go ahead then, but remember what I said. Pay attention if things don't seem right! Your instincts have served you well in the past." The four youngsters smiled. They'd finally get out and really have a chance to try out their skis.

Four days later, as they shuffled up a hilly pass on snowshoes, Joseph called for a rest and then turned to Svend, "Tell me again why this was such a good idea!"

"The girls wanted time alone with us."

"You mean that period after supper, where we build the tents and then collapse from exhaustion?"

Svend got a sanctimonious look as he replied, "Speak for yourself, old man. I have plenty of energy left at night. I have to stay awake listening to your snores!"

Agnes turned around, "Don't let him fool you, Joseph, I can't tell which of you snores louder." Karima nodded in agreement.

Svend ignored the riposte and pulled out the map they were following for the journey, the old Shell highway map of eastern Canada. It showed the rivers and general terrain features, along with highways that had existed up-time. It also gave distances between up-time towns. Studying the map and comparing it to the terrain in view Svend announced, "I think our destination is about three miles east of the summit. We should strike a southerly flowing, small river. If there's a bend to the south, we're there." He folded the map carefully and returned it to his carrying case. The hikers reshouldered their packs and started up the slope.

Three hours later, Svend's navigating skills were confirmed. They struck the river and a short trek south led them to a sheltered hollow overlooking a bend in the river. As they shed their packs, Svend boasted, "Father said

I could navigate. Just like I promised, the river and its bend. The gold deposits should be scattered all around us. We'll set up a permanent camp here, with separate lean-tos. We'll rest for a day and then start our jobs. Joseph and Karima can head upstream. The map shows a smaller stream there that appears to go through a flat area. There should be good beaver hunting there. Agnes and I will start some panning operations and once we get a lead, survey the terrain to try to locate the deposit." He pointed to a flat area sheltered by a copse of pine trees. "That looks like a good spot for the shelters. Why don't you ladies get a cooking pit started while Joseph and I gather boughs for the lean-tos?" Svend cast a skyward glance. "We'll need to hurry. It looks like we might be due for some snow soon." The four scattered and began the process of setting up their home for the next two months.

Svend had been right about the snow. They had barely finished the second lean-to when the flakes began to fall. They spent the next two days snow bound in their new abodes, enjoying themselves as only newlyweds can. By the third day, everyone was exhausted and ready to start exploring their immediate neighborhood. Joseph and Karima sorted their packs for a five-day trip into the woods to set up trap lines. As they left, Svend reminded them to watch out for sign of any Huron raiding parties.

Joseph laughed and said, "I think the only parties around here will be the ones you two have while we're gone! We'll be careful. We plan to be gone five days, but don't worry if we're late a day or two. We'll be hunting as we go and if it snows, we'll camp until it stops." Before Svend or Agnes could respond, Joseph and Karima schussed off on their skis into the woods. As they left, Agnes reached up and whispered in Svend's ear, "That sounds like an excellent suggestion, husband of mine." She took his hand and pulled him, willingly, toward their lean-to.

For the next three days, Svend and Agnes took day trips around the area, trying their hand at panning for gold and setting some small game snares for food. The morning of the fourth day dawned with a light dusting of snow falling. After breakfast, Agnes came out of the lean-to with a pack on her back and announced, "We're getting short on fresh meat. I think I'll check our snares and see what we've caught. Do you want to come with?"

Svend studied the sky. "You should be all right if you stay in sight of the river. I need to plot out what we've located so far on my map. And there's that site south along the river I want to check out further. I think that may be where one of the up-time mining operations was located. I should be back in camp before sunset."

Agnes picked up her skis that were leaning against a nearby tamarack. "I may be back tonight, but no later than tomorrow. I'll field dress anything we catch so I can pack back the maximum." She stopped and set down her skis and went back into the tent. She emerged carrying her small game crossbow. "I'll take this just in case I run into something that I can't outrace on my skis." She strapped on her skis, and with a farewell wave, headed north toward their snares.

Svend watched until Agnes disappeared into the woods. She looked like a fierce Viking maiden heading off to combat, crossbow slung over her shoulder. He went back into the lean-to to finish his notes for the map.

Before noon, Svend donned his snowshoes, slung his map pouch over his shoulder and headed downstream to the site that had shown such promise the day before. Their panning efforts had yielded almost half an ounce of gold. The pocket they'd struck had been formed by a tree root along the river bed. It was a natural seine for any gold that washed down the river. As he snowshoed along, he paid careful attention to the rock formations. They showed promise and he finally paused to chip off samples for further study. The sun had broken through and was shining warmly. He decided to pause and enjoy a brief meal of jerky while the sun shone. He sat with his back to an old maple tree and relaxed. He finished the jerky and decided to enjoy the warm sun while it lasted. Off to the west, clouds were promising that the warm sunlight would not last long. Within minutes, he'd dozed off.

◆ ◆ ◆

Two other sets of eyes surveyed the approaching weather. They also studied the lone white man who had drifted off to sleep. They checked his back trail to make sure no one else was with him. When they were satisfied he was alone, they crept up on him with their knives drawn.

Svend woke suddenly to a sharp pain on his throat, and a Huron standing over him with a knife drawn, yelling something that sounded like French. As his mind cleared of sleep, he realized a second Huron must be behind him, holding the knife at his throat. He was awake enough now to understand the first Huron's atrocious French. He was being ordered to hold still. He was their prisoner. There was no one else around.

It grated on his soul to have been captured so easily. He'd failed to follow Heinrich's instructions to stay vigilant. As the two Huron talked, he caught enough to know they were the only two, but that there was a larger party somewhere further off to the east. More importantly, they were not aware of Agnes. *I need to keep it that way!*

Svend raised his hands and said in broken French, "I understand. What do you want of me?"

The Huron that stood over him replied, "The French leader, Champlain, has offered a reward for any white man we capture in the west. There is also a reward for any proof of a *dead* white man we bring. We want the larger reward, but an uncooperative prisoner will still bring the smaller reward. Which do you want to be?"

"I'll cooperate!" Svend hoped they would simply carry him off. There was always a chance he could be ransomed if he was alive. He was alarmed at the next questions but managed to keep a straight face.

"Is there anyone else with you? Where is your camp?"

Thinking quickly, he decided on a judicious amount of truth, with some appropriate lies tossed in. "My camp is north, by the bend in the river. I'm part of a trapping party of Cree. They are out checking our trap lines. They'll be gone for a while. I don't expect them back for a week or two."

His captors whispered together before yanking him to his feet. While one kept a knife at his throat, the other bound his hands behind his back with a rawhide string. Svend tried twisting the loops, but Captain Foxe would have approved of their knot tying skills. "We will go to this camp. If you lied and there are others there, you will die." They bracketed him and proceeded north to the camp.

When they got there Svend gave a silent prayer of thanks that Agnes had not yet returned. The fire was just smoldering and the site was deserted. "See, just as I told you! No one here but me!"

The warrior in the rear dragged him over to a nearby tree and shoved him to the ground. He proceeded to tether him to the tree and the two Huron proceeded to ransack the camp. Luckily, Agnes and Karima had not brought any women's clothing along. They had both opted for pants and shirts for rough trail use. When they found Agnes's short rifle, they had a brief tussle over who would get to keep it. The taller Huron finally won out. He raised it over his head in triumph and yelled his cry of victory. The other nursed a cut lip and gave him a look of pure hatred.

Svend noticed the byplay and stored it for future possibilities. The taller warrior brought the rifle over and demanded to know if there were more like these. Svend pointed to the other lean-to and said there was a longer one there. The shorter warrior scrambled over and emerged with Svend's long rifle. The powder horn and bullet pouch hung from the barrel. The rifle was taller than he was. After another twenty minutes of wanton destruction and pillaging, the two warriors gathered up the additional treasures they'd found and cut Svend loose from the tree. They pointed downstream and pushed him off in that direction. Svend caught something about a ford further down than they had explored and that they wanted to distance themselves from any possible pursuit. All three shuffled off over the snow in snowshoes.

The next two days were a blur to Svend. With his hands still tied behind his back, he had a difficult time trying to stay up with his captors as they pushed on through the heavily forested terrain. Branches kept snagging his clothes and knocking him to the ground. They came to an area where the snow cover was heavy and each fall resulted in blows to urge him to keep his balance and move faster. On the third night, they finally decided that they had placed enough distance between them and possible trackers; they stopped and made a rude camp for the night.

Svend sank down as soon as they released his tether and leaned against a birch tree for support. The two Hurons cut his hands free so he could eat, but tied his feet together so he couldn't run. As the circulation returned, Svend felt like thousands of needles were attacking him. He rubbed his hands together and eventually could pick up the jerky they'd tossed on the ground in front of him. His captors were discussing the goods they would be able to buy with the reward they would receive for his capture. After they finished their meal, they sat close to the fire opposite him and wrapped themselves in furs to keep warm. Svend asked for a fur and the smaller warrior reluctantly reached in his pack and drew out a ragged fur for him.

Seizing the opportunity to talk, Svend asked why there was such a reward for white men. The taller Huron grunted. "The French leader wants news of where and how many whites have invaded the west. He plans to send warriors to wipe out the Danes." With that, he rolled over and went to sleep.

Svend stared at the flickering fire trying to analyze what he'd been told. Evidently, word had reached Quebec about settlers in Cree territory. If the French truly intended to launch an attack, it meant open warfare between the Huron and the Cree, and between the French and the Danes. Luke had mentioned that the Dutch warships were attacking the French in the Atlantic. Maybe this was their response to those attacks. Knowing the big picture didn't make his plight any better. At least Agnes was safe, and, when the three returned to camp, they should be able to figure out what had happened to him. Hopefully they wouldn't try something stupid, like rescuing him. Ransom was his best hope. With thoughts of war and its results haunting him, Svend slowly drifted off to sleep. The smaller Huron still kept watch to make sure he didn't escape.

Sometime in the late hours of the night, something woke Svend up. He remained stationary, not moving a muscle, trying to ascertain what had woken him. He slowly raised one eyelid and checked on his captors. The smaller Huron had fallen asleep on guard, but past experience said that any attempt to free himself would wake the Huron in a flash. It seemed to have been a false alarm. Svend started to pull the fur closer around him when a movement beyond the circle of light from the dying campfire caught his eye. He froze as he realized it was just the right height to be a bear. It had been warm the last two days and it might be a bear just emerging from hibernation. The smell of food would make him deadly to all three men. Just as he was about to shout a warning, Svend saw the glint of steel on the end of a crossbow bolt. The bolt was aimed at the larger of his two captors! He bit his lip and stifled the shout.

Ever so slowly, his rescuer slipped through the brush, aim never wavering from the larger sleeping warrior. Expecting Joseph, Svend was shocked to see Agnes step around the small pine tree. She paused and studied the ground between them. Just a few feet ahead the snow petered out and dry leaves covered the ground. Without letting her aim waver from the sleeping warrior, she reached for the knife at her waist. She pantomimed tossing the knife to Svend. Svend checked his captors' positions and then indicated she should toss it toward his feet. He curled the feet back and waited for her toss.

As she stepped into the toss, her foot caught a twig and it snapped. Both warriors stirred and when the knife struck a small rock both warriors sat up. The smaller warrior spotted the knife at Svend's feet and drew his blade. As he threw back his fur, Agnes shifted her aim. The larger warrior was tangled in his robe. The smaller Huron leaped the fire, just as Agnes loosed her bolt.

The bolt struck the warrior in his lower back and he dropped like his legs had been cut. He struggled to reach Svend, crawling with his hands. Svend managed to cut the bonds on his feet and back away from the warrior's knife strike. Svend reversed the blade in his hand and severed the rawhide cords. *Agnes hadn't been bragging when she said she kept this* sharp! His inattention almost cost him his life. He barely managed to dodge the larger warrior's killing strike. His left sleeve was cut from shoulder to elbow and blood started to instantly well up along the cut. He threw himself forward and grappled with his attacker. He made sure the fight carried them away from the wounded warrior.

While the fight was going on, Agnes drew her other knife and administered a coup de grace to the warrior she'd wounded. As Svend and the larger Huron continued to wrestle, Agnes went back and retrieved her crossbow. Winding frantically, she got the bow rearmed and waited for an opening. Svend's wound began to tell and he was visibly weakening. The warrior managed to throw him to the ground and reared back for a killing strike. The small opening was all Agnes needed. The crossbow twanged and the bolt sank into his chest, killing him instantly. Agnes dropped the crossbow and rushed to Svend.

He was trying to lever himself up with his right hand. The knife had fallen behind him when he was thrown to the ground. The blood streaming down his left arm was quickly cooling on the frozen ground. Agnes glanced at the two warriors to make sure they were dead and then proceeded to strip Svend's buckskin shirt and linen under tunic. She gathered up the furs that were strewn around by the fighting and made a crude bed for Svend. A quick examination of the cut revealed a long shallow cut that was more bloody than serious. She tore his tunic into strips and bound up the wound and then laid him back on the furs.

Svend looked up and smiled. "Took you long enough." Before she could answer he passed out. Shaking her head in relief, Agnes walked around the clearing, gathering up fuel for the fire. Casting caution to the wind, she stoked the fire until it was blazing, warming her injured husband.

Summoning what little strength remained, Agnes dragged the two Huron into the brush beyond the light from the fire. "This will have to do until morning," she said to herself. "I need some rest too." Shaking like a leaf, in a delayed reaction to killing two men, she curled up next to Svend, drew a fur over herself and immediately went to sleep.

The sun was breaking through the trees before Svend woke the next morning. Agnes was up and preparing a breakfast of bacon and beans. She spotted his movement. "Morning. How do you feel?"

"Like I was in a fight to the death … and lost."

"Naww, you made it to a draw. The other guys look a lot worse." She stared at him for a second and then raced around the fire to embrace him gingerly. "Don't you *ever* do that again! You do, and I may leave you to your friends."

Svend shuddered in shame, "You're right. I really fouled up. I completely forgot Heinrich's warning." He paused, "And what about you? Tracking two warriors alone was not the hallmark of a well thought out strategy!"

"All I could think of was you dying alone, without me."

"And all I could hope for was you not dying *with* me. I suppose we both could have planned better. I must say, when you came around that bush, I thought at first you were a bear. I nearly called out a warning to the Huron. Speaking of which, where are the bodies?"

"I managed to drag them off into the brush. I didn't know what else to do with them. The ground's too frozen to bury them."

"I recall a small pond just before we camped. After breakfast, I'll help drag them there and we can weight them down with stones and sink them. That should conceal them long enough from predators so that their friends won't find them quickly.

Agnes recoiled in alarm. "You mean there are more of them around?"

"They talked about meeting up with a larger band, but they seemed to think they were still a few days journey from their rendezvous point. If we don't linger, we should be all right."

Agnes went back to the bacon before it burned, but cast occasional glances into the woods in caution. Midway through cooking, she raced off into the brush and got violently sick. When she emerged she managed to murmur, "I think the excitement finally hit me. I don't think I've ever gotten sick like that." She finished cooking, but didn't touch the bacon when they ate.

After the meal was over, Svend flexed his arm and pronounced it well enough to help move the corpses. After an hour-long struggle, both bodies were consigned to a deep spot off a bank, with stones to weigh them down.

As they sank, Agnes murmured a short prayer for their souls. They returned to camp and gathered up all the weapons and goods they could carry. Svend was almost frantic, unable to find his map case and drawings. Agnes finally guessed what was bothering him and reassured him that she had found the case still intact at their camp. "That was how I knew you were gone. I knew you would never have left that out in the snow willingly."

It took five days to make the return trip. Svend had to pause frequently to rest. The arm was inflamed from use, but at least it didn't show signs of an infection. When they reached the camp, he collapsed on his pine needle bed in the lean-to, while Agnes straightened up the damage from the attack.

When Joseph and Karima returned the next day, they were appalled at the story of the attack. They related how they'd met another Cree hunting party on their trip and been warned of another Huron party that the Cree had met a few days to the east. They were much smaller than the Cree party and had left under threat of death. It was decided that the expedition should return to the winter campsite and then send word north about the French intentions.

Two weeks later, a lone Cree runner set out to report to Ft. Hamburg. Three days from the fort, he broke a leg trying to cross a swollen stream on a tangle of trees. The tree his leg was trapped under broke free and was swept downstream with the runner. He drowned before delivering his warning to the fort.

CHAPTER 27

May 1635, Ft. Hamburg and Sudbury

Warm weather finally drove the snows away, and the survey parties returned to the woods to prepare the sites for the initial mining operations. Heinrich was worried that nothing had been heard from Ft. Hamburg on their message that the Hurons were actively scouting with war parties. The most recent message had mentioned that a medical team would be coming during the summer with orders to travel among the natives, spreading medical knowledge and sanitary methods. He showed the message to Svend. "I guess they're not concerned about the attack, or they know something we don't."

Svend reread the message. "Father wouldn't ignore the message without a good reason. My guess is there's something going on in the east that may draw attention away from us. He and Sir Thomas had been talking about that before they left. The next time you send a message, remind them and tell them we approve of the medical team. The tribe will be happy that we've been so prompt in keeping our part of the treaty. I'll be happy to see them too. Agnes hasn't been feeling well lately. She's not sure what's going on, but she's been really tired." Heinrich stared at him, but kept his thoughts to himself.

Later that morning, after the Dutch trappers had headed east with their load of furs, the Hudson's Bay group sat down around the dying cook fire and planned their strategy for the summer. Svend led off with his plans. "I've got the site for the nickel mine staked out. I still need to check for the gold deposits. Before the attack, I found a likely spot, but I need to survey more of that area. The up-time reports said there were scattered sites all over that area. This time, we'll go armed and ready."

Heinrich stirred the fire up before finally having his say. "I didn't want to bring it up, but now might be a good time to finish our work in that area. The Dutch are heading east with their furs and if someone is still searching that area, they may draw them off. I don't like using them for a decoy, but better them than us."

Joseph nodded, "I was wondering about that. Hard on them if they run into Hurons, but they were almost bound to, considering how they insisted on returning. I think they're hoping to establish contact somewhere. They were reticent about their plans after they left here." He looked around the circle and everyone was nodding agreement. "Which brings me to our plans. When the medical team arrives, I think it would be a good idea that they meet with as many tribes and clans as possible at one time. There is an annual gathering at the great rapids that we should be able to make in late summer. If everyone agrees, I'll have messages passed that they can expect us there with the team." They all agreed. As they were breaking up to attend to their daily chores, Svend noticed that Agnes was in deep conversation with Karima.

CHAPTER 28

June 1635, Quebec

The lone Huron warrior trotted up to the western gate of Quebec. The guard slowly rose from the stool he'd been using to catch the afternoon sun after a filling meal and looked the warrior over. "What business do you have here?" His pike had drifted in the general direction of the Huron, just on general principles that the natives could not always be trusted.

"I bring a message for *Monsieur* Champlain of white settlers and trappers in the western lakes." He eyed the guardsman as one would a young child who had said something foolish.

The announcement drove all thoughts of a comfortable afternoon watch away from the guardsman's mind. The Governor General had made it very plain that *any* such message was to be brought to his immediate attention. He grounded his pike and yelled at the top of his lungs, "Sergeant of the guard! West gate! A messenger for the Governor!" The sergeant was delayed a few moments. He was still adjusting his trewes as he arrived. The guardsman sniggered at the sight. *So the rumors are true! He is seeing the widow Frontenac. The lucky bastard. She's got a nice, snug cabin and an ample bosom.* Luckily, the sergeant was not a mind reader and was hard of hearing.

The sergeant studied the warrior carefully. He was definitely Huron, or as they called themselves, Wendat, and they were in the friendly category. "Very good. I'll escort him from here." He turned to the warrior and pantomimed that he should follow.

The Huron looked disgusted. "I speak your language. I will follow." He fell into step with the sergeant as the gate was opened just enough to admit the two. All the way to the fort the sergeant tried to pry out the message but the warrior, who did grudgingly give his name as Orontony, held his tongue.

Champlain was just leaving the fort as the party approached. His eyes lit up as he recognized the warrior, "Orontony! I'm pleased to see you. What do I owe this pleasant surprise to?"

"I bring news of white settlers in the west." The sergeant excused himself, since the visitor was known to the Governor.

Champlain looked around but the receding back of the sergeant was the only other person nearby. "Did you bring prisoners as I asked? I can send someone to fetch them if they're nearby."

"Sadly no, there are no prisoners. I only bring news. I think the great Champlain will still find it of value."

"If my friend has news of worth, I will reward him. Now tell me, what have you learned?"

"My cousin and I were trapping west, near Cree country, and were attacked by two Cree warriors. One I slew as we grappled. The other, my cousin managed to knock unconscious. We bound him, and when he awoke we questioned him on why they had attacked. He said that other Wendat had attacked white friends of theirs and tried to carry them off. Their chief had warned that all Wendat should be considered enemies. We tried to get more from him, but he passed out again and never woke up."

"Where was this attack?"

"About five days journey north from the rapids from the great lake."

Champlain tried to picture where that was on a map. Just about due south from James Bay and about a third of the way north from the rapids. If that were the case, the Danes were spreading out faster than Richelieu had envisioned. It was definitely time to fortify the *sault* that controlled the Great Lakes. Bundgaard was already working on the first fort. He'd have to send some additional troops if he could scrape them together. Only God knew where he could find them, though!

◆ ◆ ◆

Four days later, his prayers were answered. A Dutch merchantman dropped anchor at Quebec with a cargo of refugees from Acadia. The Dutch had decided to return Isaac de Razilly to New France, in hopes of placating the French. He'd insisted to the ship's captain that he should stop at the site of Fort Royale and rescue any settlers who had survived the winter. Only nineteen people had remained near the fort. A few had died and others had simply drifted away in search of other settlements or friendly tribes.

Champlain greeted his deputy as warmly as he could manage and promised the refugees would be cared for. De Razilly demanded more aggressive action. "You must take measures to drive these pirates from our shores! Their presence is an affront to French honor!"

With just the opening he was hoping for to rid himself of the annoying deputy, Champlain replied, "You have brought me the means to do that. I will place you in charge of the western forces that will drive the enemies off. I have a Lieutenant of the cardinal's Guard already building a fort at the site we are calling Detroit. It is at the west end of Lake Erie. You will take a squad of ten men and whatever Indian allies you can recruit and, with the Lieutenant's men, strike out against the invaders to the north and west."

"But, but, they are not the ones that attacked me in Acadia! Why should I go west?" As he paused to catch his breath, de Razilly caught the look on Champlain's face. Insubordination was not something that Champlain tolerated, even in someone of noble birth.

"Because that is what the cardinal has ordered. I don't have the ships to settle with those in Newfoundland. They should have already been taken care of by a fleet the cardinal promised to send, but weren't. By rights, I should already have the men I need for this expedition. As it stands, all I have are you and the few men you brought with you. I will send Jean Nicolet de Belleborne with you to act as an advisor and commander of your Indian auxiliaries. You will remain at Detroit and send Nicolet and Bundgaard west to drive the Danes out and fortify the *sault* at the east end of the Great Lake. Nicolet will command that force. You are to drive them out, without mercy. Surely that should slake your thirst for revenge! Are there any further questions?"

De Razilly finally realized he'd overstepped himself. Champlain had received orders that he wasn't happy about. Isaac was his subordinate and the shit had just flowed downhill. The orders gave him no qualms, however. One enemy or another, he would have his revenge. Champlain was an old man and rumors said he didn't have long to live. A short exile in the wilderness could be endured if a richer prize awaited him. He would just have to bide his time. He had many friends at court, but that was a great distance away.

"No, Governor. I understand perfectly."

He shoved his hat back on his head and marched off. Visions of glorious conquests and shattered prisoners were already filling his head.

For his part, as he watched De Razilly go, Champlain's thoughts were less grandiose and far more practical. However it was done, by whatever stratagem or combination of forces, he was determined on one thing.

The French had lost the battle of Newfoundland. They would not lose the battle for New France.

CHARACTER LIST

Danes

Captain Luke Foxe- historical character, English explorer and leader of the Hudson's Bay Company exploration fleet, OTL died in July 1635, captain of the *København*

John Barrow- first mate aboard the *København*

Svend McDermott-stepson to Captain Foxe, artist and explorer, married to Agnes Roe

Mette (McDermott) Foxe-wife to Captain Foxe, mother to Svend McDermott

Agnes (Roe) McDermott-niece and sole heir to Sir Thomas Roe, wife of Svend McDermott

Sir Thomas Roe-historical character, originally, an English ambassador to Moghul's court and the Danish court, NTL chief investor in the Hudson's Bay Company

King Christian IV-historical character, king of Denmark, co-ruler of the Union of Kalmar

Christian Scheel- Danish Chancellor

Reuben Abrabanel-member of the Jewish Abrabanel extended family, major investor in the Hudson's Bay Company

Saul Abrabanel- member of the Jewish Abrabanel extended family, major investor in the Hudson's Bay Company

Augustus Bamberg- Factor for Hudson's Bay Company, stationed in Copenhagen

Gammel Bundgaard- ship's chandler in Copenhagen, cousin to the Minister of War, supply agent to the French fleet, spy, agent for Etienne Servien, and all around bad guy

Asmund Bundgaard- War Minister, cousin to Gammel Bundgaard

Michael O'Leary - former servant to Sir Thomas Roe, Francisco Nasi agent

Anna O'Leary- wife of Michael O'Leary, worked in Mette McDermott's dockside inn in Copenhagen, now runs the inn for Fransisco Nasi as an information collection center

Don Francisco Nasi- chief spymaster for USE

Mike Stearns- current (1633) Prime Minister of USE

Captain-Admiral Aage Overgaard- new Minister of War, after Asmund resigns

Captain Rheinwald-late captain of the *Hamburg*

Johann Strock- first mate, then captain of the *Hamburg* after Rheinwald's death

Captain Gilbert- ship captain, French fur trading ship
Lieutenant Oskar_**Mortensen-Captain of Danish submersible** *Scheherazade*
Seaman Bendt Møller-injured seaman on *Scheherazade*
Seaman Jepsen- seaman on *Scheherazade*, broke his neck
Seaman Nygaard-injured helmsman seaman on *Scheherazade*
Seaman Henriksen-acting helmsman seaman on *Scheherazade*
Commodore Hans **Jeppesen-Captain of *Aalborg***
Fister Johannsen-**First officer *Aalborg***
Fister Claussen-first mate on ***Aalborg***
Captain Nielsen- merchant ship captain with Jeppesen's fleet
James Wilson-sergeant at Thomasville
Doctor Nielsen-doctor at Thomasville
Heinrich Reinhardt-chief scout for the Hudson's Bay Company
Joachim and Kurt Hasselman-jaegers/militia with the HBC
Berndt Larson- oldest farmer in Ft. Hamburg and the farmers' unofficial spokesman

Sorrensen brothers-planned to remain at Ft. Hamburg over the 1st winter

Max Brauner and his wife Anna- planned to remain at Ft. Hamburg over the 1st winter
Captain Thomas James-historical character, English explorer, second in command to Luke Foxe, temporary administrator of Christianburg
Captain Bjornsen- *Queen Charlotte* Captain
Captain Karl Andersen-originally a Copenhagen City guard, then the Christianburg military commander, transferred to Thomasville as the military commander when that settlement was started
Doctor Mordecai Altstadt-doctor at Ft. Hamburg

French
Captain Rene Roussard- out of La Havre, captain *Der Alter Bruder,* agent for Richelieu
Captain Torcqville-Captain of the *Petite Amalie*
Cardinal Richelieu-Prime Minister of France
Léon Bouthillier, comte de Chavigny- historical character, French Foreign Minister
Paul Leval- *Monsieur* Servien's clerk
Etienne Servien-Intendant to Cardinal Richelieu
Captain Duval- in charge of French expedition to remove the Danes, captain of *Besancon*
Monsieur Giscard-officer on *Besançon*

Captain Lefebvre-captain of *Madrigal*, one of the French supply ships
Captain Dupre-captain of the French supply ship *Aceline*
Colonel Rousseau-in charge of troops to remove the Danes
Captain Jacques Le Clercq- junior Naval Captain, captain of *Dauphin*
Giscard de Villereal-late French agent in Copenhagen, died of heart attack
Samuel de Champlain- Governor General of New France
Jean Nicolet de Belleborne-historical character, OTL French explorer, commander of western detachment Indian auxiliaries
Francois le Plume-Parisian forger
Sir Isaac de Razilly-historical character, French lieutenant-general, La Have, in Acadia, deputy to Champlain

Native Americans
Faith, Hope, Charity-native adopted daughters of Samuel de Champlain
Orontony-Huron/Wendat warrior and messenger
Chief Luther Longspear- Chief of the Cree tribe situated near OTL
Ruth Longspear-wife of Chief Longspear
Adam Longspear-orphaned son of James Longspear, grandson of Chief Longspear
James Longspear-deceased son of Chief Longspear, died of rabies from a wolf bite
Joseph Longspear-younger son of Chief Longspear, traveled to England and Copenhagen with Captain Thomas James
Hurit- cousin of Joseph Longspear
Karima Hudson-Inuit, daughter of Jack Hudson, granddaughter of Henry Hudson, the explorer
Chief Keme- chief of southern Cree tribe that sheltered the mining expedition, son saved by Dr.Altstadt using CPR

English
Kirke brothers-historical characters, conquered New France

Dutch
Captain van den Broecke- captain of Dutch *fregatte Rotterdam*
Captain Tjaert de Groot-captain of Dutch *fregatte Friesland*
Unnamed Captain of the Dutch ship *Maastricht Prince*- appeared in 'The Danish Scheme', shanghaied Gammel Bundgaard for past scam that nearly killed his crew with tainted rations
Wouter van Twiller- historical character, Director General, New Amsterdam

Ships:

French

Der Alter Brude- French merchant ship, part of the French spy mission

Petite Amalie-French merchant ship, part of the French spy mission

Madrigal- French supply brig, part of the French assault fleet

Aceline-French supply brig, part of the French assault fleet

Besancon-French frigate, part of the French assault fleet

Dutch

Rotterdam-Dutch *fregatte* that escaped the Battle of Dunkirk disaster

Friesland- Dutch *fregatte* that escaped the Battle of Dunkirk disaster

Maastricht Prince-Dutch trader that Bundgaard was shanghaied on

Amsterdam Prince-Dutch ship carrying fur traders and food supplies

Danish

København-galleon under Captain Foxe's command, flagship of the Danish settlement fleet

Hamburg-four masted galleon, original Danish settlement fleet, lost in storm, salvaged by the Dutch

Scheherazade-Danish submersible vessel

***Aalborg*-Danish flagship of the resupply fleet**

Queen Charlotte-Danish trading brig

***Princess Sophie*-tender for the** *Scheherazade*

Hudson's Bay Company-OTL this was an English company, NTL it's a Danish company charged with exploring and developing northern North America

Compagnie Cente Associaes-Company of 100 Associates, a French company headed by Cardinal Richelieu responsible for New France

Treaty of Ft. Hamburg- NTL treaty that established the terms for the establishment of Danish settlements in Cree territory

Western gate of the Iroquois- the area around Niagara Falls that was the western extent of Iroquois territory

Doctor Gribilflotz-famous alchemist, NTL invented aspirins, also known as the little blue pill

Cree- lived north and west of **Lake Superior**, in **Ontario**, **Manitoba**, **Saskatchewan**, **Alberta** and the **Northwest Territories** and from Lake Superior westward

Inuit- lived almost exclusively north of the "**Arctic tree line**", the northern reaches of Hudson's Bay and the passages in and around northern Canada and Greenland

Huron/Wendat- remnants of two earlier groups: the Wyandot (Huron) Confederacy and the **Tionontate** (Tabacco people). They were located in the southern part of what is now the Canadian province of **Ontario** around **Georgian Bay**

Geographic Sites

Cheepash River- river that emptied into the southwestern area of James Bay, tributary of the Moose River

Christianburg-OTL Bell Island Newfoundland

Thomasville,-NTL port on southeast coast, OTL St. John's Newfoundland

Palais-Cardinal- A palace located in the 1st arrondissement of Paris. The *Palais* was the personal residence of **Cardinal Richelieu**. The architect **Jacques Lemercier** began his design in 1629; construction commenced in late 1632 NTL. Upon Richelieu's death, the palace would become the property of the King and acquire the new name *Palais-Royal*.

Ft. Hamburg,-South end of James Bay, site of OTL Moose Factory HBC site

Quay des Tuileries- a **quay** on the **Right Bank** of the **River Seine** in **Paris**, **France**, close to the **Palais du Louvre** and the **Quai François Mitterrand**, in the **1st Arrondissement**.

Scapa Flow-OTL site of the British Navy's major base for the North Sea, Orkney Island

Cape Breton coal mines- Baie de Mordienne OTL Port Mordien

Foreign Words

sault-a waterfall or rapids, in this story the rapids at Sault Ste. Marie

detroit-strait, in this story, the area around OTL Detroit Michigan

en flute-a naval term, meaning a warship traveling without some or all of its armament

77458949R00142

Made in the USA
Middletown, DE
21 June 2018